HCY

Out of the Blue

Out of the Blue

Gretta Mulrooney

ROBERT HALE · LONDON

ISBN 978-0-7090-8429-7

Robert Hale Limited
Clerkenwell House
Clerkenwell Green
London EC1R 0HT

www.halebooks.com

2 4 6 8 10 9 7 5 3 1

Typeset in 11/16pt Souvenir
by Derek Doyle & Associates, Shaw Heath
Printed and bound in Great Britain
by Biddles Limited, King's Lynn

In Memory of Paul Wilkins

1

The phone call comes as Liv is locking up the library, keying the security numbers into the alarm system. It is Thursday, late night opening and she is looking forward to a toasted sandwich, a hot bath and bed. Curious, what becomes a pleasure in your late thirties.

'I'm sorry to bother you, and I hope I've got the right person, but are you related to Dr Douglas Hood?' It is a soft woman's voice, hesitant, a Scottish accent.

'I'm his wife, yes.' She knows, she knows, doesn't need to ask.

'Oh, good. Nothing to worry about, it's just that, well, you see, I'm ringing you from Brighton station. I found this number in your husband's mobile phone; you know, ICE.'

In case of emergency. She'd made Douglas add it into his phone a couple of months previously, after he'd been poured off a plane at Gatwick, too plastered to remember his address.

'Yes?'

'The thing is, we found him asleep on the train. He's a bit the worse for wear. We've got him here in the staffroom and we've given him coffee. We're not sure what to do now.' There is a pause. 'He's not quite himself, you see.'

'It's OK, you can say that he's blind drunk. He must have slept

7

right through from Bedford; he should have got off at London Bridge.' She glances at her watch; nine o'clock. 'I'll come and fetch him, but it will take me an hour and a half from London. Can you keep him till then?'

'I finish my shift at midnight, so that's no problem. Is there anything else I should do or anything else I should know?'

'No, he's a quiet drunk, you don't have to worry. Probably best to just let him sleep.'

'OK. When you get here, ask for me. My name is Betsy, Betsy Duncan.'

She buys a sandwich and a carton of fruit juice at the corner shop, barely noticing contents or flavour and eats as she drives, tasting nothing. The letter she received from her father that morning is on the dashboard, in its padded envelope. She read it at lunchtime, learning of her unexpected inheritance in the fuggy warmth of Starbucks.

'Nanna took herself off to a solicitor, some fellow in Cork,' her father had written on the yellowing paper that he keeps in a box on the sideboard. 'Tim Crowley drove her in. She made a will after she'd seen a family argument on some soap opera on a neighbour's telly. Says she didn't want any falling out after she'd gone. So it's all neat and tidy, I checked on things when I was over organizing the headstone. Glenkeen is yours. You'll need to see to the roof but that's a story for another day. I'd give you a hand but Barbara's not well with her leg. Two keys enclosed, front and back door. The front door's a bit sticky and your grandmother was a stranger to WD40. You have to lift and push. You'll get the hang of it.'

She's been wanting something, *anything* to happen. Anything except this long, turgid punishment she and Douglas have been sentenced to. At night, when she lies awake listening to his stertorous breathing she dreams of running away to where no one can find her, imagines a hiding place. Once, when she was young, she had planned to run away from home after her mother told her off for dropping a crystal glass. Furious and righteous with indignation, she didn't know where she was going to go, just away. Her parents would realize the injustice they had done and pace the floor, longing for her return. Her father found her in the kitchen making corned beef sandwiches for the journey and when she coolly told him her plan, he scratched his head, saying, 'but if you run away I'll have no one to help me with the map in the car – you know your mother's a hopeless navigator.'

Her mother had come in then. Her father explained the reason for sandwich-making and the reason why Liv couldn't go. Her mother flicked a cigarette from its case and said, 'Well excuse me, but there's no way José that you can head off – who else is going to come and get the groceries with me? Your father goes into a coma in shops.'

She had looked sternly at the two of them, the sandwiches growing sweaty in her hand, grateful at being outmanoeuvred.

A kind of childish excitement at her grandmother's unexpected gift had welled up over her panini and coffee. All afternoon, her step was lighter, an unusual and welcome energy pulsing in her veins. She'd wanted to ring Douglas straightaway, but he was at a conference for the day and she didn't like to interrupt him. Now he would be too insensible to discuss it. He'd been insensible at most of the major points in her life with him: when her mother died, when she received her Master's degree, the night she'd broken her arm and he'd breathed terrible fumes over the nurses in casualty. When he's drunk, he thinks he is invincible, that he can fly, walk on water. On that ghastly night he was in magician mode and he'd fumbled incompetently with a hanky and a fiver, blind to the medics' contemptuous glances while she craved a real conjuror's skill; if only she could count to three, snap her fingers and vanish.

She drives fast, just within the speed limit, listening to the radio and not dwelling on what she will find. The ten o'clock news comes on and she listens to the usual grim scenarios, finding no consolation in others' troubles.

He is asleep in an armchair when she gets to Brighton station, snoring in a corner of the staffroom. He is pale and sweating, a bluish tint around his eyes. His straw-coloured hair is sticking up at the back in disarray. The air around him smells of a distillery. There is a yellowish stain on the front of his suit jacket. One of his shoe laces is undone. Someone – probably Betsy Duncan, a slight woman with a ponytail – has put a cushion behind his head. It adds a bizarre, homely touch to the utilitarian room and the slumped man, his gaping mouth. Liv remembers how he appeared as he left the house this morning, running for his cab; if you didn't look too closely at the skin and eyes, he was the picture of a mature professional man, briefcase clutched under his arm.

Betsy stands poised beside the chair with her hands clasped in front of her. She is wearing a dark blue uniform and a wedding ring. She seems a person with a contained, calm existence, unlike Liv, who experiences life as oozing, ragged, precarious. She is the woman with her finger in the dyke.

'He had another black coffee so it should be working through his system.' Betsy gives Liv that look she knows so well; curiosity mixed with pity and a strong dash of discomfort. 'He's lucky he was spotted and didn't end up in the sidings, that happened to a chap a couple of months ago.'

Liv wonders if she will ever reach a place beyond embarrassment. She adopts her bright tone, shaking Douglas, waking him up. He blinks at her and smiles, the dreamy, swimming glaze of vodka in his eyes and around his lips.

'Hallo my darling, what are you up to?'

10

'I think that's *my* question, isn't it Douglas? Come on, let's get home.'

He yawns, struggling to pull himself up. There are bubbly white flecks at the corners of his mouth.

Betsy walks beside them to the car. 'We get all sorts,' she says with a little laugh, as if to ameliorate the situation. 'And you should hear the mouths on some of them. It would make you blush. Your husband seems a very nice man.'

Liv closes the car door on Douglas. She wants to get away from this kindly, pleasant woman who probably has a sober, responsible spouse at home. What does it say about her that she is partnered by this inebriate? She looks at Betsy. Please, she thinks, don't be sympathetic, I can't take sympathy. She forces a smile, feels her jaw contract. 'Yes, he is a very nice man. Thank you for your help, you've been very good.'

Douglas snores deeply again on the way back, turning his head into the seat rest while she fights tiredness. His collar has turned up around his mouth like a comforter and there is a seep of dribble on his chin. She is envious of him, of the way he sleeps the sleep of oblivion while she navigates the swift currents of the grown-up world.

It starts to rain and the windscreen slicks with dirt. Douglas snuffles in time to the swishswosh of the wipers. To stay alert, she contemplates the numerous ways in which you can destroy love. You can fritter it away, through flirting and affairs. You can fail to pay it attention and watch it wither. You can poison it with arguments and bad blood. You can give up on it without even realizing, preoccupied in your own corner. You can let it slip through your fingers as you scan the horizon, believing that there is someone, something better elsewhere. Her love for Douglas, their love for each other, is being slowly drowned in a quagmire of wine, vodka and lager. There is dark, marshy water all around them,

11

sucking, pulling them down. She is clawing to escape, gasping for air.

She reaches for her father's envelope and takes the brass keys to the cottage from it, holding them tightly in her left hand. They are large and heavy, more like the keys to a mansion than a cottage. They grow warm and solid in her grasp. She clings to them all the way home as Douglas twitches and snorts, rolling her fingers on their contours; her unexpected lifebelt and possibly her salvation.

Her father hasn't been home long. He's still wearing his heavy cotton work trousers, padding around the kitchen in his thick wool socks. The air in the house is close and laced with a mothball smell and something else medicinal and sharp. He's making tea and a ham and tomato sandwich with gluten-free bread for her step-mother Barbara, who is, as she frequently is, unwell and upstairs in bed. He munches some bread and peanut butter while he layers the ham, cutting away the fat.

'I've not had a morsel since breakfast, my stomach thinks my throat's been cut,' he explains. 'There's so much work out there and plumbers are thin on the ground – well, ones that aren't cowboys and know one end of a pipe from another.'

Liv embraces him, smelling his familiar aroma of oil and rusty metal and the thick green soapy gel he uses to clean the grease from his hands. Her mother used to buy him aftershave but the scents of sandalwood and verbena never quite covered the bracing tang of the industrial strength cleanser that he works into his fingers every evening. Barbara isn't an aftershave kind of woman; she likes cheap, plain soaps, bargain basement shampoos. She's a difficult person to select gifts for; she doesn't read and rarely leaves the house, except for medical appointments. Last Christmas, Liv had bought her a handsome pill box, white and blue china and with a spring clasp.

The marriage to Barbara took place two years after Liv's mother died from a rapid cancer. Liv still expects to find her mother when she steps through the front door, sniff a trace of her cigarettes, catch a glimpse of her swift, neat feet in peep-toe mules, hear her making a cheeky comment to Terry Wogan, her favourite broadcaster. She used to have a badge saying that she was a TOG – one of 'Terry's Old Geezers'.

The house is a curious mixture of austere and cluttered these days. Comfort has given way to utility. Her father does the house-work and he's a minimalist by nature, a terrific tidier up and putter away. The reassuring bits and pieces that her mother used to leave around are gone: the pink ceramic saucepan stand, the black cat tea cosy, the pile of easy listening cassettes she liked to play when she cooked, the high stool she'd sit on, legs crossed, one mule dangling, while she waited for vegetables to come to the boil, doing the *Evening Standard* crossword. When she was puzzling out a clue, she took deep puffs on her cigarette, holding her elbow in her free hand, joining in with Patsy Cline or Dean Martin: 'sweet sweet, the memories you gave-a me'. She was a messy cook, easily distracted by a song or an anagram; 'oh sugar!' she'd yell when a saucepan boiled over, extinguishing the gas. The herbs she would sprinkle indiscriminatingly on all dishes, believing that they 'zizzed everything along' are still in their rack on the wall, dusty and stale. Liv bought her the wooden rack at the school jumble sale for eighty pence and polished it with lavender wax before presenting it.

Barbara's aids and adaptations have consumed the living space, replaced plants, rugs and cosy chairs; there are a number of metal gadgets to assist with dressing and walking sticks dotted around. A ramp has been made to the front door and there is a folding wheelchair in the hallway. The downstairs loo has a raised toilet seat and grab rail. Wrapped bandages are stacked in a fruit bowl, a row of medicine bottles ranked alongside. The house now has an anonymous, institutional look. Liv visits every couple of months and always it feels like a hospital side ward or an occupational therapy storage cupboard. She wants to see her father but watches the clock each time. Her mother acted as a bridge between them and they haven't found another crossing point for their affection. Always they end up talking about Barbara and her conditions. Her father enjoys his role as the paramedic in the marriage, speaking fluently of lipids, analgesics, bone density scans and mitral valve repairs. He makes frequent references to Barbara's knee man, heart man and allergy man. His social life comprises chats with district nurses, dieticians and physiotherapists.

Her father and Barbara wear blue and grey His and Hers cotton track suits when they are at home, fleecy lined in winter. Although Liv rarely sees Barbara, because of her numerous ailments; she reminds Liv of one of those crucial characters in TV sitcoms who is mentioned but never appears on-screen, a kind of deus ex machina.

'She's asleep at the moment,' her father says fondly, 'but I'll wake her in a while. She doesn't like missing *Coronation Street*.'

'What's up today?'

'Ah, the old hip and knee, you know, and some kind of imbalance in the ear. She never complains, though, she's one of life's soldiers.'

He puts a couple of garibaldi biscuits, the ones that he and Liv used to joke were made with squashed flies, on the tray he's preparing and Liv feels a stab of envy; they used to be her favourites, he'd give her some with her cocoa at night. She leans against the cooker, the knobs pressing into her back, aware of an ache in her shoulders. There are times, such as now, when she longs to be a child again, relinquish responsibility. She would like to rest against her father, prop herself against his solid frame but the tracksuit is off-putting; it makes him seem fussy and fusty. Her mother would never have tolerated leisure wear. Her father, she realizes, has taken up residence in another country where the mores and customs are unfamiliar to her. When she is gloomy and preoccupied with the injustice of life it seems that she has unfairly lost both parents; they have abandoned her and embarked on bewildering journeys.

Her father winks. 'Squashed fly for you?'

She smiles, hooks her arm through his. 'Thought you'd never ask.'

Barbara's voice sounds faintly from upstairs. 'Fintan, is that you? Is the tea ready yet?'

Her father darts for the tray, checks that there's a paper napkin. 'I'll pop up and then we'll have a chat about Glenkeen. Pour yourself some tea, love.'

She stays standing in the kitchen, not wanting to sit in the living-room amongst the raised chairs and footstools, the crocheted blankets that drape over Barbara's knees. She pours tea and dunks her biscuit. Upstairs, her father is murmuring. She studies the poster by the cooker, a list of foods that Barbara is and isn't permitted. They're divided into three categories, and coloured in green, amber and red; eat at any time, eat occasionally and NEVER EAT with a bold black cross by the warning. This last section includes wheat and dairy products. On the wall by the fridge is a pretty, oval art deco mirror. Her mother would always check her hair in it before she went out, lick two fingers and press her fringe down. Then she'd apply a last coat of pink lipstick, pressing her lips together and forming them into a pout. 'I'm so gorgeous, I can hardly stand myself,' she'd say in a Marlene Dietrich voice.

15

It was here in the kitchen that she told Liv of the bone cancer marching startlingly, swiftly through her body. She had been painting her nails a deep cherry and announced the prognosis as she held them out to dry. 'I can't complain, petal, I've had a good time; born in a different place I could have been gassed or persecuted or sent to a gulag.'

Liv wants to howl at someone that it's just not fair, but at whom? She drinks the tea too quickly, scalding her tongue.

Douglas wanders into the bedroom as she is packing, ostentatiously drinking alcohol-free ginger beer. He's wearing shorts and a T-shirt, signalling that he's going to spend time on the rowing machine in the basement. The can of innocent pop and the exercise are part of the theatre of life with him: Act 1, the drunken binge, Act 2, the reparation, Act 3, the one glass that will do no harm.

He sits on the edge of the bed and watches her fold and tuck. He likes to watch her, especially when she is cooking, moving between chopping board, fridge and hob, reaching for herbs and spices. He says that her movements are economical and measured, no energy wasted. She replies that all men like to watch women work, it reminds them of their mothers.

Light is falling slanted across the bed, warming the slatted oak headboard. The shadows skulking through the slats form bars on the plain cream wall. Her suitcase lies in a wedge of late sun. It is new and expensive, light dappled brown with darker trimmings a shade of bitter chocolate. The smell of virgin leather fills the room, pungent and rich. It reminds her of shops in narrow cobbled alleys in Italy and Spain, filled with expensive goods for tourists. She would have preferred her old case, a cheaper sort with dodgy locks but with handy inside pockets she is familiar with. Her old case smells of her and the bottles of duty free scent she's carried over the years, the little perfumed leakages of journeys. With its black edging, it is instantly recognizable on airport conveyor belts. She knows exactly where to put things in the frayed green case. With this one, she has to rearrange: it seems to resist her. But he has bought her the case; it is his way of accompanying her, reminding her of him. She knows this and so she struggles to fit her underwear and jeans and the new waterproof she's bought from the camping shop that tucks into a handy bag.

'Always a Mac for Ireland,' she says. 'I learned that early on.'

'I know. Those doomed picnics on beaches; just as your mother got the white pudding sandwiches out, clouds whipped in and the wind and rain started. You always ended up with sand in your teeth.'

She is constantly amazed at the things he remembers. She can't even recall having told him about those picnics and yet he knows the details of the white pudding. It frightens her sometimes, that he should have stored so many of her memories, made them his own. There are times when he speaks about her past as if he'd been there. His recollection of his own childhood is muted, apart from a few scattered, vivid scenes: his first day at school when he'd stamped on the teacher's foot, overtaken by rage at being kidnapped from home, a trip to Weymouth when he'd accidentally locked himself in a restaurant toilet and the fire brigade had to be called, the time in Wimbledon when he'd tripped up a kerb, ripped his shin and blood had soaked his shoe. When she asks him about his childhood years he looks blank and shrugs, says he can't think back that far or it is a blur. She suspects that it's a deliberate ploy because there was little joy in the life of young Douglas. Maybe that is why he collects her reminiscences, to shore up his own deficiencies.

He slips off his trainer and sock and rubs his right foot with both hands. His fingers are sturdy and capable when not trembling. His

17

thick thatch of hair makes him look younger than his years. His patients find him kind and reassuring; like all dedicated alcoholics he is crafty, pacing the booze outside of surgery, allowing recovery time. There have been nights when she's told him that she'd be better off being one of his patients, then she'd have his full attention, he'd repair her instead of inflicting damage.

His low voice is soft, melodic. 'I might not be here when you come back, if you're coming back.' He stares at his foot, flexing the toes.

'Don't say that, don't start that again. I am coming back. We agreed that this would be a good idea.'

'There's agreeing and there's knowing you have no chance at all if you disagree.'

'Everything you say sounds like a threat.'

'Then try this; have I ever told you that the day you walked through my surgery door with a sore throat, I thought you had the most beautiful tonsils I'd ever seen?'

She looks at him. He has a sudden smile and pale blue eyes, the transparent, swirling blue you are left with when you have rinsed cotton in whitening solution. She remembers that day, waking with a throat scraped with razors, trying to open her jaw wide while the kind man with a humorous mouth pointed a little torch. He had seemed so sturdy and dependable in his warm, snug surgery with potted plants on the windowsills. His shirt sleeves were rolled up to the elbows, workman-like, his tie loosely knotted and there were ink smudges on his fingers. 'Hmm, I think you'll live but you must feel rotten, you poor thing,' he'd said.

'You drew me a detailed diagram of my tonsils and Eustachian tubes, complete with labels.'

'I was trying to keep you there, hold on to you. I still am.' He shrugs. 'Who will you get to rub your back for you when you're across the sea in Ireland?'

'It'll have to go unrubbed.' She refolds a shirt, presses down on it.

He straightens up, brings his hands together briskly. 'I'll do your shoulders now, a gift before you go, they're looking hunched.'

She sits on the side of the bed while he works her muscles and sinews, stretching, untying the knots. He smells of the sweet pop and peppermint, the familiar aroma of attempted concealment. It is childlike, the way he thinks a mint or mouthwash will fool her. He gets through bottles of the stuff and keeps a spray in his pocket. She's familiar with all the flavours, their different mint, aniseed or liquorice tangs.

She watches the bars on the wall and the spaces in between. On the dresser opposite stands a wedding photograph, one taken on the steps of the registry office. Douglas had had a severe haircut that gave him a startled, vulnerable look. The day had been breezy and her hair, much longer then, had laced across his lapel. They both appeared so much younger, so unburdened, the professional couple with the confidence to dictate their own terms for the wedding; unfussy, a brief ceremony, then a meal in a restaurant hired for the evening in Putney. The dining area overlooked the Thames and they enjoyed the backdrop of a gloriously slow sunset as champagne was served and toasts made. Instead of the usual tired disco for entertainment, they'd hired a group of drummers called TomTom who they'd come across in the piazza at Covent Garden. The five men in Native American dress had beaten their thundering rhythms while the amazed guests ate dessert and liqueurs were delivered. She had relished this start to their marriage; making their own mark, declaring that they had a special, unique way of doing things. Had there been signs then, signals from Douglas that she'd missed, misty-eyed with love? She'd assumed that the whisky on his lips when they'd kissed to seal their union was Dutch courage.

19

'Do you love me?' he asks, brave enough to put the question because she has her back to him.

'I do love you. I need this break, though, and you need to get help. We can't go on like this, it's madness.'

'I'm sorry again about the Brighton thing. It isn't that awful, though, not as if I created any trouble, did any damage. I bet they get plenty of people who fall asleep on trains.'

'I'm sure they do, Douglas.' She is too tired to discuss it again, tired of all the clichés that pass for conversation. They might as well be talking in different languages.

As he smoothes her skin, the lighter strokes that mean he is finishing, she puts a hand on his forearm, hoping to soothe, to tell him that she too is sorry for the state they are in. She looks up at him, notes the frown marks becoming permanently ridged between his eyebrows. How is it, she wonders, that I love him but I can't wait to get away from him?

2

She takes the boat because she wants this to be a proper journey, with anticipation and a sense of arrival, treating herself to first-class accommodation on the train to Swansea and on-board. She is a good sailor and sleeps soundly in her cabin, lulled by the steady thrum of the engines, enjoying the rhythmical lift and fall of the Irish sea which is enjoying a late summer calm.

She wakes at six, rested, and recalls earlier boat crossings with her parents as she washes her face and brushes her teeth at the tiny corner basin. Her father liked the sea but was a poor voyager, prone to sickness at the least surge of waves. Her mother used to bring a flask of Bovril for him, so that once he stopped vomiting, the warm salty drink could settle his stomach. They couldn't afford a cabin and would sit on upright seats, her father pale, clutching a hanky and smiling with embarrassment as he sipped the beefy drink from the thermos cup. Her mother was an enthusiastic sailor and once Liv's father was settled, she'd tie a scarf around her hair and say she was off to sniff the briny. Then she'd roam the deck, smoking and chatting with other intrepid passengers. Liv would stay with her father and worry about her mother up on deck, imagining that a crashing wave might sweep her overboard. She felt the dragging, gnawing burden of responsibility for both of them. Finally, as the minutes became half an hour, three quarters, her father dozing under his newspaper, her stomach knotting with anxiety, her mother breezed back, bringing the fresh blow of salt and wind with her into the rancid fug of the lounge. She'd take her scarf off and sling it round her neck, singing, 'I joined the navy to see the world and what did I see? I saw the sea!'

Liv's father was always exhausted when they arrived at Glenkeen and would sleep for the first day while her mother and Nanna talked softly so as not to disturb him. They referred to men often as vulnerable creatures, frail within a tough outer shell. Once the journey had been dissected, Nanna would get on with her daily tasks, feeding the hens and the pig, lifting potatoes, collecting young nettles for soup. Liv's mother would light a cigarette and stand in the doorway, arms wrapped around her chunky belted cardigan, smoking and sighing. She sighed a lot in Ireland, at the rain and the breezes that whipped up from nowhere and the dampness that made her hair untameable. The smoke from the fire made her eyes sore and soda bread gave her indigestion. She was a London girl, a city girl; at night, she grew alarmed at rustlings of leaves, the barking of foxes, the silences. She couldn't wait to draw the curtains close once dusk fell. When they played cards before bed, twenty-fives and whist, she tapped hers sharply on the table, as if to reassure herself.

Liv couldn't wait to play outside. In London, she wasn't allowed out of the front door alone into mysterious streets where strangers might lurk. Her first steps across the glen were tentative without an adult shadow. Then, growing bold, she would do a handstand by the lilies, her nose brushing their sturdy leaves. Her first game always, the true mark of her arrival, was to fold her arms around her body and roll with her heart pounding down the damp grassy slope at the side of the glen. As she tumbled over the prod of stones and scrape of thistles she shrieked, giddy with abandon.

Then she would lie on her back, eyes half shut and wait for the sky to stop reeling.

She climbs the steep metal stairs and stands on deck as the boat sails up the Cobh to Cork, lifting her head to the salt spray. The rails are rusty and damp as she holds them, bending to gaze into the rushing waves. The last time she made this journey was when she was ten, the summer her mother miscarried and her father had taken his wife back to London, leaving Liv for two weeks with her grandmother. That might have been the summer when Nanna told her about the *Lusitania* sinking near Kinsale on a fateful Friday in 1915 and the poor drowned souls who were washed up on the south-west coast. 'You wouldn't get me on the wild watery ocean, child, I like me two feet on solid ground.' She'd thought that maybe that was why her father got seasick, because his mother had told him about the torpedo and all the lost souls.

The annual holidays to Cork had stopped after that, and they had taken trips in the car to Swanage and Margate, staying in small bed and breakfasts. It was getting too expensive, her father said when she asked why they weren't going to see Nanna; the cost of everything was racing away. She wrote little notes that he put in with his letters but found it hard to know what to say to an old lady who knew nothing of London. 'Just pretend she's sitting across the table from you,' her father would advise but that didn't help at all; you wouldn't need to write to someone who was in the same room. 'Dear Nanna,' she would put. 'I'm learning the violin and I'm in the school choir. I hope Susannah is behaving. I haven't got much other news.' Her father still made the journey every other year alone in the spring, before high season prices. During the week when he was away, her mother would rush Liv around London, visiting museums and churches, the zoo, Kew gardens, Kenwood House, the Tower. Her mother loved to be out of the

23

house; she was never a home bird but liked to dash a bit of lipstick on, puff a cloud of L'air du Temps around her neck and click her keys like castanets as she tucked her bag under her arm and opened the door. Their feet hardly touched the ground as they hopped on and off buses; it was good to be a tourist in your own city, her mother told her, it made you look at it differently, appreciate its variety 'because variety is the spice of life'. There was a giddiness to those weeks, a reckless energy. Once her father returned, life resumed its habitual steady pace.

Chains clang and rattle as sailors make ready for docking. The morning is bright and chilly with a clear sky. She shivers in the crisp air and zips her jacket up snug, tucks her hands deep in the pockets. The boat glides along the broad estuary, passing pastel-coloured houses and lush fields. Tractors are on the move and smoke spirals from chimneys. Gulls swoop over the boat, screeching its arrival. The engines judder and slow as it executes a stately turn, ready to find its berth. Liv feels the vibrations through the soles of her shoes, travelling along her calves. People on deck are smiling, clustering to the sides, peering to see if there's anyone they know by the quayside. The bow doors start to rise and fan open. There is a sense of occasion and celebration, the excitement of reaching the destination. She smiles too, full of anticipation now, wanting to see her inheritance.

The thin young man at the car hire desk wears a smart grey suit a size too small and covers his callowness with a flip bravura. He busily avoids eye contact and rattles through the details of the Ford. His narrow wrists jut from his too short cuffs. She focuses on them to save his embarrassment; the bony joints are pale but she thinks they might conceal a wiry strength. He speaks so fast, she has to strain to understand him, leaning forward like an old person with a faulty hearing aid. He reminds her of the jittery sixth form students who come to the reference room at the library, infecting it with their adolescent restlessness.

'Sooo . . .' he says, clicking the top of his pen with a frantic thumb, 'we have a specially reduced price of five-forty euros per month, thirty Euros deposit. Deal with an option to extend. Just give us a bell to let us know.' 'Turty euros,' he says, forgetting his attempts at a transatlantic drawl.

'Fine, thanks. Is the tank full?'

'It is indeedyo. Unleaded. Here on your holliers?'

'In a way. My grandmother's left me her cottage near Castlegray.' He won't want the information but she is interested to hear how it sounds, how it will make her feel.

'Cool.' He hands over the keys, spinning them through the air. 'Enjoy and have a nice day, Ms Callaghan. That's a heavy-looking case.'

'Yes, enough for a couple of months and all the vagaries of Irish weather.' My cares are in there too, weighing it down, she could have said, smiling and saying cheerio to him. There were always the words you spoke, concealing the ones you swallowed, those words that sank down to your chest and lay there sullenly. So, last night after Douglas finished massaging her shoulders she'd said to him, 'It will be a break for us both, a chance to think about things,' instead of saying, 'You've driven me beyond endurance, I can't believe anything you tell me because you're always lying to yourself.'

She trundles the suitcase past the huge sign saying 'Welcome To Cork'. The car park is near, only a few minutes' walk. Stepping outside, she sees that the sky has clouded now and there is a cool breeze sprinkled with rain. She halts, breathes in, feeling her tight lungs resisting, and thinks with a shiver of surprise, Home.

The car reeks of air freshener, an unpleasant citrus disinfectant and something else, like a man's spicy aftershave. She opens the window to halfway down and takes the cottage keys from her bag, laying them ready on the seat beside her, recalling her father's instructions about the recalcitrant door. She can hear Nanna saying, 'Bad cess to that old thing, it nearly has my arm ripped from my shoulder.'

She adjusts the seat and finds a map in the glove compartment, needing to check the route. The last time she'd come she had flown in unannounced, running away after Aidan dumped her. She was seeking solace in her grandmother's steady routine, remembering the cottage as a safe haven, a place removed from and untouched by the world's troubles. That day, raw-eyed, she had taken a bus from the airport to Castlegray and got a taxi to the cottage. Her grandmother had embraced her and made boiled eggs and tea, taking soda bread straight from the pot over the fire, the iron, cauldron-like container she called a bastaple. The eggs were a deep yellow, fresh that morning, the bread dark and dense. Afterwards, there was a fruit loaf, warm too from the fire, butter glistening on the plump sultanas. Liv hadn't eaten for a couple of days, since the meal she had abandoned as Aidan's words sank in. She was sick at heart, but she had felt suddenly ravenous at the sight of the food and demolished it all. Her grandmother had asked no questions, talking in her low voice about the Brennan's harvest and the Mahony's new herd as she ferried butter and milk to the table. Nanna's gift, she thinks, realizing it only now, had been stillness. When she had finally blurted out her story, Nanna had stroked her hair, saying, 'Ah, child of grace, child of grace, this old world would make your heart raw.'

She traces the route on the creased map with her forefinger as far as Redden's Cross, deciding to stop there for some groceries, and familiarizes herself with the dashboard. She'll need the windscreen wipers and maybe the lights, judging by the drifts of rain on the horizon. She starts the engine and links her knuckles, pressing down on them so that the joints give staccato cracks. Nanna used to tell her off when she did this, claiming that it would give her arthritis in later life. ' 'Tis then you'll rue the day, Olivia child,' she would say with a raised warning finger.

She couldn't claim to have been close to her grandmother; a scattering of visits throughout childhood hardly counted as an intimate relationship, yet since she died, Liv has been hearing her voice daily. She had never been Liv to Nanna, always Olivia. Phrases that she hadn't thought of for years spring into her head: 'The man who made time made plenty of it.' 'Every little helps, as the old woman said when she weeweed in the ocean.' 'That'll do nicely for the dinner, as the fox barked when he skelped the chicken.'

She fishes her mobile from her bag and rings home, hoping that the answer phone will be on. She's relieved when her own voice replies, inviting her to leave a message. She tells Douglas in that light tone she can't help using that she's arrived, everything is fine and she'll ring tomorrow. 'Look after yourself,' she adds.

When they were first in love, she'd sing to him: 'Take good care of yourself, you belong to me.' And she had buttoned up his overcoat, smoothing the lapels down, telling him that someone had to look after the doctor or he wouldn't be able to look after all the others.

The burden of the call lifted, she exhales, taps her foot on the floor, switches the phone off and drives out of the car park, towards the rain-laced west.

At Redden's Cross she pulls in outside the grocery store. It has been recently decorated, judging by the sheen of white paint but the sign is the same: O'Donovan's General Provisions and Post Office (Fish Bait Sold Also). She'd always loved those brackets. The rain has passed, slanting eastwards and the pale sun is glinting on the chrome of a tractor parked at the side of Crowley's pub across the road.

Stepping out of the car, she moves to drape her bag bandolier-style across her chest as she would in London and realizes that there is no need; not much chance of a grab-and-run here. She hangs it on her shoulder and pushes open the door of O'Donovan's, setting the bell ringing. The shop has been modernized so that it is now in the style of a mini market with the post office section in the corner, but the floor is still dark oak and the Guinness clock hangs over the counter. Jim Reeves is crooning mournfully in the background about distant drums.

She smiles at the young girl with pigtails behind the till who grins back, gap-toothed and carries on reading her comic. Taking a basket, she collects basic foodstuffs: tea, milk, bread, eggs and cheese and two tall bottles of water. The fridge holds some reasonable wine and she selects a bottle of Chenin blanc. She notes that bean sprouts and tofu are now being sold and wonders if Nanna ever tried them. Matches, she thinks, and firelighters; her father said that there should be plenty of turf in. She picks up a box with a picture of a roaring fire on the front: 'light in the wrapper, no more oily fingers!' it says. She feels a trace of disappointment. She'd always liked the whiff of paraffin from the white blocks.

As she is finding her purse a stout woman wearing a smart beige short-sleeved shirt and trousers bustles through from the back of the shop and replenishes the stock of cigarettes behind the till. Her upper arms are sturdy and mottled, her dyed blonde hair cut short around her square face.

Liv takes a breath. 'Mrs O'Donovan?' she asks.

The woman turns, tugging her shirt down. She is wearing a dark orange lipstick on her plump lips and heavy mascara. 'Hallo, yes,' she replies.

'I'm Liv Callaghan.'

Mrs O'Donovan claps her hands together. The motion sets the loose flesh on her arms wobbling. 'Well, I should have known.

28

You're very like your father, you have the green eyes and all. Are you just arrived?'

'Yes, on the morning boat.'

'Well, isn't that something! I haven't seen you in ages.' She looks Liv up and down appraisingly.

'No; last time I visited you were away, in Lourdes, I think.'

'Oh for sure, I was, so. Didn't I have a touch of the old women's troubles and I went to see would Our Lady take pity on me.' Mrs O'Donovan drops her voice. 'I'm sorry about your grandmother. It was sudden, her poor old heart just gave way. But wasn't she a great age, she used to say she'd had a good innings.'

'Yes.'

'And you'll have come about the cottage, and her after leaving it to you.'

'That's right.'

'Well, isn't that something. I heard that from your da when he was over. It's so long now since we saw you, you were always her pet. She mentioned you whenever she came in. And isn't it a shame you couldn't come for the funeral.'

Liv feels guilty heat flush the back of her neck. 'Yes, I'm afraid I couldn't make it.'

'A liver infection,' Douglas had said, writhing and sweating on the sofa. 'Got to check into hospital for a couple of days, nothing a blast of antibiotics won't sort out.'

Mrs O'Donovan nods. 'Ah for sure, she was so proud of you, with the university education and all. And you're beyond in London all this time?'

'Oh yes, that's where I live.'

'That's lovely, lovely. Ah, she often mentioned the times you used to come down with her and Susannah. She said she'd have to ask you to walk slower, she couldn't keep up with your young limbs.'

'Hold on there, child, you have me winded and poor old Susannah will be ready for the bacon factory if you carry on at that lick,' Nanna would say.

Liv wonders if Mrs O'Donovan is thinking that this grand-daughter who's come to claim the house hasn't bothered to visit for years but the woman is smiling.

'Who's Susannah?' the little girl asks.

'She was Mrs Callaghan's pig, her pride and joy,' Mrs O'Donovan explains. 'This is my granddaughter, Carmel,' she tells Liv. 'She helps me mind the shop sometimes.'

'You say it Carmel, Gran,' the child says reprovingly. 'You say it the Spanish way.' Her grey eyes are huge, rounded and solemn, heavy lashed.

'She takes notions,' Mrs O'Donovan explains, making a help-less gesture with her hands. 'Carmel was always good enough round here before but sure I suppose times change.'

Liv smiles. 'Hallo,' she says to the girl, gesturing at the comic. 'I used to read *Bunty* when I was little.'

'It's not my absolute favourite,' Carmel informs her. 'I prefer *Look Lively* but I have to wait until Dada comes from Castlegray with it.' She has a precise way of speaking, weighing the words in an adult manner.

'Do you remember Maeve, my daughter – Carmel's mother?'

'I don't think so. . . .'

'Ah, for sure, you probably wouldn't. She was just a baby the last time I saw you in the shop. I expect she was asleep; she was an angel of a baby, she never gave me a moment's trouble and she slept through the night. Not like Madam here!'

She looks adoringly at her granddaughter who wrinkles her nose back. Jim Reeves is droning another melancholy verse about lost love. Suddenly, Liv's skin is prickling and she needs to run from the plunking guitars and saccharine lyrics.

'Well,' she says, 'I'd better make a move and get sorted out.'

Mrs O'Donovan smoothes her hair and rearranges her shirt collar. 'Anything at all you need, just come in. It might be a bit chilly up there, but I see you have the makings of a fire. Your father checked that everything was shipshape when he was here after the funeral. And he's still at the plumbing.'

'That's right, but retiring soon, I think. Barbara, my stepmother, isn't in good health.' She lifts the carrier bag. 'I expect I'll be in again tomorrow, I'm sure to have forgotten something.'

She keeps moving away, wanting to be gone but Mrs O'Donovan follows her out, holding her hand palm upwards to the fine drizzle that is falling. 'That's in for the rest of the day now, I'd say. The forecast says we have the makings of decent weather coming. 'Twould be good to have some fine days before the nights draw in. Isn't that a handy little car you have.'

'It's easy to drive, I thought it would be useful to have one.'

'For sure, you couldn't do without. Are you here long?'

'A couple of months, probably.'

Mrs O'Donovan makes an O of surprise with her lips and sticks her thumbs in the top of her trousers. 'And do they give you them kind of holidays in England?'

'Some of it's holiday, some of it's a sabbatical.'

She waves goodbye from the car and turns left by the pub. She is tired by so much dialogue. At home, she has got into the habit of economical conversation. The fewer words you speak, the less likely you are to be asked the awkward questions that probe your dull secret like a drill bit on a worn tooth: 'I saw Douglas at the bus stop, is he anxious about driving after his accident?' 'Your husband was looking a bit pale when I met him in the market, I suppose he's had that awful flu virus.' She is always aware of her fixed, bright smile, the false buoyancy of her voice when she replies. She is the master of the swift glance at the watch and the need to hurry

31

away and has a ready battery of excuses to refuse social invita-
tions. It is understood that she is doing a PhD and needs to study
in her spare time.

She reflects on the information that Mrs O'Donovan extracted
from her, smiling to herself. Nanna wouldn't have approved;
Eileen O'Donovan, she always claimed, had a curious mind and a
careless tongue, a deadly combination. It was best to keep your
business to yourself and plough your own furrow, her grandmother maintained; that way you had no grounds to fall out with
your neighbours. It is the path she follows herself in London, Liv
thinks, shifting down a gear to negotiate a bend. But here, without her heavy history at her shoulder, she can afford to be more
open. She thinks how Mrs O'Donovan speaks, the way her rolling
accent and easy phrasing tease out a response, her statements
disguising questions. The interrogative comment. She tries it
herself, adopting the Cork brogue, making a splashing sound with
her lips; 'and ishn't it . . . and you're beyond . . . he's shtill in the
plumbing.' Best of all, she thinks with relish, is a 'touch of the old
women's troubles'. She smiles, then chides herself for being an
oversophisticated Londoner.

As she negotiates the deserted, twisting lanes she feels her heart
give a little lift. She spreads her fingers wide on the steering wheel
and moves her shoulders up and down. The sun has ventured out
again, despite Mrs O'Donovan's forecast and there is a rainbow to
her left. She hears the rush of water, smells its brackishness in the
air. The hedges are high, filled with the red blaze of fuchsia. Now
and again between the hedgerows there is a teasing glimpse of the
Atlantic glittering in the distance, like a mirage. Crossing the
hump-backed bridge over the river, she counts to fifteen and there
it is perched at the top of the glen, a low white cottage with dark
green door and windows. Glenkeen; beautiful glen. Before her
father had a driveway tarmacked up to it, the only access had been

via steep steps, which were often treacherous with moss. A snatch of a song comes back to her: '. . . a-down by the glen side I saw an old woman, a-plucking young nettles, she ne'er saw me coming . . .' The sound of her voice startles her. It is a long time since she's sung. Douglas mentioned that to her a couple of months back: 'When we first got married, you were always singing around the house, it was like living with a lark or a nightingale.' She'd looked at his rueful face, the flush on his cheeks, flinched at the trace of yesterday's beer on his breath.

'I suppose I must have had something to sing about,' she'd replied, turning away, leaving one of those sour atmospheres that regularly taint the space between them.

Slowing the car, she drives in and parks to one side, near the little semicircular hut that used to be Susannah's dwelling. She stands, turning to look back down at the empty road beneath, letting the cool moist air lap her skin. Running her fingers along a dripping laurel bush by the front door, she sucks rainwater that tastes of peat – a smoky, dank flavour – and runs her fingers along her forehead and down to her neck. The little pulse in her throat is steady. She listens; silence.

The door gives way to a determined push, creaking and complaining. Liv rests her case against the wall and crosses to the wide hearth. There is a half-burned log in it, maybe the very one her grandmother had thrown on the evening she died. The cottage smells as it always has, of sunflower seeds and child-hood holidays; a dry, savoury scent of turf, bran and floury potatoes.

She walks around. Little has changed. Oil lamps provide light, water will have to be fetched from the well and food cooked over the fire. The tin tub for washing is hanging on its hook by the back window. The only concession Nanna had made to modernization was allowing Liv's father to lay the driveway. She only agreed to

33

the latter after she slipped on her way down to the well and sprained her ankle.

There is one large room downstairs with a pine dresser opposite the fire and a round oak table covered with an oilcloth. In a corner by the fire is the sofa her grandmother slept on, rarely venturing upstairs. An eiderdown embroidered with yellow primroses covers it. The open tread staircase leads up from one corner of the room to two bedrooms above. She goes up, raising dust that sets her sneezing.

The bigger front bedroom holds an old metal-framed double bed and a washstand, the type with a china bowl set into the centre. In the fireplace is a jug of dried grasses and lavender. She turns in a circle, letting the room grow familiar, noting the patch of damp in the left-hand corner of the ceiling where it meets the outside wall. On the mantelpiece is a small, scratched pink and beige case, like an attaché case, with the name Lady Anne on the lid in raised gold lettering, dulled with age. She takes it down, places it on the bed and opens the rusting clasps. Inside she discovers a radio nestling, with pink facing and chunky beige dials. There are batteries beneath the back panel. She twists a knob on top and it crackles to life. It is tuned to a French station and she holds it as she tests the bed, which is covered in a vast billowing eiderdown, similar to the one on the downstairs' couch. The broadcaster murmurs away anonymously, liltingly. The bed is firm, the eiderdown snug, if damp to the touch. Guitar music starts and she carries the radio to the back bedroom, which is empty except for some burlap sacks that would once have held chicken food, and a row of hardback books on the window ledge. She examines the titles; several Dickens, *The Mill on the Floss, War and Peace* and *Dubliners*.

She fingers the lace curtain aside and looks from the side window at the acre of land that stretches behind the cottage.

The earth has been turned ready for the winter frosts in a few beds near the back door. Her grandmother would have been planning early potatoes, Liv guesses, searching her memory for the names of those she had favoured; Kerr pinks. Their floury skins parted as they were cooked, revealing a purplish blush. They were served with a hunk of pale creamery butter on an oval blue and white plate, featuring a bonneted lady in crinoline at its centre. The plate is on the kitchen dresser, the centrepiece, middle shelf.

The rain is slanting again, steadier now. She will save a trip to the well for the morning, a treat to anticipate, and make do with bottled water. She shivers, switches the guitar music off and heads to find something warmer to wear.

She wakes suddenly, having lain down on the sofa for a few minutes' rest and realizes that she has slept for nearly two hours. Leaping up, she craves a cheerful fire.

The shed is stacked full of turf, not the sanitized briquette version sold in the shops but dark rough chunks with crumbling edges. Against one wall is a row of logs with thinner kindling piled in a basket. She carries several armfuls of these into the kitchen and sets a fire, building a wigwam of sticks on top of the firelighters and hunkering back on her ankles to watch it catch. There is an old bellows in the corner and she pokes it cautiously into the firelighters, wheezing air to encourage a blaze. She brings the eiderdown from upstairs and hangs it on the back of a chair near the fire; it is heavy, dragging on the floor and she sneezes again as she spreads it out to catch the heat.

The sun is slipping down the rim of the sky, casting long shadows. She brings the two lamps before the fire and checks that they both hold paraffin, then pumps them, unscrews the glass and lights the wicks. The glass covers scratch back into place as the flames flare blue, then settle into a steady glow. This had been her evening task during childhood visits; the official lamp lighter. It had symbolized the freedom of the cottage and the glen, where she was allowed to roam at will, chat to passers-by on the roads and handle matches.

Her fingers are ash coloured from the fire and the blackened wicks. She rubs them on her jeans and pushes up the sleeves of her angora cardigan, stroking the heathery colours. It is delicate, warm and very expensive. Douglas had bought it for her after one of his 'episodes' as he refers to them. She always receives something special when he feels particularly shameful; a digital camera, a leather jacket, handmade gloves. She keeps all these gifts in one drawer, the guilt stash as she calls it privately, rarely using them. Somehow, the reason for them being in her possession sours their value. He packed the cardigan when she wasn't looking. She thinks of his puffy face, his hamster cheeks, his eyes made bloodshot and squinty by the fluid and toxins in his bloodstream. He is a handsome man grasping a map of self-destruction in his trembling hand. Driving her to Euston, he had promised that in the next month he would go to all the AA meetings: 'This time it's for real,' he'd told her.

She pushes her hair off her face and holds her hands out to the yellow-red flames, the angry flare that she always thinks of as the colour of a pacing tiger's eyes. Food, she decides; bacon and eggs and strong tea. 'A cup of tea you could cut with a knife,' Nanna would have said.

She goes to bed as light is draining from the sky. Dark comes swiftly. In bed, she snuggles under the warmed eiderdown. It breathes out a woody, smoky scent. She listens. An owl's wild cry sounds once, breaking the silence. The high moon touches the curtains with a pale beam. For the first time in ages she relaxes her guard, thinking, this is mine, mine alone. She reaches a hand out, dimming the lamp until the blue flame flickers away. The comforting shade is complete. For a while she lies, gazing into the formless shadows. Then, fumbling for the radio, she switches it back on and is lulled to sleep by the sombre voice of Jacques Brel.

3

Aidan sees her leave the shop, swinging the plastic carrier bag to and fro. She has her back to him but immediately he recognizes that confident, tripping walk; she holds herself so straight, bobbing up and down with each step, the motion making her shoulder bag rotate. Her coffee-brown hair, a shade that he used to compare to a milky cappuccino, is shorter, shaped to her scalp. He tracks her to the car, telling himself it isn't possible, everyone has a doppelganger. Then she turns, in profile and he sees that face mapped with freckles, her sunglasses pushed up, holding the fringe of hair back. He watches as she settles her bags and drives away.

He grabs the box of vegetables and fruit from the back of the van and clutches it to his chest. He is surprised that the first rush of emotion is anger, a hot flush like those his mother-in-law regularly complains of. Then a dry-mouthed shock; what is she doing here – has she come seeking him? He takes off his glasses and rubs his eyes. It has been a long morning since the downpour that drenched him as he was setting out the stall. He has been damp for hours and now his bones are demanding a hot shower but he has to get Carmel to the dentist.

He recalls then that Liv had once mentioned family in Cork, a grandmother she had stayed with sometimes as a child. Liv had commented that her grandmother suffered with toothache and treated herself with oil of cloves because she was terrified of the dentist, who she called a butcher worse than Sweeney Todd. He could picture the place where she had told him, an Italian café on Fulham Road where they went to eat cheap tomato risotto and drink red wine that rasped their throats. It was where he'd blurted out to her that he wanted to break it off, that he needed to explore life, find himself, have adventures. 'Aren't I an adventure, then?' she'd asked, shoving her fork violently into her food, gulping from her glass. There was cheesy Eurovision music playing, an upbeat nursery type tune – *lalalala* – and he knew he'd done it all wrong, was annoyed with himself and then with her because he couldn't find an answer for her and she was staring at him, willing him to look her in the eye.

Carmel has spotted him and is waving, hopping from one foot to the other outside the shop door.

'Carmelita, Carmelita, you couldn't get no sweeter!' he calls.

'Dadda! Did you get my comics?'

He hefts the box. 'I did, don't I always obey orders? Come and give your old man a kiss.'

She skips over, gawky, so skinny that Maeve tells her that if she stood sideways, she'd be invisible. She flicks her pigtails and squeals as he kisses her.

'Your nails are filthy and you've a big stain on your shirt. Gran'll say you look like a navvy.' She pulls her finicky face, the one that makes her look middle aged.

'Honest dirt, baby girl, that's what it is. The bag with your loot's in the back. I'll just check in with Gran, then we'll get going. Have you got homework?'

'I did it inside. Sums. I'll stay here and read. Can you get my satchel?'

'What did your last slave die of?' He smiles their old joke at her

39

and she retorts, quick as a flash.

'Not obeying orders promptly.' She wriggles in the back of the van. 'It smells of onions in here, and it's all mucky.'

He shrugs and heads for the shop. He caught his thumb on one of the carrot boxes earlier and it's bruised, twingeing. He hopes he won't lose a nail. He has to duck through the shop door. When Maeve first brought him back from Manchester to meet her mother, his height had been the source of all the well-worn jokes; 'How's the weather up there?' and 'Tell us what's over the horizon!' Then, when he'd informed Eileen O'Donovan that he was giving up his computer design job to cross the Irish sea and sell vegetables in Castlegray market, she'd declared that he must have softening of the brain from all the time he spent with his head in the clouds.

'Hallo, Eileen. Everything OK? I brought the carrots, salad stuff and apples.' He greets his mother-in-law from the doormat, wiping his boots carefully. He can see that she has just retouched her lipstick; her teeth gleam brilliantly through the orange. He wonders if Liv noticed that Irish dental hygiene has progressed.

'Fine. Carmel's a joy to have, as always. She wheedled a scone but I said not to eat too much in case the dentist needed to do an injection. She has such a small appetite. She promised me she'd try and eat more vegetables. Still and all, I suppose 'twould be no good if she was like you, big and muscular.' She gives him a coy look, head slanted.

'Well, thanks, it's back to usual routine tomorrow so it'll be Maeve fetching her in the afternoon.'

The shop is the same as always, yet different. Maeve believes that a place can be disturbed by emotions, by the feelings we carry with us, unaware. He listens to her, indulging her, thinking, mumbo jumbo. Now he thinks that maybe he senses a change that Liv has brought, like an alteration in temperature. His scalp is

40

chilled. Or maybe the change is emanating from him? Stop it, he tells himself, it's been a long morning, you're tired and you've had a shock. He nods and makes to go, then turns back, steadying his voice. 'There was a woman coming out as I pulled up. I haven't seen her around here before.'

Eileen O'Donovan neatens chocolate bars in front of the till. 'That'll have been Liv Callaghan, she's old Mrs Callaghan's grand-daughter, the woman who used to live over at Glenkeen. I don't suppose you'd have met her.'

He shrugs, looks out of the window.

'Well, anyway, Mrs Callaghan left your woman there the cottage. She's over to view her inheritance. She was in here making friendly. Didn't show her face here for many a year, mind, but that's the way of things. She'll be here for a while, she says. Trouble follows that family, they're all as mad as hatters, the Callaghans, always have been.'

'How do you mean?'

Eileen holds a hand up and ticks off on her plump fingers. 'The great-grandfather drowned himself, there was an aunt who went roaring mad and there's an uncle over near Castlegray with strange ways who married a Protestant.'

Aidan laughs. 'Marrying a Protestant doesn't mean you're certi-fiable.'

Eileen gives him a knowing glance. 'That was only the start of it. Anyways, I suppose Liv Callaghan will tart the cottage up and make a quick killing, sell it to some Germans or the like. More customers for your stall, wanting aubergines and such. Were you busy today?'

He circumvents the possible trap of the innocent-sounding question. 'I think the weather was against us but it wasn't bad at all.'

She sniffs. 'Well, you're a highly educated carrot seller, that's all

I can say. I never heard before of a graduate weighing spuds for a living. Maybe the three of you can drop over for a bite of dinner on Saturday, the new priest is coming.'

He is always disconcerted by her swift changes of subject. 'I'll check with Maeve.'

'Oh, do come,' Eileen says, head tilted to one side again, cajoling. 'It's so nice to have little family occasions, and so important. Now that you've decided to live here, we must make the most of it. That's what I said to Maeve when she was so upset at the upheaval and all your things were packed up ready for the lorry; every cloud has a silver lining. We must all pull together.' She comes towards him, gliding across the shop, tapping his arm, a little too close for comfort.

'If we can . . .' he says vaguely, waving a hand and dislodging hers. His heart sinks at the prospect of having to eat one of Eileen's huge meals while she pumps a new clergyman for information and gives them unwanted advice on the rearing of her granddaughter. He wants to get away, think over this information he's been given about Liv. Eileen is chatting on about the new priest, something to do with West Africa and Aids and how she's going to be raising money for doctors there.

He is seeing Liv that last time she walked away, all those years ago, her freckled arms glowing from sunbathing on Hampstead Heath earlier in the day, her head high, refusing to glance back. He'd admired her for her courage, felt gratitude that she hadn't raised a storm. In her haste to get away from him, she'd left the book she was reading on the café table, *Under The Net* by Iris Murdoch. He has it still on a bookcase with her writing inside, her careful Italic script, executed in the turquoise ink she used. *Liv Callaghan*. Some joker in her year, bored during a lecture, had written underneath. 'If this book should dare to roam, box its ears and send it home.'

In the van, he listens to Carmel as she tells him about history being the story of civilization and a Roman poet who described the sea as wine dark. They had drunk a deep red Merlot in the Fulham Road, it had a label with swirling lines that Liv said looked like a girl dancing, with her head thrown back. He smiles as his daughter mentions how the Romans constructed a tortoise shape for battle.

'Do you know the rhyme, Carmelita?' he asks. 'Julius Caesar the Roman geezer, conquered Britain with a lemon squeezer.'

'*Dad*,' she says crossly, undoing and redoing a plait, 'you never take anything seriously.'

'I'm dreadful,' he agrees. 'Then there's the well-known lines; *Caesar et erat, Brutus et sum iam, Caesar sic in omnibus, Brutus sic intram.*'

His daughter sighs. 'Yes, there there, father. You do talk rubbish.'

He glances at her in the rear-view mirror; she has her head in her comic and is chewing the end of a plait. The centre parting in her hair exposes her small, delicate skull. He drives carefully, feeling suddenly wild, as if he's had a couple of glasses of rough Merlot. He hasn't thought about Liv for years but now, he remembers, she would have instantly understood the lines. She had a passion for Latin and in particular for Catullus. Before she walked away that evening of his shame, she had grasped the table, reciting: 'But fools do live and waste their little light, And seek with pain their ever-during night.' Then, there had been tears filming her eyes. But when she laughed, her mischievous, gurgling laugh, the freckles at the corners of her mouth blended, dancing.

In the late afternoon he pulls up in front of the bungalow, thinking how much he dislikes this house. It sits, squat and unlovely, fronting the road. He had wanted to buy an old place on the road out of Castlegray and do it up but Maeve had prevailed, keen on a modern home with double glazing. Given that they were going to be on a tighter budget, they needed a place that wasn't going to spring any nasty surprises, she'd argued, no damp or wood-worm.

He tries to like it but can't. He finds it featureless, soulless. Sometimes, he almost drives past it because it looks like so many others in the neighbourhood. The rooms inside are big and boxy. Despite the insulation and fierce heating, the place somehow always has a whiff of something mouldering. The furnishings are chintzy and floral, chosen by Maeve, who likes pale yellows and rose tints. There is an abundance of swagged curtains, plump cushions, side tables and knick-knacks. He frequently bumps into ornaments, catching them just before they topple, or stretches his legs and collides with a figurine. Maeve had tended to the fussy when they set up home in Manchester but he had managed to rein her back, achieve a balance between his love of simplicity and her penchant for embellishment. Here, with her mother egging her on, there is no stopping her. He is also aware that there is an unspoken trade-off now; she has reluctantly tolerated his change of work and loss of status and income and in return the house is her territory.

Maeve is stirring a casserole when he walks into the kitchen. Carmel has already dashed into the living-room, where she is watching cartoons. He sniffs the air, registering that he is raven-ous. Maeve smiles at him, gazing up from under the Alice band that holds her long, thick hair back. She has to wash it at night because it takes so long to dry. He can still feel it damp on the pillow when she lies beside him; the apple scent of the shampoo she uses permeates the bedroom, lingering on the bedding.

'I thought I was cooking?' he says, thinking of the steak and salad he'd planned.

'I got back a bit early, Reagan was delayed at court and he rang and said I might as well head off. How did the dentist go?'

'Fine, all routine. The brace gets fitted next week. She's quite excited at the prospect now, there seems to be some kudos attached to having one.' He kisses Maeve's cheek, her pale, clear skin and peers into the saucepan. It holds a cream and green-coloured substance. 'Smells good.'

'It's a recipe I saw last week, chicken with celery and coriander, a Martha Stewart.'

A few years back, after her husband died, Eileen had spent time with a cousin in Philadelphia, where she had become a fan of Martha's. From time to time the cousin sends her magazines that she passes on to Maeve. He always knows when one has arrived because there is a new dish, flower arrangement or home decoration courtesy of the guru of American domesticity.

'Good old Martha,' he says heartily. 'Is she out of jail now?'

'Yes, the poor woman. I haven't ruined something you'd planned?'

'No, no. To be honest, it'd be great to have a hot shower while you dish up.'

'Bad day?'

'No, just long, you know. I'll be ten minutes. By the way, your mother said something about dinner on Saturday.' He watches her stir and add more seasoning. Martha's recipes always seem too fussy to him, too many layers. Yet somehow they are also bland in a way he can't put his finger on. On the wall above Maeve's head is a tapestry that Eileen made for them, a homily picked out in pink against a background of cream and blue flowers, reminding him that home is where the heart lies. He hates it, he always has, everything about it is false and sentimental.

'I'll ring her later.' Maeve strokes her right eyebrow. Like her mother, she has small hands with plump, almost stubby fingers. She is conscious of this, thinks them ugly, so her nails are beautifully shaped and painted with the palest pink varnish. They are her one true vanity; she has a manicure outfit and sets about them every Saturday morning, filing, cuticle softening, varnishing. Always she wears her gold watch on her left wrist and a bracelet on her right, to draw attention away from her hands. Next to hers, his hands look gigantic and battered. He's always sucking out splinters or digging at them with needles. She tastes the sauce and offers him some on the end of the wooden spoon.

'Mmm,' he says, puzzled by the flavours. 'Is there cream in it?'

'Low fat yoghurt. It's good for the heart.' She laughs, waving the spoon at him. 'I want to make sure you live to a ripe old age!'

In the bathroom he runs his aching thumb under cold water, tilts his head to look in the mirror. Now that he is no longer a suited executive but a self-employed trader, his chin is allowed to have stubble and he delights in not shaving every day, even though Carmel calls him Mr Hedgehog. His hair is longer, unconditioned, wind blown, its curl coming back. He has lost the processed, urbane image that used to look back at him, has shed it like a skin, with the constricting colour-matched shirts and ties. His skin is rougher; he looks both younger and weathered. He feels a real person again, enjoys the solidity of his upper arms where the muscles have developed from lifting and carrying. As a family, they've taken a big gamble but it's paid off. When he reads the papers these days, he sees dozens of articles about burned out professionals downsizing to achieve quality of life and he always points them out to Maeve; a bit of extra self-justification never hurts.

He stands in the shower, letting the hot water ease his muscles. It is the best feature of the house, strong and rushing, with four settings. He likes to start on moderate, then work up to full power. He reaches for soap, working it across his chest, resting his palm in the centre to feel his heartbeat. It is thudding dependably. 'He had a heart scare,' someone said about another stallholder who hadn't appeared for a couple of weeks. He'd heard a woman in the pub describing her daughter's miscarriage, saying 'me heart is scalded.' The heart, the heart; everything you put in your mouth now was judged by whether it was good for the heart. What is good for his heart? he wonders. Does his low-fat, low-cholesterol, polyunsaturated heart lie here, in this modern bungalow? It's a long time since it has beaten fast, thudded with expectation and desire. When he was waiting to meet Liv it used to flutter and knock against his chest. What was that cheesy ballad she knew – 'your fingers touched my silent heart and taught it how to sing.'

The soap smells of Maeve's pale skin, of apricots and the moisturiser she uses. She is like a summer fruit, soft and pleasant. When he met her in his firm's personnel department, typing up a contract for him, he liked what he came to think of as her refreshing, old-fashioned simplicity. She didn't obviously weigh him up, play games about when they would meet, have a need to visit the latest clubs and bars. She liked to stay in mainly, have sofa suppers and watch films, relax in her deep cushions. Such domesticity was a relief after numerous flings with career women who always had schedules and deadlines, who liked late, exhaustingly prolonged restaurant dinners. Maeve obligingly fitted in with his schedules, accommodated her life to his like a shoe made to fit. Some of his male colleagues said they envied him, finding himself someone so pretty and uncomplicated; he became pleased with himself, thinking that he was a lucky and clever fellow. He realized how comforting Maeve would be to come home to and had reached a point in his life when the idea of comfort was as attractive as her ready smile and easy manner. Her astonishing, flattering conviction that he was an intellectual as well as a business high-flyer led him quickly and easily to the belief that she was The One.

The spray bombards his eyelids. He shakes his head, inhaling

47

steam, feeling his lungs expand. Maeve is a good person, he can't find a bad word to say about her. She has agreed to him giving up a highly paid job with an international company to sell fruit and vegetables, honey, eggs and jam on a market stall in a little country town. He can only do that, balance an unpredictable income because she works as a secretary at Riordan's, bringing in the steadier wage. He knows that she regrets the life they had in Manchester and still hasn't come to terms with the disruption he has caused. In her gaze, he sometimes sees disappointment, an unguarded yearning for the man he used to be, the one she proudly boasted about when she phoned her mother; sharply suited, high earning, smelling of aftershave, glowing with a corporate sheen. She has made the best of it all, she never complains; sometimes, he wishes she would, then he could fight his corner.

She is a reliable woman. Her heart is constant and lies dependably in their home. He should be counting his blessings.

He turns the shower to the pulse setting. His mind is flooding with memories, scenes and images he hasn't thought of for years. Liv used to sing to him in a theatrical fashion when they took baths together, Mario Lanza songs her mother was keen on: '. . . you are my heart's delight and where you are, I long to be . . ' Or she would treat him to songs from the shows, musicals that her parents had taken her to over the years: 'The Street Where You Live', 'I Could Have Danced All Night', 'The Black Hills of Dakota'. She knew all the words, the composers and original singers. She'd taught him 'Baby, It's Cold Outside', so that they could duet with him taking the Dean Martin role. The bathroom in her flat was damp and always chilly, the steaming water the only way of keeping warm. The old gas heater popped and gasped when they topped up the hot water, the flare of the pilot light hissing. He would pretend to count her freckles, her sun dust as he called them.

He shivers and squeezes his eyes, switching the shower to maximum, hoping the drumming water will drown his thoughts. Inside the thundering spray he sings, tentatively at first, then louder.

I have often walked down this street before,
But the pavement always stayed beneath my feet before,
All at once am I several storeys high
Knowing I'm on the street where you live.

As the cascade beats down on his head he laughs, eyes still tightly closed, seeing rushing stars and myriad lights, a pulsing galaxy of caramel freckles, that unforgettable tripping walk.

In the morning Liv wakes to bright sunlight and thinks of the well, smiling. She carries a mug of tea made with bottled water and the empty galvanized bucket along the little path made of stepping stones curving away to her right behind hawthorn bushes. The stones are worn and smooth with moss growing between the cracks. She follows them past the bushes and through a sea of swishing ferns, deep green and still licked with morning dew. She holds her hands out on either side and they tickle her palms, leaving traces like moist cobwebs on her skin.

The path leads her past oak and elder trees, via a dense tunnel of fuchsia and blackberries, then turns through a narrow gap and down worn steps into a grove encircled with more blackberries, fat-leaved rhododendrons and tall lilies. In the centre of the grove is a well, surrounded by more interleaved stones, built up in a couple of layers around it. A tall hazel tree throws dappled shade. The sun sparks on the stones, catching the surface of the water, illuminating tiny flies dandering above it. The blackberries are ripe and she picks and eats a handful, tipping them into her mouth.

49

They taste of earthy red wines.

Kneeling on the ground, she lowers her face towards the water. It is deep and clear and fresh smelling, a natural spring. She plunges her hand in. It is earth cold, tingling. As a child she had imagined the fathomless source it came from and always it had filled her with a delicious fear. Kneeling by it, she would close her eyes and bend forward, thinking what it would be like to fall in and drift down through the chilled depths towards the earth's raging core.

Her grandmother had treasured the well as an almost sacred place; provider of pure water but also of protection and healing. She would sprinkle the water over her aching shoulders and rub it against Liv's throat to protect her from recurring tonsillitis. When Liv's mother had shingles, Nanna had sent her a bottle of the water to dab on her abdomen but she had poured it into a plant pot, saying she preferred the doctor's medicine to Juju. Always, Nanna carried a small bottle in her pocket, in case she felt unwell or sensed ill will or danger. It was an ancient well, she explained to Liv; it had been there long before the house. The hazel tree signified its special qualities because there was a hazel by the well at the centre of the world. This tree had dropped its berries into the water and to eat a hazel berry meant that you gained wisdom. All wells were linked to the central one and this meant that magic could occur at any of them. That was why the fairies often stopped by wells and had their meetings in the trees and bushes around them. 'The people these days is full of science and brain work but there's more wisdom in that water than in all the books in the world,' she'd advised, as Liv's mother threw her eyes up to the ceiling.

Liv scoops the well water into her mouth, shivering with the shock of its icy purity, then drinks and drinks with abandon until her mouth is numb, paralysed, and her face and hair drenched.

50

She laughs, a loud, reckless note. A passer-by might mistake her for a fairy on the rampage, one of those her grandmother had often referred to. She'd a wealth of verses and stories about them visiting wells and dairies; they were usually mischievous beings, out to hoodwink, irritate and tease, the delinquents of the spirit world. At night in the kitchen she would sing as she scraped leftovers into the pig bucket:

With tip-toe step and a beating heart
Quite softly I drew nigh,
There was mischief in his merry face
And a twinkle in his eye,
'Twas Tic Toc Tic his hammer went
Upon a weenie shoe,
Oh I laughed to think of the purse of gold
But the fairy was laughing too.

Liv shakes her head back, sending a cloud of spray rattling into the bushes, then lies on her stomach, her arms propped on the stones, staring into the restless water. The sun and high clouds move across the surface, a constantly changing pattern of light and shade.

She turns on to her back, shifting her shoulders to get comfortable and closes her eyes, the stones now acting as a pillow. The well sings quietly to itself, a constant, delicate melody. The ground is warming slowly under the sun. She can hear it breathing, stretching, stirring itself, releasing a loamy aroma. She dozes, the well murmuring behind her, little whispers of reassurance.

A cloud passing across the sun stirs her. She stretches, bones clicking, as if rediscovering their natural arrangement. Finishing her tea, she steps around the well to a hollow at the base of a furze bush and parts the grass to see if the stones are still there. They are; small white chips of shingle specially collected by her father from the beach at Owenahincha on one of her parents' wedding anniversaries. He'd used Liv's plastic sandcastle bucket, a yellow one with moulded turrets to carry them back. That evening, she and her mother had watched as he'd levelled the ground by the furze and arranged the stones: MOLLIE AND FINTAN. Her mother had said it was the nicest gift she could have imagined. 'Your daddy's one of life's real romantics,' she'd said to Liv, holding her on her lap, making sure she blew her cigarette smoke away from her daughter's eyes.

She traces her fingers along the stones, removing weeds. Once, she had asked her mother how much she loved her and her mother had said, 'You know the well at Nanna's? I love you as deep deep deep, deeper than the well and even more than that – deeper than the deepest ocean.' Standing by her mother's coffin, she had understood suddenly, in a way that made her want to cry out, that a world was lost to her.

She rearranges the grass around the stones, restoring them to their hiding place. Then she fills the water bucket and makes her way back, her right arm dragging with the weight.

She crosses the paved area outside the kitchen and puts the bucket down by the door. There are terracotta tubs with flowers and herbs but they all look ragged and in need of attention. An archway through a trellis leads to the main vegetable plots. A spade is stuck in a ridge of upturned earth, leaning at a perilous angle. The soil is a dark, cocoa brown, the colour of the milky paste she'd mixed the previous night from a packet she'd found in the kitchen cupboard. A wheelbarrow half full of stones and shards stands next to the path, mulched leaves piled around it. She kicks through the leaves, gripping the spade and standing it up straight, slicing it deeper into the soil. The wooden shaft is warm and rough like dry skin.

Another trellis and archway takes her to an area of overgrown fruit bushes and semi-jungle, where the juicy grass is brushing her calves. Turning and looking back through the archways, she sees order being stealthily overtaken by confusion. She is no gardener but she knows, from a time long ago when her father had appendicitis, how quickly nature wrenches back control; his small garden became unruly within a month.

The path vanishes and she walks on through thick grass and bracken, her shoes becoming soaked until she reaches a low bank and steps with a stile crossing into a field with cows. She climbs to the top of the stile and catches her breath; even now, the vista can surprise. There, at the end of the sloping field is the glistening sea, reflecting the blue of the sky. From where she stands, she can believe the illusion that she could run down the field, straight into the waves. She holds her arms across her chest and stands, entranced.

As she watches the swelling tide, she thinks of the first time she and Douglas went on holiday together. They took a package trip to Rhodes to celebrate their engagement and he confessed to her, as they walked down to the beach in blazing heat, that he couldn't swim. She had been astonished because to her, he'd had a privileged childhood, rooted securely in 'old' money; father a surgeon in the army, mother an ex-debutante – one of that breed who had been 'presented' to the Queen – who bred Labradors and had her own London property, a vast and gloomy mansion flat off Eaton Square. Douglas had been educated at Harrow and Oxford. Summers were spent in Switzerland and Gibraltar. The family home was a huge house in Sussex with acres of land, gardeners and domestic staff. He could ski, ride, play cricket, polo and golf but was frightened of being out of his depth in water. He'd informed Liv, in that mechanical voice he always used when speaking of his mother, that when he was two years old she'd thrown him into the sea off Brighton, just as she'd done to his siblings, to encourage him to swim. Unlike his brother and two sisters, he'd panicked and gone under, felt the water pressing on his skull, drank his fill of salt as he screamed. Afterwards, he'd developed a stammer that came and went until he was a teenager. Even then, telling her the story, it returned as a hesitancy, a pause between words and it occurred to her that he spoke in this way when he was in his mother's company.

Liv had spent a good deal of the holiday encouraging him into the sea, reassuring him that the shallow coast was perfectly safe. At the end of the fortnight, he was happy to doggy-paddle as long as the tips of his toes touched the bottom and she stayed near him. Watching him, she had enjoyed feeling nurturing, protective but later, when she reached the lowest ebbs in the marriage, she resented being trapped in the role of mother. I'm a mother with no children, she would reflect as she made excuses for him, forgave him, waited up for him, cleared up the trail of debris he caused.

She had never been able to warm to his mother, a brisk, excruciatingly thin woman who regarded Liv as a downmarket addition to the family. 'Haven't heard from you for a while, since you blew in with that dreary bird,' she'd written to her son after their first visit, which had been an endless, chilly spring weekend of croquet, mysterious horsy business and tasteless meals eaten in a freezing dining-room. The days and nights had been filled with the yapping and scrabbling of dogs that Liv feared. She had been glad that Douglas rarely visited his parents, preferring to keep his distance. They visited now once a year, at Easter and she thought of it as her duty, similar to the doctrinal laws she had obeyed in her childhood when communion and Mass had to be attended.

Bending, she picks up a handful of scutch grass and soil, crumbling it in her fingers. This, she thinks, is what I want: simple days and nights. Today I'll clean the house and poke about in the garden, see if there are any vegetables I can use, pick blackberries. I might see if they do an evening meal in Crowley's. I'll make cocoa and go early to bed and wake early. I'll plan each day as it comes. No waiting for a key in the door and a smell on his breath, no half truths and evasions and lies, no watching him push food round on his plate and missing his mouth, no having to look at the sheer heart-stopping stupidity of the smile on his lips.

She lifts her face to the breeze and lets her unhappiness lie quiet, like a calmed baby who will grow fractious again when it wakes to the difficult business of living.

4

She's itching and blinking from dust, in need of a bath. She has spent the day cleaning the cottage from top to bottom, dusting, sweeping with the heavy brush, scrubbing floors. She has washed all the kitchen crockery, cleaned the windows, cleared out the fireplace and rinsed the curtains. She explored the shelves beside her grandmother's bed/settee, sniffing the bottles and tubes of medications for rheumatism. They smelled of camphor, menthol and pungent eucalyptus. The eiderdown on the settee is impregnated with the same sharp scents and she imagines that Nanna must have rubbed them into her limbs before sleeping.

Carefully, she wipes off the books in the back bedroom and examines the yellowing pages. On each flyleaf are the initials O.F. The copy of *Bleak House* has a flattened Sweet Afton cigarette pack as a bookmark. Her grandmother had never liked cigarettes, or the devil's weed, as she'd called them. That was why Liv's mother had always smoked standing at the open door, or out in the glen.

It's a long time since she's done so much hard physical work; she and Douglas have a cleaner who visits once a week and sees to all the chores, including the ironing. She is grimy, aching, happy.

She lights a fire, cranks the big cast-iron pot from the back to the middle of the hearth and fills it with water, placing the tin bath ready in the centre of the kitchen. While she waits for the water to heat, she pours a glass of wine from the bottle she's kept chilling in the well. It's delicious, all the more so, she thinks, for being well earned. She relishes the taste, the relief of being able to open a bottle without having to worry that it will be an overwhelming lure, without having to hide it at the back of a cupboard or behind a bookcase.

Her father cleared most of Nanna's personal papers after her funeral. In the dresser drawer Liv has found a small photo album. She sits by the fire with her wine and turns the pages, looking at black and white images of people she doesn't know. There are various groups, the women in dark clothes, the men in suits. A nun is at the front of some of the groups, waving at the camera cheekily.

There is one photo of Liv and her grandmother holding hands, taken by the well; Liv aged about five in a ruched summer dress, Nanna garbed in her usual black, a tall woman with a full bosom, straight shoulders and capable hands. Around her grandmother's head is one of the scarves she always wore, wrapped bandana-style, framing her high forehead. Every Christmas, Liv's father would buy one in Debenham's on the high street and post it in a padded envelope. It was always the same style, silk and in her preferred colours of blue or cream with a rose print. The bandana lent her an exotic air of a hippy or woman from the east who had wandered into the glen. Liv couldn't recall ever seeing her without it, even at bedtime. She is sure that her grandmother slept in it.

She holds the photo closer, scrutinizing it. Both she and her grandmother look solemn, squinting in the sunlight. She has only distant, fleeting memories of the visits; hot potatoes bursting on a plate, milk cans wedged in the well, a sudden shudder of fear as a bull's head loomed through a hedge, steam coiling from fresh cow pats, collecting eggs still warm from the hens for breakfast, her grandmother singing as she fed Susannah and chanting a rhyme as she helped Liv undress at night in front of the fire.

> Dan, Dan, the dirty old man, washed his face in a frying pan,
> Combed his hair with the leg of a chair
> And threw his britches up in the air!

Her grandmother's hands were rough from work, but warm, and when Liv was washed and in her nightdress, Nanna would hold her face and plant a kiss in the middle of her forehead, saying, 'Now, Alannah, it's time to sleep the sleep of the just.'

She touches her grandmother's face with her finger. I hardly knew you, she thinks, I was always too busy to come and see you and yet you left me your house, this refuge.

When the water is bubbling she transfers it by saucepan to the bath, a laborious process that takes a good ten minutes, topping it up with cold. No wonder she'd never seen her grandmother bathing. She lies in the tub with the pink radio on a chair beside her, listening to an Irish station. There is a discussion about the phenomenon of returning emigrants coming back to a country they'd left a long time ago. 'It's history revolving,' a Professor Coughlan is saying. 'Life is, if you like, a carousel and what goes around comes around; every nation has its time, when it takes a step forward on the world stage.'

She imagines an Irish dancer, one of those girls she used to see attending the Maura O'Dwyer academy on Saturday mornings, stepping forward from behind a curtain and commencing a jig.

She supposes that's what she is in a way, a second-generation returnee. She'd asked her father if he wanted Glenkeen and he'd shaken his head vigorously. 'I'm too long away,' he'd said, 'there's been too much water under the bridge, I wouldn't want to be going back. And anyway, Barbara can't be travelling these days, she gets too tired. Your grandmother wanted you to have it; it's a gift of love. You could make something of it, you can do whatever you want, it could just be an escape hatch.'

She'd looked at him then, wondering how much he knew, what he might have told Nanna in the letters they exchanged but he had busied himself with the washing up.

She lowers her shoulders beneath the hot water. Sheer bliss. When she uses the soap, it creates a riot of soft lather. The day's activity had driven away thoughts, but the usual regrets and anxieties surface as soon as light starts draining from the sky and evening steals in. She has read that babies and old people often grow restless and disturbed as dusk approaches. Douglas has told her that there is a name for it in older people with memory problems – sundowner syndrome. It is the time when all the frettings of life's ragged edges encroach, the shadows of loss and longings, the whisper of things left undone. In his surgery, he briefs worried relatives who describe their elderly parents pacing the house, inconsolable, twisting their hands with worry, then passes them to the specialist nurse in the memory clinic. It seems to Liv that they suffer from a surfeit of memory rather than a lack of it, that they know only too well how the demons of the dark have their snares coiled at the ready.

This is the time of day when she recalls the disastrous milestones of her marriage such as the January evening Douglas phoned from the police station to tell her that he'd crashed the car. She was already worried at his lateness, glancing at the clock, getting up from watching the TV to peer through the curtains at the fierce, icy night. The weather forecast had advised motorists to stay off the roads unless their journey was absolutely necessary. *Pride and Prejudice* was on the TV, but she couldn't concentrate on Olivier's Mr Darcy and when the phone rang, she knew that it would be bad news. Douglas had sounded tinny, thin voiced. She felt as frozen as the glacial air outside as he told her he'd been breathalysed and photographed.

A police car had dropped him home and he had stumbled through the door, glazed still with drink, a clotted cut over his right eye and blood on his shirt collar. Bathing the eye with warm water and antiseptic, she had turned her face from his fume-laden breath. He was trembling, his skin warm and yeasty. There was mud on his trousers and coat sleeves and the hem of his coat was ripped. He looked and smelled like one of the street people who hung around outside the tube, mumbling their pleas for money. She gathered that he had driven into someone, that both cars had been written off but that miraculously, the other driver had also sustained only cuts. 'He must've been over the speed limit too, don't see why I get to take the rap,' Douglas had grumbled. Patting his brow with cotton wool, she had wanted to shake him, to hit him and return the violence he was visiting on her, on their lives.

'This can't go on, I'm not going to be your nurse when your liver packs in,' she'd told him the next morning, her voice snaked with bitterness.

But of course it had gone on, the dreary litany of 'just another glass, I can give up tomorrow if I want, it's just a question of determination'; the weekend health farm bookings for detox; the purchase of cases of spring water and mounds of grapefruit and oranges; the steady hum of the fruit juicer; the diets involving raw vegetables and pineapple; the use of medications that induced vomiting; the days when he looked paler, more frail than some of the patients who crossed his waiting-room. She had witnessed the good intentions, set up like the pins in the bowling alley, ready to be knocked down by the next seductive, brimming glass.

She wrings out the hot flannel and drapes it over her face,

hiding from the demons under the steaming veil. She dozes briefly, while the radio drones and the fire sparks and murmurs.

Her phone rings and she starts, slopping water over the side of the tub. She switches the radio off with a dripping hand and reaches for it.

'You get a signal OK then, down in the glen – or is it on or up in the glen?' Douglas says after a pause. He is speaking slowly and carefully. Familiar fingers pinch at her heart.

'Yes, no problem with a signal. How are you?'

'Oh . . . OK. Going to have something to eat in a min. I miss you.'

'I miss you too,' she says, a half truth. 'I've been really busy, cleaning mainly. I was just having a bath.'

'How d'you do that?'

'With a tin tub and a lot of difficulty. Four star it isn't.'

'Well, you wanted to go.'

'Yes, I did. I wasn't complaining.' She stares at her white legs beneath the water.

'You settled in, then?'

'I've made a start. Everything takes a long time; fetching and boiling water, cooking over the fire. It slows you down. It's good.'

'Sounds amazing . . . oops, sorry, phone slipped.'

'It's early yet for you to be drunk, you must have left the surgery in good time.'

'Hmm, not too busy today, just the average arthritic hip or two.' He clears his throat. She hears an intake of breath, can picture him trying to focus. 'Listen, I've rung AA, going for my first visit tomorrow night.' He has put on his wheedling voice.

'That's good, Douglas, it really is.'

'I'm trying, you know?' he mumbles.

'I know.' She stares into the fire, into the tiger flames. He seems a very long way away. She is glad of that. 'Let me know

61

how it goes, won't you?'

There is a fumbling. 'Sno big deal,' he says. 'I just have to get myself there, I can do that. A couple of sessions should see me right, no need for months of torture and self-recrimination. Don't want to change one habit for another, become one of those teetotal bores.'

She feels the dragging weight of his excuses like a stone around her neck. 'Yes, of course. Listen, I'm getting a bit chilly now and you need to eat. I'll ring you later tomorrow night, see how you've got on.'

'OK. See ya later. Love you.'

There is a crackling as he fades. He'll have bought a takeaway that he will fiddle with, eating a few forkfuls, spilling drifts of chicken tikka on the table as he misses his mouth. Finally he will give up, shoving the plate away and concentrate on his pack of beer or bottles of Frascati. She misses him, but in the way you would miss a nagging ache that you'd temporarily quietened with painkillers. No, that isn't even it; she mourns him, she is quietly grieving for the man she met and married, the man he used to be, the one who treasured her before the pale and amber liquids in the dewy glasses enticed him away and replaced her as the love of his life.

She shampoos her hair briskly, digging her fingers into her scalp to stop the scalding tears that spring, leaking from the corners of her eyes, and rinses it with clean cold water from a jug.

She has dressed and is contemplating the best way to empty the heavy tub when there is a light knock on the back door. A well-built man with eyebrows like wild hedgerows is standing with his hands in his pockets, whistling.

'You'd be Liv Callaghan,' he says.

'I would, yes.'

'The freckles are the same. I heard you were over.' He has on a dark suit, a mustard-coloured knitted waistcoat and a trilby. His white hair is luxurious and wavy and somehow familiar. It is in stark contrast to the ragged dark of his eyebrows.

'I think I know you but I'm not sure,' she confesses.

He holds out a hand. 'I'm Owen Farrell, your great-uncle – Bridget's – your nanna's – little brother. We haven't met for years. Last time I saw you, you had your leg propped on a chair and you were putting calamine lotion on your hives. The itching was driving you mental, you were twitching like a cat in a bag.'

She shakes his large hand, the size of a shovel. 'Come in,' she says. 'Are you the man who used to smoke Sweet Afton and are those your books upstairs?'

'Very probably. Bridget looked after me once when my Achilles tendon went on me. I was a runner back then, ran for the county. Anyway, one day the old Achilles went twang and Bridget said I needed feeding up. I'd try and blow the fag smoke out the window above but I'd say a lot sneaked back in.' He takes his hat off and scratches his head. 'What books did I leave?'

'Dickens, Tolstoy, George Eliot.'

'They're the companions to see you through, all right. I used to be able to read for hours but the eyesight's not so sharp now. The Achilles tendon's in great shape, though.' He looks around the kitchen. 'It's a long time since I was in here. It hasn't changed a bit. Bridget wasn't your one for the shock of the new.'

He sounds like Nanna, quiet voiced. He has the same deep set, dreamy eyes and rangy frame and what she thinks of as a countryman's walk, slow, from the hip. He picks up a brass bell with a stag's head handle and rings it.

'She got this in the flea market in Cork. I bought a boomerang the same day but I lost it soon afterwards in the fields beyond the house; it failed to come back. We went for tea and cake afterwards. I ate my first walnut whip, my first walnut too. The cream on my tongue was like velvet but I didn't care that much for the walnut, it was fusty tasting. It was my twelfth birthday, my first trip to the city. I thought I'd died and gone to heaven.'

'She must have been quite a bit older than you?'

'Seventeen years. I was an afterthought, my poor mother thought I was the menopause. When she found out she was pregnant she went to see the priest and he told her I was an extra blessing from God.' He shakes his head, grimacing. 'I'm not sure any of the family would have agreed with him. Bridget was more like my mother than my sister. This place is yours now.' He takes out a tobacco pouch and extracts a thin home-made roll-up. 'Mind if I light up?'

'No, go ahead. Nanna left me the cottage. It was an unexpected surprise. You don't mind, do you?' It suddenly occurs to her that this great-uncle might have come to raise an objection.

He shakes his head, trimming the end of the cigarette of its ginger tobacco shreds before lighting it. 'God, no.' He draws in deeply. 'Not much of an inheritance though; I'd say it would take a fair bit of work to make it sound. Are you going to keep it?'

'I honestly don't know yet. I'm still getting used to the idea of it being mine. I'm going to spend a bit of time here, get the feel of the place. It's so peaceful.'

'You think so?' He stands with a hand on the mantelshelf, looking into the fire, pushing a crackling log further in with the heel of his boot.

'Yes, don't you?'

'Well, now. I'd guess that peace is what a person brings to a place as much as anything. Make sure this fire's damped down before you go out and when you go to bed at night, the draught works well here. D'you know about raking the ashes?'

'No, what's that?'

'If you want the fire to stay in, not have to light it again the next

64

morning, heap a big pile of ash over some hot turf. It'll stay in and next morning you can put the bellows in under the ashes and apply gently; abracadabra, you'll have a flame before long.'

She listens carefully and to the laughter that touches his voice. It stirs a memory of blue smoke rings drifting through the window. 'I remember you now,' she says. 'You told me that the blue in blue cheese was made by cheese worms and that when the police put you in custody, it meant you had to stand in a bowl of custard.'

He throws his head back and laughs. 'What a terrible fellow I was, spinning stories like that to a child.'

'We were sitting at that table, having boiled eggs. Nanna told you off and warned me I was to take no notice of you. Then she threw the window open and ordered you to lean out with your cigarette.'

'She was right to tell you to ignore me.'

'I didn't eat blue cheese for years because of those worms.'

'I hope you forgive me now for depriving you.'

'I'll think about it. It was very traumatizing, you know.'

'Oh, I can imagine. Now, d'you want a hand emptying this?' He nudges the tub with his boot.

'Would you mind? I was wondering how to deal with it. I'd planned to drag it outside.'

'No need for that. It's the least I can do after terrorizing you in your early life. Open the door for me.' He picks the tub up by the handles, hefts it outside as she pushes the door back and throws the water in a wide arc over the bushes, then puts the tub upside down on the gravel. 'There, now.' He gestures at the heavy sky. 'We had a grand July this year, but August was a washout. They're threatening a sudden blast of summer now, so you might still get the benefit. The farmers could do with it, certainly.'

'I thought I might swim tomorrow,' she says.

He gives her a look. 'Jaysus,' he says, 'you English are half daft.

65

That sea would chill your bones – it's the Atlantic, remember. Next parish America.'

She laughs. 'I'll give it a go, even so. I used to swim down on the strand when I was little.' She can recall exactly the gritty, stinging sand particles in the breeze that always blew inshore, the jellyfish that floated in every July and made her run from the sea, frightened that their pale bodies might touch her, the shock of the cold green water against her goose-pimpled legs.

'Well, it's your funeral, as the magpie said to the worm as he ate him for breakfast. I'd best be on my way, I've a dog who needs his evening walk.' His cigarette has stuck to his bottom lip and he peels it off. 'If you want to visit, you're welcome. I'm just at the westerly edge of Castlegray, the house called Lissan. I could make one of my famous fry-ups.'

'Thanks, I will,' she says. 'Oh, before you go, would you take a photo of me, outside? I just wanted to mark this . . . this well, I suppose it's a kind of homecoming, isn't it?'

She fetches her camera and he snaps her quickly by a pot of scarlet geraniums. She likes the way he is businesslike, no fuss.

'Nice camera,' he says, examining it.

'Yes, it was a gift.' Another item from the guilt stash.

'There,' he says, handing it back. 'It makes a welcome change from all the sombre photographs of emigrants back down the years; tears and lamentations on the quayside. A great sign of the times, the old country opening up again. Now, I must love you and leave you.'

'Your hat,' she says, darting in for it.

He flicks the brim and fits it on his head. 'I felt for you,' he says, 'scratching at your skin. I used to get the hives too, when I was a child, big hot weals that would blister. At night they'd have me demented. I'd be poking them with a stick. My mother would give me sulphur tablets to cool and purify the blood. I still get itchy skin in spring and at the start of winter, I'm a seasonal creature.'

'Me too,' she says, 'little runs of itchiness, there one minute, gone the next.'

'We must have fiery blood, you and me.' He glances at her, smiling.

'Hives are an allergic reaction. You'd be given antihistamines now,' she tells him.

He takes a final suck of his cigarette and throws the stub into a bank of ferns. 'That's too clinical an explanation, too neat by a mile. I prefer the idea of hot blood. See you then, maybe.'

'Thanks for the help with the tub and the tip about the ashes,' she calls as he makes his way down the path.

He raises his hat and waggles it without looking back. On the road at the foot of the glen is a bright blue car. Inside, she can just make out a dog, its nose poking through the open window. It leaps up as it sees him approach, paws pressed to the glass. She watches until he's vanished from sight, remembering how one autumn, hives had come up on the soles of her feet and she'd walked barefoot on corn stalks after the harvest to find some relief. The sharp blades of the stubble had pierced the blisters and freed bright red ribbons of blood. Nanna had made her soak her feet in cold water in which she dissolved potassium permanganate crystals; her skin was stained a pale purple, the colour of ripe plums, for weeks afterwards.

She turns back into the cottage. Fiery blood; what does she know of Owen? Something had happened in the family, that was all she could recall. She remembers that summer when her mother had lost the baby who would have been her brother or sister and she was left with her grandmother; Nanna sitting by the fire, legs akimbo, a lamp by her side, reading a letter, whispering that her tyke of a brother had the heart across her and would live to rue the day. 'He'll find he's treading the sorrowful road after what he's done.' She had wanted to see the letter, curious to know who had written it and why Owen would find the road sorrowful but her grandmother had thrown it into the hissing fire and poked it sharply down until it was consumed to grey ash.

In the evening, after she had gone to bed, Liv heard the door closing and watched from the window as her grandmother made her way down to the well in the dusk, her shawl gathered around her shoulders. Bats swung above her head in a criss-cross dance, vague shapes in the half-light and Liv felt anxious at being alone. She got up and quietly followed her grandmother, sensing the tension in her back. Peering from behind the bushes, she had seen Nanna circling the well, round and round in a clockwise direction, her rosary playing through her fingers, whispering her prayers. Suddenly, she missed her parents and darted back to the cottage, running up the stairs and pulling the bedclothes up around her head.

Once, when she had been constructing a family tree for a school project, she'd asked her father to go through her grand-mother's side. He had counted off the names: Bridget, Dennis, Fergal, Oona. She had written them in, then asked what about Owen, wasn't he the youngest? Her father had pulled at his mous-tache, tested a wobbly chair, saying it needed mending. She had looked at him, puzzled, pen poised. Wasn't Owen the baby? she'd asked again. Her father had nodded, saying he'd better see to that chair before someone took a tumble from it. So she had written in the name, Owen, thinking again of the sorrowful road, imagining it as a thorny country path like the boreen that ran from Nanna's to the Moran's farm. The boreen was bumpy, bordered with this-tles, nettles and tall fat dandelions. When she walked it with her father he slashed the weeds and branches aside with a blackthorn stick, saying sternly, 'down, down, false pride, discourses die,' which was a line from a hymn they sometimes sang on Sundays.

She pictured Owen becoming tangled in the brambles as night was falling, without a stick to beat them back, wishing that he hadn't done the thing that made his road sorrowful.

She decides to go to Crowley's for supper. She lights a lamp and leaves it in the window to guide her back. Remembering Owen's advice, she closes the damper on the fire. Taking a torch, she sets off down the glen. The sky is almost dark, retaining just a faint flush of high, pink clouds and the air is sweet. A line of cows is lumbering along the road, calling mournfully, a young boy urging them, brandishing a stick, wobbling in oversized welling-tons. She waves to him and turns to Redden's Cross.

Aidan is meant to be doing his monthly accounts. He is in the study, the smallest, north-facing bedroom. The spreadsheet is open on the screen, the computer humming comfortingly. A spat-tering rain has started, weeping down the window. He shivers; unless the promised Indian summer arrives, they'll have to turn the heating on soon. The radiator in this room makes a grumbling sound like a low level complaint. He's bled it but can never find a remedy. It resists him, like the rest of the house. Despite his best efforts, the back door always sticks, the kitchen lino curls up at one edge and the dining table maintains its wobble. He is convinced that the house is built on a slant.

He totals a column. Nearly a year into his new business, he is making a modest income. The truth is, accounts, balance sheets and tax returns don't interest him much. It's the bustle and activ-ity of the market that makes his days, the frenetic early morning pace of the traders as they dart around in the dewy street, their shouts and calls, curses and laughter, the flavour of scalding, strong tea and a smoky frankfurter from the mobile café when the lorries have been unloaded, the cacophony of sounds from the country and western, traditional Irish and rock music sellers. Often as he grasps his mug with fingerless mittens and shivers with pleasure at the heat and the tart aftertaste of tannin, he thinks; just over a year ago I was staring at a screen in an air-conditioned, sterile office and drinking a coffee I didn't even register the taste of, eating muffins I wasn't hungry for. Now I have this keen, vitalizing air that hasn't been breathed by scores of other people and my stomach is desperate to be filled. He loves the way all the market people gradually unpeel, shaking themselves, slapping their arms, shedding layers of clothes as the dawn chill evaporates and the day comes into its own.

But above all, there is the pleasure of setting out the stall. He relishes the shapes and colours of the vegetables and fruit he sells, the cold earthy smell of the carrots, parsnips and celeriac, the slight scent of drains from cauliflower and broccoli, the hot glow of tomatoes and aubergines, the speckled skin of cidery apples. The pale ridges of celery remind him of corduroy. He likes the feel of the produce in his hands, the weight and contours, the ribbed skin of radishes and the rough whiskers of spring onions. The white turnips with the purple blush are coming in now, little cousins of the hefty orange swedes that smell acidic as you cook them, but are sweet on the tongue. You have to be careful with the little, soft-coated tangerines that will be arriving in the coming months, they bruise easily, their skin as tender as Carmel's. On the stall, they nestle cosily in their tissue wraps, orange and cream winter blossoms. He likes to polish peppers until they gleam and arrange his produce seductively; last October, his range of colourful pumpkins from pale cream through Hazelnut, burned terracotta and biscuit brown had brought admiring glances. He had constructed a witch's profile from pumpkin and turnip slices, with a hooked courgette for a nose. There had been a photo in the local paper for Halloween but it hadn't shifted much extra produce. He isn't sure the Irish are ready for pumpkin pie.

He runs his fingers around the edge of the keyboard. He has been dreaming about Liv and thinking of her; she is invading his sleeping and waking. The night before he'd married Maeve, he'd dreamed of her and woke, feeling hot and guilty. He had willed and secured the loss of her through recklessness, fear and bad judgement. Always, her memory is framed by the *what if?* question. He knows that this is also immature, that the past cannot be revisited and shouldn't be, for good reasons. He knows that he shouldn't consider the life they might be having now, the freckle-faced children they could have shared. Sometimes, though, it is hard not to hanker after what you've carelessly thrown away. And he hasn't sought the past; it has appeared before him, a living, breathing past, existing in a cottage in a glen just a few miles away.

A picture forms of the first time he saw her and he smiles. A friend who knew Liv through the university madrigal group had invited him to dinner with her, commenting that she made the best lemon meringue pie in the galaxy. They might never have met otherwise; he was in the final year of his Law degree, she in her second term reading English. Her flat was in Kentish Town, the tiny basement of a tall Victorian House with peeling paintwork and windows that rattled when the wind blew. He had been startled at the sight of her standing in the kitchen, balanced on her left leg, right foot swinging. She was wearing a bright pink cotton dress which made her freckles seem like exclamation marks. He had experienced an instant flash of recognition; he'd never felt that since, that sudden and complete yearning. She had been so unnerved by him that she accidentally tipped the lemon meringue pie she had just taken from the oven into the sink. The rescued, crumpled remains were eaten in bite-sized pieces, the pastry, filling and meringue a glutinous but wonderful-tasting mess with only a slight, occasional hint of washing-up liquid. Later, as he walked home, he had licked his lemony fingertips and wondered if she had freckles all over her body and when he might find out.

They had been together, inseparable, for almost a year. Her thin, muscular frame fascinated him; she was boyish and gutsy and he found her resolve mesmerizing. He felt that he would never want to be parted from her and yet somehow it was the strength, the fervour of the bond between them that came to terrify him. Dissatisfaction with himself had made him end the relationship; a deep unease that he had studied the wrong subject, the unspoken belief that there might be, must be other challenges, other experiences to be had, including other women to love. He felt himself to be unformed, needing breadth and density in his life and he fretted that his passion for her, the passion between them would wane and they would be trapped, opportunity flown, roads closed. He didn't want to complete his studies, marry, settle down into domesticity. Some of his friends were doing just that, consulting their parents about mortgages, looking at flimsy houses on estates in bleak suburbs where the mud from the building sites still spattered the kerbs and rows of shops offered bargains of the week. They were living their parents' small, ordered lives, as he saw it and the prospect of this repetition made him yawn with fear. He wanted to travel, breathe the air of other continents, wake to hear languages he didn't understand and Liv had another two years of her course to complete. Then his childless aunt died, leaving him twenty thousand pounds and the balance tipped; surely it was meant, a sign that he should trust his instincts. Right timing and wrong timing, he had persuaded himself as he agonized about how to tell her.

On a visit to his parents he discussed his predicament with his father, in that veiled, oblique way that men approach such conversations. He chose dusk, under the trees in the back garden so that he could try to hide his shame from this man of integrity whom he held in such esteem, he could barely approach him. He couldn't hope to emulate his father, who was a litmus paper of all that was honourable and scrupulous.

Aidan senior had come late to parenthood, fifty-two when his son was born and he was a gentleman of the old school, a barrister who experienced life in black and white, no room for blurring and evasion. He took no prisoners where behaviour to the fairer sex was concerned. When his son had stumblingly mentioned difficulties in his love life he leaned on his walking stick and pursed his lips. 'Be clear about your intentions. If you're going to break with the girl, do it quickly and cleanly; if you're not, marry her. Don't prevaricate, that's sheer self-indulgence.'

He finally spilled his decision out callously over a meal in the café with the numbing pop music playing and a lurid oil painting of sunset over Lake Maggiore on the wall by their table. There were no shadows, no concealing dusk to ameliorate the hurt in her open gaze.

'I just don't understand, what's wrong, is it me, something I've done or said?' She'd rubbed her eyes, as if trying to wake from a nightmare.

'No, it's not you at all, it's me, I'm not sure what I want or who I want.' And afterwards, in far-flung places – Shanghai, Boston, Mexico city, Bombay, he had looked in misted, speckled mirrors and disliked what he saw. He had been her first lover and he thought of himself as a predator. She had challenged him even in his leaving of her and he knew there would be a price to pay although what that price would be or when he would pay it was unknown.

He pushes the keyboard aside and draws a notepad towards him.

Dear Liv,

This will come as quite a surprise to you. I saw you leaving the shop at Redden's Cross a few days ago. My mother-in-law runs it. I couldn't believe my eyes at first, I had a shock. I still haven't recovered from it. I understand that your grandmother left you her cottage nearby. I thought that I would send you a note as we might very well meet by chance at some point. It would be good to see you, if that would be OK with you. Isn't it strange, how paths do cross in the most unexpected . . .

A fierce lash of rain hisses against the window. He glances at the clock, starts; time has vanished. Maeve is at her evening class and he has to pick up Carmel. He tears the page from the pad, dislodging a loose sheet that Maeve has jotted a shopping list on: washing up liquid, loo rolls, strong cheddar, sliced ham, sage and onion mix, hair grips, ankle socks, intensive moisturizer. The last item is for him, to replenish his cracked and torn hands. At the bottom she has drawn the round smiley face that she finishes all her notes with, a kind of reassuring flourish to herself. Her handwriting is girlish, with curlicues on the loops of her Ls and Gs. She'll have written it with the pen Carmel gave her for her birthday; pink lights flash on the end when the nib presses the paper. He reads the plain script of their intimate, daily routine and tastes the sourness of deceit in his throat. He tears up his note and shoves the shreds in his pocket, grabs his van keys and hurries out.

5

The barman in Crowley's has informed Liv correctly that their cheese and mustard baked spuds are hard to beat. He'd handed her the menu and looked at her, head on one side, as he rubbed the bar with his dishcloth, and said she looked as if she needed a bit of belly timber. She had felt strange and oddly looked after and dangerously weepy. The potatoes had arrived with a vivid carrot and tomato salad that reflect the colours of the fire near her table. The skins are crisp and the cheese is Gruyère and wonderfully elastic.

The pub is quiet this early on a Wednesday evening. The television is on above the bar, David Attenborough stalking big cats. A couple of old men in dark suits sit hunched in a corner by the fire, voices rumbling. The one time she'd visited Ireland with Douglas, a long weekend in Dublin and Wicklow, they'd joked that the same old men travelled around the bars, paid by the Irish Tourist Board to pose scenically with their pipes and flat caps. Why has she never brought him here, to the south-west? They could have visited Nanna, she could have shown him the places she'd played as a child, where she'd made dens, mixed magic potions down at the well, breathed an air dramatically different to Haringey's. She knows why; he had that cool English attitude to

75

Ireland, encouraged at his public school, an amused eye that viewed it as the land of the little people, Celtic mists and fey story-tellers. His parents had an Irish handyman at their country pile in Surrey who they always referred to as Macnamara. The first time she'd met them, his mother had said, 'Oh, isn't Callaghan a wonderfully Irish name.' Later that night, Douglas had crept along the hall to her bedroom and reassured her that beneath his mother's cool exterior lay a heart of ice. He whispered that his sister had told him that when he was a baby, his mother used to leave him out in all weathers in the pram to toughen him up. Liv had pulled him to her, astonished, wanting to warm him and make up for his infant deprivations. Later, when she heard about his semi drowning off Brighton, it was another piece of a bizarre jigsaw.

The pub door opens, letting in a gasp of rain and a turf-scented breeze. Mrs O'Donovan and Carmel run in, laughing and shaking themselves.

'Johneen, can you change a couple of notes for me?' Mrs O'Donovan asks the barman. 'Lord God, I just had my hair done today and the wind's after playing merry hell with it.' She peers in the wide, engraved mirror over the bar that advertises whiskey and reshapes her fringe.

The barman pings the till open, one handed, and pulls out notes. He holds the twenties that Eileen O'Donovan has given him up to the light, turning them this way and that, pretending that they might be fakes, winking at Carmel. Liv guesses that this is a regular routine. 'Ah, you're always a glamour queen to me, Eileen, aren't you the rose of Redden's Cross.'

Carmel sniggers and her grandmother gives the barman a knowing look. 'Never mind your old palaver, Johneen Crowley.' But she has her head to one side, appreciating her reflection.

When the transaction is complete, she looks around and sees

Liv across the room. She gives a little wave and moves over, Carmel alongside. 'And how are you going up there?' she asks: 'Getting along all right?'

'Fine, thank you. I've been cleaning all day so I thought I'd treat myself to a meal. The food's lovely.'

Mrs O'Donovan scans her plate. 'Oh, for sure. I'll tell my son-in-law. He provides Johneen with all his fruit and veg. You couldn't get fresher.'

Carmel is pulling her grandmother's sleeve. 'Gran, maybe the lady will know.'

'Know what, pet?'

'About the general knowledge questions, especially the book one. Do you know about books?' Carmel asks Liv, tracing a line of moisture on the tabletop.

'I should, I'm a librarian,' Liv answers.

'Ah now, don't be bothering Miss Callaghan, she's trying to eat her dinner,' Mrs O'Donovan says, propping a hip against a chair and folding her arms across her chest. She is wearing an identical trouser and shirt outfit today, but in a lime green. There is something about the cut and quality of the material that make Liv think she buys her clothes from catalogues. Her own mother had been a catalogue fiend; bulky parcels had constantly arrived and been despatched from the house. She had maintained that there was nothing like trying things on in the comfort of your own home and would make Liv and her father sit while she paraded different dresses and suits for their inspection.

'That's OK, I've nearly finished eating anyway. And call me Liv, please. What's the question, Carmel?'

'It's in my homework. Who wrote *The Call of The Wild*?'

'Jack London.'

Carmel beams. 'Wow, that was quick – you should be on *University Challenge*!'

77

'You're welcome. What's the other question?'

'We got some of it; it's what's the seven wonders of the ancient world? We got The Hanging Gardens and the Pyramids but then we were stumped.'

Liv laughs. 'My mother used to say that it was one of the seven wonders of the world that I ever got to school on time. Now, let's think.' She ticks them off on her fingers. 'The Colossus of Rhodes, the Statue of Zeus, the Temple of Artemis, the Mausoleum at Halicarnassus, the Lighthouse at Alexandria. That makes the seven with your two.'

'Thanks, that's great, isn't it, Gran?'

'Oh yes,' Eileen O'Donovan says brusquely, 'the wonders of education for those lucky enough to have the advantage.'

Liv blinks. Is she supposed to apologize for knowing? 'My pleasure,' she says and because of that remark she adds, 'Any other answers you don't know?'

'No, that's the lot. Are you in a big library?'

'Pretty big, it serves a London borough.'

'Do you get to read a lot?'

'Not as much as I'd like. I'm hoping to catch up on some books while I'm here.'

'Oh, for sure and you should have the peace and quiet anyhow, up there alone, not a soul to bother you,' Mrs O'Donovan says.

'I hope so. I had my first visitor today though, my uncle.'

Mrs O'Donovan straightens up, her pencilled eyebrows arching high with surprise. 'Would that be Owen Farrell?'

'That's right. It's ages since I saw him.'

Mrs O'Donovan nods. 'It's a long time since he's been to Glenkeen, that's for certain. Did you hear that, Johneen?' she called to the barman. 'Owen Farrell was up at Glenkeen today.'

The barman scratches his nose with a tea towel. 'Ah well, it's not a no-go area these days, I suppose. Times change, and isn't it just as well that they do.'

The television blares the evening news and several customers hurry in, calling greetings. The pub is suddenly busy and humming. An old man throws another lump of turf on the fire, creating a shower of sparks that glint scarlet in the mirror behind Johneen.

'We must go, Carmel's daddy will be here soon but can I interest you in a raffle ticket?' Eileen O'Donovan says, reaching into her shoulder bag. 'It's for a health centre in West Africa, I run it every year, they're only a pound each.'

'We get photos from the nurses,' Carmel informs her, 'and this year we're buying them proper toilets and showers.'

Liv gets out her purse. 'Of course, I'll take a couple.'

'The prizes aren't great, but sure it's the cause that's important,' Eileen O'Donovan says, handing over the tickets. She is standing very close. Liv moves her chair back.

'First prize is a big basket of my dad's stuff from his stall,' Carmel adds. 'It comes with a lovely red ribbon round it. Last year someone said it was like a work of art, they said it could be in that place in London, that gallery where they had the bricks.'

'Tate Modern,' Liv tells her. 'Well, I'll keep my fingers crossed that I win it – you never know, I might sell it to an art dealer and make my fortune.' She folds the tickets, thinking how fortunate it is that Carmel's huge limpid eyes save her serious face from looking fractious.

Aidan pushes open the pub door and peers in. The warmth bathes his face, misting his glasses. The malty scent of stout washes over him. There was no reply at the shop and Eileen likes a chat with Johneen in the evenings when trade is slow and she gets fidgety. She is a woman with a low boredom threshold. As he looks around, using his fingers like windscreen wipers across his lenses, he sees them across the room; Eileen and Carmel with their backs to him and Liv with head bent, zipping her purse. She is wearing silver ear-rings with inset blue stones that sway as she moves. Her ears are small and neat; she has a habit of tucking her hair behind them before she eats. The breeze catches his shirt, chilling his damp scalp. He backs out, letting the door slam and hurries across the road to his van. Climbing in he sits, staring through the oily windscreen at the rain and the blurred lights of cars turning at the crossroads. He has parked on this spot hundreds of times but he's never before noticed that the gate at the side of Crowley's has a lion's head on the right-hand post. He thinks how easy it is not to see the obvious.

Leaning forward, he grips the steering wheel, rubbing the clammy, familiar ridges. He says her name in the safety of the cab: Liv. It sounds like a caress. He repeats it, over and over, tapping the wheel, chanting so that she has become a mantra. He knows in that moment, with a sense of delight and desolation, that he has never stopped loving her. He has been travelling and living and marrying and becoming a father and all the time she has been there like a subtle melody that plays through your days without you noticing. And now his love has become a destitute refugee, looking for acceptance, hoping for shelter.

His life seems strange to him, as if he barely inhabits it. His reflection in the windscreen is indistinct. Forgetting his daughter, the homework she will have, the spaghetti he's supposed to be cooking, he starts the engine and drives aimlessly around the roads. To be moving is not having to think. He's the man who is supposed to have had his mid-life crisis; certainly, he knows that that's how Maeve interpreted his change of career. He'd heard segments of the sotto voce phone conversations with her mother, when she thought he wasn't listening: '. . . they say that men have hormone swings too, I read an article about it in *Cosmopolitan* . . . he says it's as if he's driven into a brick wall . . .'

The rain withdraws, slowly and stubbornly, the sky washed and soft. The hedgerows are drenched. He passes the sculpture to the dead of the Civil war and a small Celtic cross at the side of the road, marking where a woman was killed by a runaway tractor in 1947. The van drifts along, guiding itself.

There is a deserted, decaying house a couple of miles on. The man who had lived in it was a bachelor with no relatives. There's talk that a Dublin family might buy it, if they can get a grant to do it up. He turns in to the track and stops by the barred gate. Pushing his way through the tangle of brambles and dog roses, he walks to the back. Sheep have been here, nibbling the sweet grass down to short tufts, leaving their droppings. He bends double, letting his head hang between his knees, arms dangling so that the sound of blood in his ears will drown out the confusion roaring through his brain. He breathes noisily in and out, great whooshes of air. His diaphragm rises and falls. He thinks back to the yoga he practised in Bombay and tries to concentrate only on that intake and exhalation. Then he sits on a wooden chair that's been left next to a rusting lawn mower and presses his hands to his thighs to stop them trembling.

The day is set fair, the promised fine weather arriving stealthily during the night. Liv wakes to a clear sky and a bold sun. She throws the bedroom window open and holds her hands out, as if she could catch the drifting sweetness in the air. Isn't it something, she thinks, to be responsible for nobody but myself, to have to account only for myself. There is a thin mist at sea, hanging lazily on the horizon but this will burn away by mid morning. The breeze is salted, tangy and the earth, still warm, is taking its final breaths before hunkering down for the winter.

She has a routine going now, the days measured; trips to the well morning and evening frame the hours in between. By the water, she listens carefully to the murmuring and drinks deeply, hoping to imbibe some badly needed wisdom and regeneration.

First thing, she breathes life back into the fire and breakfasts on eggs or bread and blackberries from the garden. Then she washes, kneeling in front of the fire, dipping the flannel into a dish of hot water. Every other morning she washes her hair, rinsing it outside, shaking it dry in the sun. The soft water is making it glossy, taming her natural frizz. When she looks in the mirror she sees someone different; it is as if she has been freshly ironed. The well is working its magic, she thinks. Each morning she handwashes her underwear from the day before and hangs it on the line stretching across the heavy beam above the grate. All her clothes are scented now with peat, as if she spends her time stoking bonfires. She tidies the kitchen and wanders outside, exploring for vegetables and fruit.

For lunch she has bread and cheese, sitting on a chair by the honeysuckle that frames the back door. She washes the food down with creamy milk. The bread is nutty, heavy, the cheese sharp. She likes the solid sensation in her stomach. She reads for a while, then dozes in the sun. When she wakes she goes for a swim and floats, gazing at the unusually blue sky. She is eating bulkier food and more than she's used to, yet she feels lighter, unburdened. There are times when she finds herself smiling for no reason.

For her evening meal she eats the thick soup she has made in the biggest pot; every day she adds another handful of vegetables and lets it simmer away. She reads again with a lamp at her elbow until her eyes grow tired. She makes cocoa to take to bed and lies in the dark, sipping.

There is a hypnotic quality to this routine. She deliberately leaves her watch in the dresser and judges the hours by her hunger and the light. Her thoughts are abstract and random. At times her mind is almost still. She rarely thinks of Douglas. These hours and days have the rhythm of childhood, a time when the hardest lessons were how to tie your shoe laces and the moon riding the night sky outside your window was undoubtedly made of green cheese. It strikes her that she is living her grandmother's existence, without the hard work and that this is the true inheritance.

Today is going to be different; she is planning to visit Owen. She props the window open, heads downstairs for coffee and sets off for the well, selecting blackberries on the way. The seeds hide between her teeth and she seeks them with her tongue, crunching them. Kneeling, she drenches her face and listens to the spring's musings. The shape of her head is reflected back, wavering. She recalls her parents kneeling at night in the living-room for the rosary; her mother always looked up trustingly at the picture of the holy family, her beads held out before her, her father would lean over the back of a chair, head down, rosary dangling as if he didn't hope for much. She has a notion, like a nerve that twitches involuntarily, inexplicably, that at some point in his life her father lost his energy and confidence. Barbara suits him because he can hide behind the curtain of her ailments. She is also frightened of Ireland and its troubles and this is fine with Liv's father, who visited Glenkeen even less frequently after his remarriage.

On the way back to the house she picks more blackberries, for Owen. She assumes that a man who can do a fry-up might stretch to a blackberry tart or crumble. In the middle of the night she had woken and retrieved a whisper of information that Owen married but it didn't last. She doesn't know how she came by this information or whether it is true – maybe it had been the cause of her grandmother saying he would travel the sorrowful road or it was in one of the letters that used to arrive from Nanna or from Uncle Brendan who is Father Brendan, running a parish in Saskatchewan. Her father would read aloud from these letters over breakfast, snippets of news about Castlegray, people who

83

had moved away or died, or the successful whist drive that
Brendan had recently organized. But there were times when he
would stop, shoot a significant glance at her mother and turn the
page. Then, once Liv had left the room, she would hear them talking in low voices; *spsss spsss spsss*, like the noise that came from
the tap when her father was replacing a washer. Sometimes she
would move near the door and listen but could only ever catch
phrases – 'the waters broke early . . . and never another word
exchanged . . . they had to send for the doctor . . .'

Certainly, a talent for fry-ups could indicate a bachelor life;
when she visits today, she will see for herself. There are bush
tomatoes in a plot near the back door and she picks ripe ones,
putting these in a carrier bag next to the blackberries.

On her way to Owen's house, she posts the note she's written
to Douglas. She can be kinder to him on the page and when writing, she feels a nicer person. And he likes letters; ruled by the
computer on his desk in the surgery, he grumbles about the
Internet and shoddy punctuation.

I'd forgotten how enchanted this place is; the air is sweet and
the silence pure. I shouldn't have stayed away so long. I am
swimming in the sea. The forecast Indian summer has arrived
and the water is a shock at first, but then warm enough.

I've had a chance to explore the garden now. I found potatoes and a purplish green bean, spinach, onions and a big
bed of tomatoes, the small sweet kind. My very own harvest.
I have a big soup/casserole on the go all the time.

I'm going to see my great-uncle Owen who has a slightly
abstracted air. He's a bit like a north London intellectual to
look at. Some kind of scandal surrounds him from way back,
the kind that means your name isn't mentioned.

The cottage is pretty shipshape for now and with Owen's

84

advice I've got the knack of keeping the fire in which saves on labour and firelighters, although sometimes it takes too long to rekindle and I cheat. The place will need some work doing longer term, though. It's nice to lie in the sun and daydream about it. Reminds me of when we were buying our house and we sat up late at night, doing drawings of how we'd arrange things, have the fireplaces put back, knock through the kitchen and scullery. I never expected our life together to turn out like this. I don't understand why it has. There are times when I've thought that I must have disappointed you in some way, that the drink fills a gap I've left.

I want you to succeed at AA. You're muffled in a cocoon, there's a dense, impenetrable blanket wrapped around you. If you can imagine a life without a drink then you can have such a life. Please try.

I'm happy here. I'd forgotten the simple trick of being happy. I'm sure we had it once.

Don't forget to pay the window cleaner.

On the way to Castlegray she passes modern bungalows and cultivated gardens, a place selling tourist goods with a tea shop attached, a building with a plaque saying it had once been a national school and is now a craft centre selling pottery and tweed. Nearing the town, she stops at a garage and asks for Owen Farrell of Lissan. A skinny man with thick glasses is sitting on a camping stool at the side of the petrol pumps, drinking from an enamel mug and reading a newspaper. He nods, telling her to carry on straight for a mile, then right at a T-junction and she'll find the house up on the left on the corner, a couple of hundred yards past the creamery.

'It has wrought-iron gates, tall yokes. If you're going up there, would you fetch his shopping? I've it ready inside. It'd save me a trip.'

She says of course and he disappears, returning with a large cardboard box which he places on the back seat of the car.

'Could you tell him as well for me that Jimmy'll be up to look at the septic tank Monday week?' He scratches his head. 'Would you be the niece from London?'

'That's right.'

'Yes, he said there was a young girl over. Well, good luck, now.'

She follows the directions and turns at the junction on to a single track road. She sees the sign for the creamery, with a smiling cow like the one on a French cheese and drives on slowly. The gates are old, tall and open, leading on to a long driveway bordered by trees. His blue car is parked outside the house, a substantial, traditional double-fronted building – handsome, imposing, even. She is surprised, having been expecting a cottage or farmhouse.

She hefts the box from the car and knocks at the front door but there is no reply. When she looks in at the two front windows set on either side of the door the place seems empty. The room on the left is lined with bookshelves and dotted with armchairs, the one on the right holds a large dining table and chairs. She walks around the side of the house, along a narrow path, to the back door. The corners of the box are rubbing her arms. The back door is open. She knocks and waits but there is no response. She pushes against it and walks into a turf-scented, square kitchen which is so full of light, she blinks.

The dog is asleep in a basket by the range and Owen is sitting at the kitchen table by the window with his back to her. He has earphones on and is reading a book. She moves across the stone-flagged floor and he looks up as her shadow falls on the book.

'I didn't know petrol pump Peadar had taken on new help,' he says, removing the earphones.

'Yes, his rates are impressive and he referred to me as a girl. He said to tell you that Jimmy will be here to look at the septic tank on Monday week.' She puts the box on the table.

'Typical, putting things on the long finger.'

'Sorry?'

'The long finger; putting something off, postponing things, mañana; the curse and blessing of this country.' He tilts his chair back, closing his book with his nicotine-stained fingers. 'So you came and you got directions from Peadar?'

'Yes, and I brought you blackberries and tomatoes from Glenkeen.' She looks at the book. It is the story of Albert Speer, Hitler's architect. She'd read it several years back, when Douglas was on a more rigorous than usual bender and she'd wanted complete distraction. She knows the detailed framework of her life, the hows, whys and whens in terms of Douglas's liquid intake. Owen sees her glance.

'Herr Speer,' he says. 'I think the woman writing about him fell in love with him.'

She nods. 'When I read that book I understood for the first time how very sexy Hitler was, I appreciated what drew people to him. Before that, I'd only ever seen him as a demon or a strutting fool.'

He looks at her with approval. Today he is wearing a green waistcoat and brown corduroy trousers. With his glasses perched halfway down his nose and his wild shock of hair, he looks as if he is about to give a poetry reading in Hampstead. He picks up a cushiony plastic tube, like one of those executive stress toys, and works it with his left hand, squeezing and relaxing.

'It's a fascinating story, but I have to listen to Verdi while I read it, to balance the taint of it all, the flavour of corruption. Take the weight off your feet.' He gestures at a chair.

She sits, pushing the box further along the table. He draws it towards him and peers in. 'Ah yes, the usual gourmet fare; soups, pilchards, sausages. Oh, and some surprise tinned artichokes. You know, I don't really need the delivery any more. It was handy a couple of years back one winter when I had terrible bronchitis and was as weak as water. Now I can't bear to cancel because Peadar always puts in something unexpected to see will I say anything. Last time it was dried bananas, the time before that, coconut milk.'

'And do you – say anything?'

'No, that's the joy of the game. But one day when Peadar drops in, you see, I'll make him an artichoke sandwich or put coconut milk in his tea and he won't know what it is but he won't be able to ask and then we'll be square. You have to make your own amusements in the countryside.'

The dog gives a loud snore and twitches noisily.

'That's not much of a guard dog,' Liv says. 'I could have been a burglar.'

'Toby? Sure, he's nearly as old as his master and half deaf.' He turns in his chair. 'Toby! Toby! Cats, the place is awash with cats! See?' he says, as the dog sleeps on. 'A hopeless article. Now, I usually have brunch around noon. Will you join me?'

'A famous fry-up?'

'That's it. One of those inside you, you won't need much for the rest of the day.'

While he juggles bacon, sausages, eggs, white pudding, potato bread and tomatoes in a vast cast-iron frying pan, she follows his instructions and lays the table. His cupboards are wide and deep and smell of allspice. He burrows for bread in Peadar's box and saws slices, holding the loaf against his chest and cutting towards himself.

'You look very like your mother,' he says, dropping the slices roughly on a plate.

She puts the salt and pepper cruets on the table. 'Mrs O'Donovan at Redden's Cross said I look like my dad.'

He snorts. 'What would that old biddy know.' He mimics her. 'Oh, for sure, aren't you terrible like your daddy?'

Liv giggles, delighted to find someone who speaks in the same codes as her. 'Why does she talk like that?'

'She went off to America a while back, came back with startlingly white teeth, a new hairdo and that "for sure" affectation. You have your mother's expression – and the freckles. How long has Mollie been gone now?'

'Seven years, nearly. I miss her every day. She was so lively, a buzz came into a room with her.'

'I remember. She had the gift of making laughter. And your father remarried?'

'Yes. Barbara. She's a pleasant enough woman and Dad's content with her. She has quite a few health problems and he likes looking after her.' She leaves a pause, then says, 'When I mentioned in Crowley's that you'd called on me, there was great interest. Mrs O'Donovan's eyebrows vanished into her hairline.'

He forks spitting sausages. 'I can imagine. I hadn't been to Glenkeen for . . . how old are you?'

'Thirty-eight.'

'Nearly thirty years, then. Long time. Now Toby, Toby! Are you going to have a sausage?'

The dog opens one eye, yawns and turns around before settling back to sleep.

'He's too well fed.'

She stands with a bottle of ketchup in her hand, perplexed. 'Do you mean you didn't see Nanna in all that time?'

'Ah no, we met up every Christmas Eve in the town for a pot of tea and a chat. You know, neutral territory.' He shakes the pan, flipping bacon over. He is an extravagant, messy cook. He is frying in butter and spattering grease on the hob. He skips a mushroom high in the air with the wooden spoon and catches it in his mouth. 'Perfecto. We're ready to roll now. Have we butter?'

Questions are jostling on her tongue. 'We have. I'm starving, I had some blackberries ages ago.'

He hands her a heaped plate. 'There now, that'll put hairs on your chest.' He pours strong, dark tea from a teapot with a knitted cosy.

She tucks in. It is cooked to perfection, the bacon and sausage crisp, the tomatoes browned, the eggs firm but runny. She dips bread into the egg yolk.

'Oh,' she exults, 'it's wonderful. You know, I've been for some posh meals in London but this is hard to beat. What is it with men and fry-ups? My husband, Douglas, has to have one every Sunday morning, even in a heatwave.'

He spears a tomato, holding his fork in the air. 'It's slow-burn food, so it keeps you going while you're out hunting and gathering.'

'And what do you hunt and gather?'

'Not a lot these days. Most of the land here is rented out. I dabble a bit in antiques, buying and selling and I still go up to Dublin occasionally and do some work, radio stuff mostly. But even as an actor, you suffer the invisibility of age, especially as we have such a young population.'

'You're an actor?' She puts her fork down and takes a gulp of tea, scalding her tongue.

'Yes, on and off, over the years. More off than on.'

'I had no idea.'

'No? Well, I've no idea what you do.'

'I'm a librarian.'

'So, we both have careers in the printed word. More tea?'

She holds her mug out. 'I know almost nothing about my father's family. My mother was an only child, adopted, and her parents were dead, so that's a simple story. But the Callaghans and the Farrells; my father's hardly ever spoken about them.'

Owen stirs three spoons of sugar into his tea. 'I suppose when you emigrate everything changes for you, distance is inevitable. And it works both ways – the people left behind may know very little of the emigrant's family. I didn't know you had a husband called Douglas.'

She curls her fingers around the warm mug. 'Yes, he's a GP.'

'And what does he think of your legacy?'

'I'm not sure, yet. Listen, I have to ask; what's the story about you and Glenkeen? There are lots of hints and allusions. I can remember a letter and Nanna being upset. Why did you meet her on neutral territory, did something happen?'

He wrinkles his nose at her, waves a dismissive hand. 'Ah, that's old history, best left well buried in an unmarked plot. This country's blight, clinging to what's past. Move on, that's my motto.'

An expert herself at avoiding the tricky interrogator, she understands that she has trespassed, and is embarrassed at her rushed questioning. 'What have you acted in – any films?'

'Just a couple, bit parts, you know – the traffic warden or the man outside the tube station who says, "That's OK, guv", when someone's trodden on his toe.'

'Oh, so you acted in London?'

'A couple of times. Last time was in the early seventies.'

'Did you stay with us, I can't remember.'

'No, I was in a B and B in Hammersmith, near the river. I used to watch the rowers in the early morning. I loved the Thames. My landlady was a Jehovah's witness, she used to try and convert me over breakfast.' He nods at her plate. 'That hardly touched the sides.'

'Food always tastes good when someone's cooked it for you.'

'So how are you faring in your cottage?'

91

'Fine. I'm sleeping deeply, I haven't slept so well for years. And I'm finding time to read. Time to just *be*.'

'Ah yes, company's good but so is rich solitude.'

She seizes the timely cue. 'And you, have you ever married?'

He lines his cutlery up on his plate, balancing the handles. 'I married, yes. It didn't work out. We've been apart many years. My wife lives five miles away.'

'And do you see her?'

'No. Or only by accident. Sometimes I see her in the car with her brother, or maybe across the street in Castlegray.' He's looking thoughtful, mellow, so she risks a further question.

'Did you have children?'

'No. That's a regret. I haven't had much talent for loving, though, so maybe it was for the best.' He rubs his chin and looks at Liv. 'It's strange, you know, I miss Edith, my wife, more now than I did after we parted. I never expected to miss her so keenly after so many years.'

She nods, not knowing what to say. 'I remembered something else about you last night,' she tells him. 'There is a gramophone at the cottage, a wind-up one with a horn and you told me that a man called Charlie lived in there and sang the songs. I used to put sweets down the horn for him in case he was hungry.'

'Just as well I didn't have children, they'd have turned out head-cases.'

The cooling frying pan gives a sigh and settles on the hob. Toby wakes, licks his coat and pads to Owen, laying his muzzle on his knee.

'Well now, Toby, what do you think of our visitor from over the sea? Isn't she a breath of fresh air in our male stronghold?' He holds out a scrap of bacon rind and the dog licks it efficiently from his palm.

'I was thinking,' Liv says, gathering crumbs from the table and dusting them on to her plate, 'you could give petrol pump Peadar artichoke tortilla, that would floor him.'

Owen pats Toby. 'You see,' he confides to the dog, 'she's a kindred spirit, a fellow voyager on the ship of life.'

6

The afternoon is hot with a light breeze as she drives back. The car speeds along the roads, the sun glancing through the windows, warming her face. There are drifts of dandelion in the air, white dancing fluff. They look like hope. When she arrives at the cottage she takes her swimming costume from over the fire and makes for the sea. It is a ten minute walk, with a narrow path at the bottom of the second field that leads down steeply to the deep cove. She has seen no one else here. The sand is smooth, no other footprint. The sea is calm, whispering in. Far out, on the horizon, is a tanker. It looks becalmed. She slips into the water, shaking her head at the slight chill, walking until she is up to her waist. The sand shelves away slowly; as she feels the clammy kiss of seaweed on her calves she launches forward and swims out towards the tanker. She floats, wondering where the great vessel is heading. The sun shimmers on the water, creating diamonds in the tips of the waves. From nowhere slides a memory of being in Rhodes with Douglas, falling asleep on a beach after drinking retsina and eating glossy spiced olives. He had to be careful of his pale skin becoming sunburned so they sprawled under a canvas umbrella. Just now, she misses him, wishes she could have that man again, the one who used to make her laugh with stories of eccentric patients, the one who taught her how to do handstands and back flips in the sand and could do uncanny impressions of Cary Grant and Jack Nicholson.

After a while she grows terribly thirsty; Owen had been liberal with the salt and the sea spray on her lips makes her dry.

Once out of the sea, she hops over the stile that leads back into the garden, thinking that she will have a glass of water and then a nap. It is warm enough to lie outside. As she passes the tomato bed she sees a man at the back door. He has his back to her and an envelope in his hand. The bright sun is in her eyes and she can just make out his shape, the check plaid of the shirt he wears outside his jeans. She steps to one side, into the shade of a rhododendron and sees the head, drinks in the stance. He is wearing a workman's boots, high around the ankles. Owen's fry-up lurches mutinously in her stomach and she swallows. Her tongue is parched.

'Yes?' she calls, her voice sliding, like an old woman's.

He turns and stands still, cradling the envelope in two hands before him. 'Hallo, Liv.'

'Aidan.' She holds on to the damp bundle of costume and towel. Water is trickling from her hair, sending a chill along her neck.

'I'm sorry to give you a shock. I was about to leave you a note.' He has grey hairs over his ears. He wears glasses, fashionable dark rectangles. The breeze catches the edge of the envelope, rustling the white paper. A grasshopper clicks nearby.

She hasn't felt faint since the age of nine, when she'd keeled over after Mass one Sunday in the churchyard and been sick amongst the daffodils. She'd been worried because she had vomited up the Host – the guilt had invaded her sleep – and the next week in confession, she had informed the priest that she'd sicked up God. He'd reassured her that God would understand that this had not been a deliberate rejection of His body and blood.

'How?' she asks, and her voice reverberates in her head.

'I live in Castlegray. I saw you at Redden's Cross.' He shrugs.

'You live here?'

'Yes. I moved here two years ago.'

'God. I mean, that's just . . . incredible.'

'I know.'

'I'm . . . well, let me open the door. I can't think in this sun.'

She turns, goes in. The kitchen is shaded, the fire a quiet glow. Her T-shirt and shorts are sticking to her. I must look a fright, she thinks. Her knickers and bra hang there brazenly over the fireplace. She feels panicky. There is a fist now in her stomach, squeezing and turning.

She falls back on the social nicety her mother would use in such a situation; usually when the priest called and she wasn't decent. The worst occasion was on an afternoon when her mother had been using a depilatory cream on her legs, a thick pink layer, and Father Dorkan's broad figure had loomed outside the front door. As he pressed the bell her mother had quickly washed her legs, using the shower head frantically so that it sprayed all over the bathroom floor. The pungent smell of the cosmetic, of decaying roses, filled the house. Father Dorkan had wrinkled his nose and grimaced. His eyes had taken in her mother's bare legs, the skin inflamed from a rough towelling.

'I wasn't expecting visitors,' Liv says now.

'I'm sorry to arrive like this. In a way, I was relieved that you were out. I was going to put this note through the front door.'

'Just as well you didn't try. The letter box is stuck. The postman leaves stuff inside the shed if I'm not in. Not that there's much post. I've been swimming.' She fingers her hair, squeezing the ends.

'Is the sea warm enough?'

'Not really, but it's so inviting and I love to swim, but I hate the chlorinated pools of London.'

'You still live there?'

'Yes, I've never moved, since university. I had no travel bug.'

There is a silence. A log shifts in the fire.

'Would you like a cup of tea? I'm dying for a hot drink after the cold water.'

He looks at his watch. A lock of hair dangles over his forehead and he pushes it back impatiently. 'Thanks, that would be good.'

She rakes the fire and throws clods of turf on, pulls the kettle over and while it bubbles, takes the tin of tea from the mantelpiece overhead. While she fiddles with the teapot, he moves to the front window and looks out, arms folded across his chest. He blocks the light and while his back is turned she snatches her underwear from the line and shoves it behind a cushion on the settee. God, she thinks, this is like a drawing-room comedy and nothing like a drawing-room comedy at the same time. She makes the tea clumsily, spilling leaves on to the hearth, splashing hot water over her foot. The shock brings her into herself, calms her.

They pull two chairs to either side of the fire and sit there drinking their tea. If anyone looked through the window, she realizes, they'd think we were Darby and Joan, together for years, indulging in our afternoon ritual. She looks directly at him, returning his gaze.

'I feel sick, as if I'd been punched in the stomach. That's the second time in my life you've made me feel like that; once with a goodbye and now with a hallo.'

He sits the way he always sat, the way big men do, leaning forward slightly, legs apart and forearms resting on his thighs, balancing his teacup in the air. 'I can only say that I'm sorry and I am. I was cruel. I'd have understood if you'd refused to let me in, let alone making me a cup of tea.'

97

'I'd always make you a cup of tea. Of course, you don't know what I might have slipped in it. You could be sipping with the Lucretia Borgia of county Cork.'

He drinks and pulls a face. 'Ah yes,' he nods, 'bitter almonds.' He puts the cup down on the grate, touches the bellows. 'This is a lovely cottage. I like the way it stands high in the glen. It gives you the feeling that you can breathe.'

'It beats London at the moment, that's for certain. This is where I came when you dumped me. I stayed for a week, holed up, licking my wounds. Isn't it strange that you should appear here, of all the places we could have met?' She wants to lash him with hurtful words; she never had a chance before. She's shocked at herself, that so much rancour could have survived the years and spill from her tongue, unbidden. There are things it's better not to know about yourself, better not to trawl the deep-shelved caverns of your own enmity.

He winces, shaking his head.

'And where do you live?'

'Castlegray. That's where I live and work.'

'What do you do?'

'I sell fruit and vegetables.'

'And do you enjoy that?'

'Yes. I had – well, a kind of breakdown a couple of years ago, I was in a bad way. I had to change my life.'

'Did your past catch up with you?' Now *she* winces at herself. 'I'm sorry, that's a nasty thing to have said. I'm in shock, seeing you like this. I can just about hold the cup steady.'

'I know. I only appear a bit steadier because I've had a week's headstart, time to think. It's all right, you haven't said anything I don't deserve. You've not said anything I haven't said to myself, many times.'

They both sip their tea in a kind of truce.

'And you, Liv, how has your life been?'

'Eventful, not always as I'd imagined it. I find that I'm happy here. I sleep and I don't recall dreaming. In London, my sleep rampages with busy, technicolour dreams. I wake up stunned some mornings, it can take me half the day to straighten my head. Here I'm pacing myself, taking my time, breathing. I'd forgotten how to breathe.'

He looks at her, nods, a peaceable glance. She thinks, he understands what I'm saying. How come it's so easy to talk to him after all this time? 'Where did you go, Aidan, when you left London?'

'More like where didn't I go! India, South America, Australia and lots of other places.'

'I used to think that maybe one day I'd get a postcard, a phone call. You never thought of getting in touch?'

He sighs, shifting his shoulders. 'I thought of it, of course. But I reckoned it wouldn't be fair on you. What would I have said? Life changes shape. I liked to think that you were better off without me.' He gulps the last of his tea, glances at his watch again.

'Don't let me keep you,' she says, making her voice chilly. 'You seem anxious about the time.'

'I do have to go now, I have to fetch my daughter. I called on impulse. I didn't know at all if it was the right thing and I didn't mean to stay.' He rises and takes his van keys from his pocket, jingling them by his side.

She stays sitting, keeping by the fire's warmth, protected by her own hearth.

'I'd like to leave you the letter anyway,' he says. 'I wrote at least half a dozen that I threw away, like some awkward teenager. My mobile phone number is in it. If you want to get in touch with me, I'd like to see you again. But I'll understand if you don't. I thought I ought to warn you that I'm around because we'd bump into each other eventually.' He walks to the door, opens the latch and stands half-turned, looking down. 'Since I saw you last week, I haven't stopped thinking of you and how I treated you. I still love you, for what it's worth.'

She listens to his footsteps growing fainter. She pours herself another cup of tea and stirs the fire. She sits for a long time, until the sun has moved away and the tea dregs in her cup are completely cold. Leaning forward, she takes the poker and writes her name in the ashes at the front of the fire, as she had in childhood.

The letter is on the dresser, her name on the envelope in his neat, precise writing. When they first met he wrote to her every day on cream vellum notepaper, a thick, top quality brand that absorbed the ink, securing it. His outpourings of affection had bathed her in love. She still has all that correspondence tucked in a box in the loft at home. She reaches for this letter, written on plain white paper, a functional note, and takes it to the window.

Dear Liv,
I've made a number of attempts at writing. I've found out that you're staying here. I live nearby. It's a long story. I'd like to see you. I'm married, with a daughter.
My number is below.
I wouldn't just like to see you, I'd give anything to see you, talk to you.
Aidan

How dare he come here, disturbing my peace, she thinks; he'd give anything to talk to me but he couldn't wait to get away again. Back then, when she'd run here for consolation, she'd have given anything to see him at the door. When she heard a car down on the road, she'd look, hoping foolishly that it might be him, that

100

he'd changed his mind, knowing it couldn't be because he didn't know where she was. The loss of him had been a physical pain, all the bones in her body aching. In this kitchen she had sobbed as her grandmother stood behind her, rubbing her back and murmuring comfort without knowing why the solace was needed; *shush now, alannah*. How she had yearned for him, willed him to change his mind and come for her and now it is as if time has snarled, dislocating the years and her longing has finally summoned him out of the blue. She laughs, a brief yelp and curls her fingers into fists, digging her nails into her palms.

She folds the letter firmly, pressing on the creases and puts it in a jug on the dresser. Her skin is salt scored, itching. Suddenly, she is starving. She cuts a wedge of cheese and munches into it as she sets the fire blazing, draws the big pan full of water over the flame and drags the bath from its hook, screeching it across the floor. Then she turns the radio on loudly, filling the kitchen with blue-grass, hoedown music, blotting her thoughts out with the busy banjos and sliding fiddles.

Late in the evening, she phones Douglas from out in the garden. The air in the kitchen seems secretive and close. The answerphone is on but he rings back within minutes.

'I heard the phone ringing as I got to the door, but I couldn't find my key. I thought it was probably you.'

'I wondered how things are going, how you are.'

'You mean have I been drinking?'

'Mainly, yes. It is the big subject isn't it? It's the main reason why I'm here and you're there.' She's cross with him now, for the distance between them. She pulls a piece of bark off a woody shrub, rolls it roughly in her closed fist.

'Well, since you ask, things have been going OK. That means I haven't had a drink for six days. I've been going to a meeting every night since you left, more or less. And on Friday, I'm book-ing into a kind of health farm in Hampshire for a month. My mentor suggested it. He asked if I had any support at home and when I said no, he said he thought Hyde House would be a good idea.'

She bites back a retort to the comment about no support. He always becomes snide when he is on the wagon, the strain is too much. He's lost the knack of being nice and sober. 'What happens at the health farm?'

'A combination of medication, detox, exercise, massage, good food and vitamins, counselling. I've got the brochure here, it looks very swanky – big swimming pool with jacuzzi, leafy grounds etc. I expect there might be a rock star or two there drying out.'

The tomatoes are giving off a feral scent in the dusk.

'You sound optimistic.'

'I am. And I know that it's crunch time.' Long pause. She knows what is coming, braces herself. 'I don't want to lose you, Liv.' The acid tone has gone now, replaced by contriteness.

'I know.' He never seems to recall that she's heard it all before, that his voice is an echo. Every time he says it, he makes it sound fresh, genuine, heartfelt. She knows that to him, it is.

'You could try sounding a bit more enthusiastic. I've never done anything like this before, this is a big step, you know.'

'Oh, Douglas, you have no idea how much I want you to succeed.'

'Well . . . anyway, how are things with you? What's happening in the Cork countryside?'

She splinters bark under her thumbnail, feeling the sharp needle in the tender skin. 'Not much. I've been to see my uncle Owen, been swimming, you know, just relaxing.' She has done nothing wrong, yet she is feeling treacherous, duplicitous. A man has stood in the kitchen and said that he loves her still. The words are hovering in there, dancing in the lamplight, ready to whisper betrayingly down the phone. 'So, will you let me know how you're doing at this Hyde House place?'

'No, that's the thing, part of the deal is you don't talk to anyone on the outside. I can write, so I'll send letters. You won't hear from me by phone till I've served my time and the sentence is done. So, wish me luck as you wave me goodbye.'

'You know I do. How have you squared it at work?'

'Just said I needed a break. I've got a locum in, so they're not too bothered. It'll do them good to have to manage without me.'

She imagines that they will be more than glad to manage without him. He's only tolerated because it's a poor, inner city practice that struggles to attract doctors. She is mindful of the Christmas celebration at the practice, the glances from other GPs and the flinty-eyed receptionist as Douglas grew more loquacious and staggered into the notice board. In the end she had lured him out with talk of a takeaway, huddling him into his coat and scarf, manoeuvring his arms as if he was a large, recalcitrant child. She supported him across the icy car park to a waiting taxi, pouring him into the back seat, hoping that no one was looking out of the misted windows. She has no idea how he's survived this long, breathing mint-coated fumes on to patients. He is practised at keeping all the balls in the air, a soused juggler.

She has drawn blood under her nail. She rinses it in water from the rain barrel. She feels a tremendous shamefaced relief at the thought that she won't have to talk to him for a month. Time off for good behaviour, she assures herself; I've been doing as long a sentence as him. The air is cooling rapidly and she is glad of the warmth as she steps into the kitchen.

She found the old gramophone, the one that Owen had spun tall stories about, on a shelf in the back of the tool shed, amongst the spades, rakes and hoes. Beside it was a cardboard box of records. She lifts it on to the kitchen table and opens the lid. There is a fluff covered needle in the heavy round head. She cleans it carefully with a damp cloth and winds the handle tight. The records are the ones she had played many times while her grandmother stirred the fire or sat at the table, peering at the *Cork Examiner*. They are in their card covers, mottled with damp and spots of mould.

She looks for and finds her mother's song, 'My Blue Heaven'. There had been a warm night when the back door was open and daddy long legs drifted in, lured by the light. Her parents had danced to the song, holding each other, swaying, then her father stooped and swept Liv up in his arm and they had moved as a threesome, she with an arm around both of their warm necks. Her mother had been to the hairdresser that day and she smelled of soap and acrid perming solution. She said a perm was the only way to keep her hair halfway respectable in Ireland. With her curls, she looked girlish and jolly. 'Bubbles,' her father had called his wife, singing as they turned around the floor.

Just Mollie and me
And baby makes three
So happy in my blue heaven

He nuzzled Liv's neck with his nose as he sang about baby making three and she laughed as his moustache tickled. Afterwards, it had been bedtime and her father had gone around the house, collecting the daddy long legs, cupping them in his hands and ushering them outside because she screeched if one dangled near her in bed. She watched him, amazed at his bravery, shivering as she imagined their legs brushing against his skin.

She puts the record on. It hisses, the needle catching for a moment and then the familiar crackle begins. She sings with it, dancing her own dance, her outstretched arms casting shadows on the walls.

You'll see a smiling face
A fireplace
A cosy room,
A little nest
That's nestled
Where the roses bloom
Just Mollie and me
And baby makes three
So happy in my blue heaven.

On her way to Castlegray, Liv stops at Redden's Cross to post the small padded bag to Douglas. Eileen O'Donovan weighs it, examining the address.

'A little gift?' she asks, putting on a pair of glasses to peer at the scales.

'That's right.' She pauses. 'It's for my husband, a bottle of water from the well at Glenkeen.' She has rinsed out moisturizer from a plastic bottle and scooped it through the water. She's not sure why she's making the gesture. Maybe it's just a way of sharing her good fortune, the peace of her days. The clear liquid, she suspects, also holds her own unease.

Eileen gives her a shrewd glance. 'Is he sick, then?'

'He hasn't been that well recently, but he's on the mend.'

'That's two euros thirty-five. For sure, your grandmother always swore by the power of that well water. She'd take it round to sick people. The priests aren't always keen on it, they think it's superstitious I suppose, a bit pagan, but plenty of the older people here put their faith in it. There's plenty of stories of it curing illness. I've heard it has a lot of calcium in, or maybe it's fluoride, I can't recall.'

'Well, it was just a thought anyway.'

'Oh, and a lovely one. Your grandmother will be smiling up in heaven.'

She's not sure if Nanna will be smiling, knowing that there were mixed motives involved in the packing and posting.

'And you're not bored up there in the cottage, all alone?'

'No, it's wonderful to have time to myself.'

'Oh for sure, I suppose after the big city, it would be a real change, true enough. If you fancy it any time, we have a social evening in the parish hall two Thursdays a month; there's a bit of poetry reading and singing and such and we have talks. Maybe you could do one for us sometime, about London?' She franks the parcel and places it on a stack beside her.

'Maybe, I'll have a think about it.'

'That's great. You're getting a good colour, anyway, you have a real country bloom in your cheeks. Your husband won't recognize you when he sees you.'

She finds her way to the gallery easily, following Owen's directions. It is just off the main street in Castlegray, in a tall terraced house painted a washed Mediterranean blue with white geraniums flowing from window boxes. With the high, hot sun, she could be in Italy. Owen's friend Lucinda is having an exhibition, he'd said and if she wanted to drop by about twelve for a gander they could have a bite of lunch afterwards. Inside the front door there is a small hallway covered in posters, featuring displays of art works; ceramics, jewellery, watercolours, sculptures. A young man directs her upstairs to the second floor when she asks for Lucinda Montgomery's exhibits. Her footsteps ring on the bare varnished boards as she ascends. All the walls are painted white and the place smells of convents, of lemon polish and soap.

She hears their voices before she sees them. The second floor has been knocked through into one room with skylights so that light streams in. She has an impression of huge canvases covered in dark, swirling colours. Owen and Lucinda are sitting close together on a window seat at the far end, sipping champagne.

The sun makes shimmering haloes around their heads.

'Ah, you made it!' Owen stands and holds out his hand, introducing her to Lucinda.

'So nice of you to come.' Lucinda rises. 'We had a mild rush about an hour ago but it's gone quiet now. Some bubbly?'

She accepts a flute of champagne while Owen draws a chair up for her. Lucinda is a tall, light-boned woman about the same age as Owen. She is lean and well toned, her hair cut in a gentle bob and quietly coloured a pale straw. She has an upper-class English voice, a lazy drawl. She wears a tailored linen suit in pale green, the trousers flaring over navy blue boots and her bony fingers are weighted with huge rings. Owen is dressed in his same Hampstead literary outfit, complemented with a purple bow tie. Liv feels grubby in jeans and jumper. She hadn't expected to find such classy dressing in a country market town; she hadn't expected to find a woman like Lucinda. She is glad that she's washed her hair but conscious of the lingering turf scent in her clothing.

'What do you make of our superb Indian summer?' Lucinda asks, gesturing at the sun. Her hands are older than her face, wrinkled, with distended veins.

'It's not what I expected.'

'The mad girl goes swimming,' Owen tells her.

'And why not?' Lucinda asks. 'You used to go all the time, with Edith.' She nods to Liv. 'His wife, you know?'

'Did I?' Owen says vaguely, rolling his champagne between his hands. 'Ah well, that's when I was young and easy under the apple bough. More of this lovely stuff.' He refills the glasses. 'A toast. To dancing in the dark!'

Three sips of champagne and Liv is feeling bold. 'I'm afraid I'm a bit scruffy. I don't have anything smart to wear with me,' she says, 'and everything is impregnated with the smell of turf from the fire.'

107

Lucinda and Owen exchange glances and smile.

'But that's perfect,' Lucinda tells her. 'My exhibition is called *Ireland's Spine*.'

'Peat bogs,' Owen nods, taking a deep draught from his glass. 'Lucinda has been painting peat bogs and turf for a year now. You could be seen as a walking work of art, Liv.'

'Well, that's something I've never been called.'

'Take a look around, then we can lunch, I'm feeling hollow.' Lucinda sweeps the gallery with an arm.

They carry on talking while she circles the room. The paintings are in oils and heavily textured. The predominant colours are browns, moss greens and pale purples. There are giant expanses of peat bog, flat and grass-patched under pale cloudy skies; one has a small railway running through it. Some canvases depict ridged sections of sliced turf, gradations of chestnut to cocoa brown. She knows little about painting but she wants to touch them so reckons they must be good. There are no people in the desolate landscapes. Lucinda's self-containment makes this unsurprising.

'Whereabouts did you go to paint?' she asks.

'The bog of Allen. I got webbed feet, no Indian summer there.'

'You don't paint people?'

'Not there. They don't belong there, even though they harvest it. There would be bodies though, down below the turf. People have drowned on the bogs, they can be treacherous if you leave the paths. A dog, a greyhound, went missing one day when I was there.'

'Come on,' Owen says, collecting the glasses. 'I'm dying for a fag and I can't smoke in the caff. There's a great place just near for sausages and chips,' he tells Liv. 'I know the woman who makes the bangers and the man who grows and sells the spuds.'

He shepherds them down the stairs, singing, 'Give us a bash of the bangers and mash me mother used to make'.

They walk along in the sun, Owen between the two women with his arms linked through theirs. 'Is there anything to beat being sandwiched between two lovely women in Castlegray on a warm September day?' he asks rhetorically.

They turn into the bustle of the main street. It is market day and the sun has enticed a crowd. They pass stalls selling clothes, leather goods, cheeses, jewellery. There are tempting smells of bread and roasting chicken. There's a hubbub of conversation and a group clustered round an electrical goods stall where the trader is calling, 'Come on now, ladies and gents, lads and lasses, make me an offer I can't refuse – just fifteen of these DVD players left!'

Liv feels the warmth of Owen's arm and is glad to have found this uncle that she hadn't even known she'd mislaid. Not to know you have lost something and then to discover it must be one of the most amazing experiences, she thinks, an unexpected gift. Being alive is good; the sun on her face, the Atlantic air borne in on the breeze, the to-ing and fro-ing of the market, the whirl of a fast jig from the accordion player by the music shop. She gulps it all in. It is a champagne day, the taste of life fizzing on her tongue.

Then there he is, suddenly, holding a box full of tomatoes. Although it is baking, he is wearing a cloth hat and a body warmer over a T-shirt. His broad forearms strain with the weight of the produce. Heat sweeps her neck.

'Now,' Owen says, 'here's the man whose spuds we're going to eat. Aidan, hallo, how's your belly off for spots?'

He turns, sees and nods. She looks away at the stall with its heaped produce and mossy green trimming. It looks cool under its blue and cream striped awning. She notices the thought that has gone into it, the way shapes are juxtaposed, bulbous fennel against tapering carrots, still with their feather fronds. She concentrates on the display to cover her confusion and avoid his eyes. On

109

a side table are jars of jam and marmalade with home-made labels and gingham tops. She reads the labels: blackberry, damson, plum and orange with lemon zest.

'Hi there,' he says, resting the tomatoes on a knee.

'And Carmel, I spy you too,' says Owen. 'Should you not be at school? Will I contact the child chaser immediately?'

The girl is sitting on a stool at the side of the stall, eating a red lolly. She grins, pointing. 'I've been to the dentist for a brace.'

'Ah, I'll let you off, so. Aidan, this is my great-niece Liv, and she is great too, a woman who likes a fry-up. Liv, this is Carmel, Aidan's wondrous daughter. Aidan, you know Lucinda?'

'I do, yes.' He puts the box down carefully, wipes his hand on his jeans and extends it. 'Hallo, Liv.'

'Hallo.' As their skin touches she knows him again, the feel of him, his texture.

'I've met your daughter already, at Redden's Cross, with her grandmother.' The skills for dissemblance learned through the years with Douglas serve her well now; as the jigsaw pieces of Aidan's family come together she maintains a steady expression.

Owen reaches and takes a tomato, rubbing it on his sleeve and biting in. He wipes spraying seeds from his chin with his cuff. Carmel stares at him, open mouthed, her tongue strawberry red.

'Mmm, the real McCoy,' he tells Aidan, 'not those hothouse yokes. We've been to Lucinda's exhibition and now we're going to the caff. Will you join us?'

'No, thanks. I can't just now.'

'We're waiting for Mum,' Carmel says. 'She's just getting the messages.'

'She's here,' a woman calls, arriving with two carrier bags. She puts them down, smiling. 'Isn't it lovely and warm? Oh Carmel, you shouldn't be having that lolly after the dentist!'

'Daddy bought it.'

110

'Hmm. Hallo, Owen, Lucinda.'

Owen bows. 'This is Liv; Liv, meet Maeve, wife of Aidan, mother of Carmel.'

'Hallo.'

'Pleased to meet you.' Liv smiles and watches as Maeve leans upwards to kiss her husband's cheek, then tucks her hand under his arm. She looks very young, diminutive, her honey-coloured hair pinned back with a plain barrette, her face scrubbed and open. She reminds Liv of the earnest women at university who belonged to Christian movements and met at guitar strumming house groups to pray and discuss their faith. Like them, she is dressed in a curiously old-fashioned way, in a blouse with lace at the collar and a pleated tartan skirt. On her feet are court shoes with tiny bows.

'Do you like jam?' Aidan asks Liv. 'I made the plum myself. I've been told it's delicious.'

She picks one up, pretends to examine it. 'Yes. I'll buy a pot for my breakfast. How much?'

'Two euros. Do you need a bag?'

'No, that's fine.' His fingers brush hers again as she gives him the money and she blushes, sure that everyone must notice.

To her relief, Owen declares that he must have lunch, his stomach thinks his throat's been cut. He escorts Liv and Lucinda along the street to a café. It is busy but they find a table and order sausage and chips. The tea comes in a huge brown pot and Owen pours, moving the spout energetically up and down so that the liquid froths in the cups.

'Is Aidan making a living, do you think?' Lucinda asks Owen.

'Getting by, I'd say. He puts his all into it. I didn't know you'd met Maeve before.'

Lucinda takes a mouthful of tea. 'God, that's good. Just the once, at the stall. She was holding on to Aidan that time too. It's easy to see who's the lover and who's the loved there.'

The food arrives, sausages laced with French mustard and sea
salted chips with little pots of mayonnaise. Liv eats while Owen and
Lucinda talk about the gallery and people they know in Cork and
Dublin. She watches them, wondering if they are more than friends.
Owen has an ease with women, a warmth that any woman would
find attractive. She dips her chips in mayonnaise. They are hot,
plump and delicious, coating her tongue. Aidan has grown these
spuds. She pictures him digging them up, cleaning them, stacking
them in bags, his shoulders moving. He had always been an orderly
person; he used to clean her cooking pots, getting rid of all the
grime, rejecting her claim that the old charred remains added to the
flavour. She fingers her palm where he touched her, his hand warm
and roughened. She is replete with champagne and hearty food. A
delightful anarchy fills her. Here's to space and liberty, here's to
spring water and a quiet cottage, here's to bangers and chips and
tea that lines the stomach, she toasts silently, raising her cup.

The hubbub of the café recedes to a background hum. She sees
him again, standing by the cottage door, half turned, saying words
of love. In her mind's eye she pictures the first time she ever spotted him, weeks before he was brought round to dinner and offi-
cially introduced. She'd never told him about that sighting, had
kept it to herself like a tiny, hidden jewel. He was sitting at a table
in the university library, taking notes, his index finger holding a
vast law book open. He had stopped writing for a moment,
rubbed his chin and gazed into the middle distance. What a beautiful head, she'd thought, taking in the dark curls, the line of jaw,
the firm mouth under the moustache which was both ridiculous
and attractive. He had stroked the moustache absent-mindedly,
gently, between two fingers and she'd shivered. It was the first
time she had truly felt the shock of desire. Then a girl had come
up to him, leaned over him, whispering and she'd turned away,

disappointed. And so when he had appeared before her suddenly in her own flat she had been astonished, her hands turning to helpless, flapping objects. Now it takes all her self-control not to flee into the street and cry out to him.

Owen scrapes his chair back and heads to the toilet. Lucinda licks her fingers and declares herself completely 'pogged'.

'This is when I unconsciously reach for a cigarette,' she says. 'Damn and blast this smoking ban.'

Liv nods although she thinks privately that the ban is a long-awaited miracle. 'Have you known Owen long?' she asks.

'For ever, it feels like. Edith is a distant relation of mine, something twice removed. I met him when they were courting.'

'How come he has that big house?' Liv asks her. 'I mean, the Farrells never seemed to have much money, they worked on other people's farms and my grandmother's cottage is lovely but basic.'

Lucinda smoothes her hair back. 'Edith gave him that house when they separated. She was left several properties by her mother so one for Owen made no difference.'

'But I thought he left her? That was generous of her.'

'She is mad about him, was even after he did the dirty. Maybe it's a way of keeping him close by.'

'And what is this dirty that he did?'

'Oh the usual, an affair.' Lucinda takes a napkin and wipes a smudge from the toe of a blue boot.

'And they don't see each other?'

'No, except in passing. It's a just-up-the-road long-distance marriage. They never divorced, you know, even though they married in the Church of Ireland so they could have done.'

'Why not?'

Lucinda shrugs. 'The mysteries of other people's relationships are many and unfathomable. That sounds like a quote but I think I just made it up.'

113

Liv is suddenly tired. Lucinda's scent is musky and close. She longs to lie on her plump eiderdown back at the cottage, set the radio to a whisper and close her eyes to the world.

Owen is making his way back to them, greeting various people as he moves past tables. He seems to know everyone, exuding bonhomie.

'Saturday night,' Lucinda says. 'Are you busy?'

'I shouldn't think so.'

'Come to my nephew's birthday bash, then. It's in the hotel, just around the corner.'

'Well, I'm not sure . . .'

'What aren't you sure about?' Owen is looking down at her, balancing his chair on two legs.

'I asked Liv to come to Paulie's birthday. Do come.' Lucinda nods firmly at her.

'Now Liv, you must loosen those foreign English corsets,' Owen says, winking. 'No ceremony here and no strangers. It'll be great fun. The mustn't-miss hooley of the season!'

'All right, then.' She smiles. 'How can I refuse?'

'Spoken like a true Irishwoman!' Owen spins his chair and sits astride, facing the back.

She likes the description, likes to think that she can pass as one of the indigenous tribes. And why not? Half of her belongs here, half of her genes were shaped through centuries in the glen. Maybe, after all, there is a rare, unlooked-for chance of another life, another way of being.

7

She reads a letter from Douglas as she rakes the fire, waiting for it to spring to life. She loves the sharp rattle of the poker, its wake-up call. The letter is written on headed notepaper, blue on white: *Hyde House Therapeutic Community*. She sees a bright, airy room, a desk with a small vase of flowers in front of a window, looking on to broad manicured lawns, the notepaper in a drawer with envelopes and biros. Douglas has written in his own pen, thick upright strokes. His handwriting is clear and evenly formed, as far as it could be from the stereotypical doctor's scribble.

My dearest, my very own Livvie,

I arrived yesterday morning, hungover, having spent the previous evening on my last hurrah. I came in the door with a throbbing head but a hopeful heart. The place is a country house style hotel in beautiful gardens. Looks and smells like a cross between a convent and a spa. My personal counsellor while I'm here is Kia. She's from Tasmania and she's, like, you know, *cheery* and her voice goes UP at the end of every sentence. She asked me, if I could wake up tomorrow and not be an alcoholic, how would I feel and what would my world look like? I said that I'd feel as if a stone had been taken from around my neck, that the world would be in colours again instead of a misty grey and that my wife would love me again and I would be able to love her in the way she deserves. She nodded. I suppose she's heard the like many times.

I'm in a group of eight and we've agreed the rules of our journey. I can't tell you those, they're confidential. I've had a sauna and a swim and I've drunk pints of water and fruit juice. I'm wobbly now and scratchy without the prospect of a drink for the evening so I'm going to go and have a walk and read. I've missed reading, it will be nice for the words to stay on the page and not blur. I've brought novels and poetry, that book you got me last Christmas. I wasn't much company for the festive season, was I?

I'm sorry for all the grief I've given you. I don't deserve you but I will, I will. Write and tell me what you're doing. I picture you sitting cross-legged in the glen, eating in your slightly abstracted fashion, a mug of tea at your side, playing with your fringe as you bend over a book. What's the news on your uncle Owen – did you find out the back story, is he a rapscallion of the worst order? I do hope so.

Kia agrees that it will be hard to let the colour flood in again; that misty grey is so pleasant. I put my most worrying question to one of the therapists here; what am I going to do with my life if I'm not drinking? He said; how about starting with loving your wife?

I do love you and I'm sober and I'm going to stay that way.

Douglas

She runs her hands through her hair, lifts and lowers her shoulders. The letter tires her, her spirits sliding. She recalls the feathers of dandelion fluttering around the car and wants to hope for the best but is frightened of hoping. Hope is tricky, slippery; it's a

116

door opening and then slamming in your face. The time at Hyde House will be tough for him, but easy compared to the day to day battle waiting on the outside. Well, she thinks, at least he's safe, he'll be having healthy meals and he can't come to any harm for a couple of weeks. She blows on the fire, rakes it again and banks it with two big clods of turf.

Carmel is doing her homework, sitting cross-legged on the living-room floor, her tongue poking between her lips. Her pencil case has spilled open, rulers, rubbers and her twin pencil sharpener in the shape of the owl and the pussycat lying by her side. Her Russian hamster, Boris, races on his wheel inside the small plastic palace that houses him, a complicated three storey affair with transparent tubes, layers of sawdust, toys, feeding tray and drink-ing bottle. The cat ignores the hamster, knowing its home is impregnable and brushes insinuatingly around Carmel's legs, trying to distract her. Finally it gives up as she shakes her pigtails and nestles beside her elbow.

Maeve has finished her regular evening phone call to her mother, when they tell each other about the minutiae of their days. 'Indeed, Indeed,' Maeve echoes soothingly as her mother relays some real or imagined slight. Now she is reading a magazine, sitting in an armchair with her feet on a stool. She rubs one foot on top of the other when she relaxes, creating a faint scratching not unlike the hamster when it gnaws on cardboard. Her favourite Ronan Keating CD is playing. She produced a particularly strange supper called Pork Carnival, another Martha recipe featuring pork and walnuts with pasta and an undertaste Aidan couldn't identify.

He has washed up, dried and put everything away. He then wiped down all the kitchen surfaces, bleached the dishcloth, emptied the waste and compost bins and descaled the kettle. Anything to keep moving. Now the muscles in his legs are twitch-

117

ing, the ache that his mother used to call growing pains. He paces up and down with the dustpan in his hand, staring out of the kitchen window. It is westerly facing, laced with late sun. Their corner plot has the biggest garden in the row but it still isn't anything near spacious enough for him to grow everything he wants in order to abandon the wholesalers, achieve a totally organic stall; spuds take up a lot of room and aren't much of an earner but he can't give up on them, they're too popular. The back of Liv's cottage faces the same way and he imagines that she might be standing now, looking out on the last of the orange light. The pictures in his mind are vivid; she has the turquoise scarf around her neck that she'd been wearing earlier in the day, a glass of wine in her hand. She is squinting slightly, her eyes light sensitive. Her freckles are paler before dusk, waning with the day.

The evening is fine and clear and full of promise but the house holds him in a tight clench. He sees that a new item has appeared on the kitchen wall, a pale blue ceramic plaque bordered with forget-me-nots and a motif in curling script saying *A Round Tuit*. Stepping closer he sees the small print; *this is to remind me that one day I'll get around to it!!* It must have arrived in the parcel from Philadelphia this morning. Another bit of twee American clutter. He drifts into the living-room and straightens a picture, fiddles needlessly with a curtain rail. Just being able to stretch is a relief.

'Daddy, you're in my light,' Carmel says crossly.

'Sorry.'

Maeve looks at him, smiles her sweet smile and mouths a kiss. She's reading something about a TV personality. How has he ended up married to a woman who devours magazines about obscure celebrities?

'You're restless tonight, sweetheart,' she says.

'Am I? Must be the weather.'

'It's odd, isn't it, to have this heat all of a sudden? We had to put two fans on in the office today, it was so close. I envied you being outside.'

'You were adding to global warming, using all that electricity,' Carmel admonishes her.

'Was I? What could I have done instead?'

Carmel thinks. 'Put something cool on your neck, a damp flannel or some ice maybe.'

'But I can't type and answer the phone with ice on my neck, sweetheart. I don't think Mr Riordan would appreciate damp marks on his court reports.'

'It's what Mrs Driscoll tells us to do when we get too hot. What do you think, Daddy?'

'Hmm? I think an ice pack's a good idea. But you still have to run a freezer for that so you're damned whichever way, I'd say.'

'It's your generation that's costing us the earth, with that kind of attitude,' Carmel moralizes.

Maeve gazes adoringly at her daughter, always impressed by her precocious statements about the world.

'Well, Carmelita, when you give up your iPod and your computer, I'll take your criticism more seriously,' Aidan tells her. 'In the meantime, I've still got some energy left, despite the heat – I think I'll pop out for a while.'

'Oh, where?' Maeve tucks her finger behind a page.

'There's a few orders I need to check on. Business is picking up, you'll be pleased to hear. No rest for the wicked!' He forces the bravura into his voice. 'I won't be long.' *The first lie; I believe it's supposed to be the easiest.*

'Can I come?' Carmel looks up. He knows the brace is necessary and Maeve has been right to insist on it but he hates the savage look of it, the way it resembles some torture implement.

He squats down and straightens a constricting bow on a pigtail.

He loves to free her hair at night and brush it so that static tingles. They pretend that she is being electrified, that they'll be able to power the house off her. She puts a hand up automatically, as she always does, to pull his earlobe.

'No, Carmelita, you finish your homework and talk to Boris. I'll be quicker on my own.'

'Will you be back to read me a story?'

'I will. What are we having?'

'I've started *Long Ears*. I'm on chapter three.'

He seizes his keys and leaves the house before he can change his mind. He revs the van and drives, heading for the glen. He stops a mile or so away and gets out. He hesitates, a hand on the door. All is silent, as if in that split second, the world is hesitating with him, breath held for his decision. There are risks you have to take to prove you're alive. He starts to run, slowly at first, gathering speed until he has settled into a steady pounding. The thud of his feet matches the beat of his heart and the chant in his head: Liv, Liv, Liv. He feels an unaccustomed flow of energy as his muscles warm. The light is gentle now, the sky scuffed with palest pink shreds of cloud. The perfumes of the evening wash over him, soft and insistent. Closing his eyes momentarily, he raises his arms and believes that with the next step he might launch off and fly. He runs his hand over a wild honeysuckle as he passes, releasing its fragrance and tears a branch off. He swerves into the glen and breathes deep on the steep slope to the front door.

Through the darkening window he can see her dancing, arms held out, moving in the lamplight. The shadows she creates on the walls follow her like obedient servants. She is clothed in a loose, dark kaftan and her skin is pale against the fabric. The lush strains of an orchestra drift on the air. He stands, watching as she circles, dips, sways from side to side. A spark hisses from the fire and she rubs it with her foot, making the motion part of the dance. He rests his forehead against the windowpane, swallows. The paint of the frame is scored, rough against his skin and beaded with evening dew. He rolls his head from side to side with her glides, knowing that he is about to leap into the void, glad of the solidity of the wood and the chipped, uneven gloss.

He raises a hand and taps loudly. Liv looks up and stops, hands dropping, then clasping before her. Now she resembles a priestess, the celebrator of some ancient rite. She moves slowly to the window and puts a hand up to his, spreading her fingers, matching the shape of his outstretched palm. For a long moment they stay, unmoving. Then she opens the door and looks at him.

'I'm here, Liv. It took me a long time, but I'm here.'

She reaches out for him. All he hears is 'yes'.

They lie before the fire on an eiderdown, turned towards each other, the branch of honeysuckle tucked between them. He strokes her arm from shoulder to wrist and back again, loving the wiriness of her, the angular line of her jaw. Her kaftan is bunched under her head. The fabric is soft, springy, a mixture of dark and lighter greens. He is guilt free, soaring, intoxicated by the ferny scent of her skin and the downy texture of her freckles.

He rubs the kaftan, admires its weft. 'This is lovely; you looked like a white witch through the window.'

'Douglas bought it for me in San Sebastian. I always think it looks a bit ecclesiastical.'

'Douglas is your husband?'

'Yes.'

'Do you love him?'

'Yes, an exhausted, faded kind of love. Do you love Maeve?'

'Yes, an apprehensive, guilty kind of love.'

'Do you love me?'

'Yes. I must have all down the years but didn't know until I saw

121

you again, walking away from the shop at Redden's Cross. It was as if I'd been in a Rip Van Winkle slumber.'

'When was that, when you saw me?'

'The day you arrived.'

'This is hard to believe. My stomach is doing somersaults. It's a small world here, Eileen O'Donovan being your mother-in-law.' She is conscious of her insides squeaking and groaning, like an orchestra tuning up.

He moves an ear to her midriff. 'I can hear it, having its own conversation. My right eyelid twitches these days when I'm nervous. It's been on overdrive the last weeks.'

She peers. 'Oh it is, the skin is crinkling! It used to be your right eyebrow, you'd worry it with your fingertip when you were anxious until there was a bald patch at the edge. Before your dissertation had to be in I thought you'd wear it away completely.'

He sighs, relaxed. 'I've no nerves now. I'm where I want to be.'

They are talking quickly, tripping over words, replying hastily. She wonders is it because they have so much to say after so long or because they both know his time is limited, measured? She pushes the thought away. The reality of his being here is almost too much to absorb. She strokes his hair back. It's still full bodied and strong.

'When did you get rid of your 'tache?'

'Oh, around 1988, in Buenos Aires.'

'You travelled in faraway places for a good while, then?'

'For several years, then I got a job in Manchester. I met a guy in Bucharest who was starting up a computer company. He offered me work back in England. I found that I had an unexpected aptitude for computer language. You finished your degree?' He's always worried that she might not have, could have dropped out after the trauma of his leaving. Just another of the little guilt debts that have kept him awake at night and ambushed him in his dreams.

'Oh yes. Then went into libraries. I manage one now. Where are you supposed to be tonight?'

'I remember that about you, the way you slip in the unexpected, incisive question. I'm out checking orders; I do home deliveries, boxes of vegetables.'

'I tasted your jam. It's delicious. Did Carmel write the label?'

'Yes. I make the jam, she readies the jars and sees to the wax discs and the labelling.'

'She can look very serious.'

'I know, she was born with a grave expression, as if life was a burden she had to shoulder. Then she had terrible colic as a baby, it went on for months. She used to look so miserable. Sometimes I think the pain leached away some of her capacity for joy.' He used to walk her up and down for hours as she squirmed and moaned, holding her over his shoulder, rubbing her hot little back. 'Don't worry 'bout a thing,' he'd sing to her, shifting her to the other side when his neck began to ache.

Liv sits up to throw another chunk of turf on the fire. They lie, watching it smoulder and catch flame. She rests her hand on his thigh, claiming him. She feels that he is a glorious reward that she has long awaited.

He feels the heat on his skin and is glad of it. He has goose pimples of pleasure and fear all over his body, little rushes of amazement. This is what he has missed, the way she speaks directly, the strong glint in her eye, her bullshit detector. She had never let him get away with anything until the night he'd told her it was over, and then she'd been too stunned to put up a fight. She'd steadied him; he knew he was prone to flights of fancy and she had been an anchor. A pity he hadn't understood that back then.

'Look at your hands,' she says. 'They're rough. Your skin is peeling on the thumb.'

'I'm always scraping them on boxes.'

She takes his right hand and massages it, working along each finger, pressing the joints. 'You said something about a break-down. What happened?'

'I'm not sure. I started to feel as if I wasn't me, somehow. There were days, weeks, when I didn't seem to be breathing. The office was like a jail, somewhere I'd been sentenced to.' He stops; he's never told anyone the next part. Liv carries on silently smoothing his hand. 'Well, there were some allotments I used to see on the way into work every day. They looked so quiet and green; some were a bit overgrown and shady. It struck me that there'd be no spotlight on me in there. I'd worked for a while during my travels in a market garden near Rouen and I knew I had a talent, one that I'd forgotten somewhere along the way, for growing and selling produce.

'One morning I started driving to the office but I didn't arrive. I stopped at the allotments and chatted with an old chap who spent all his time there. The rain came on so we sat in his shed. It was a little home from home; two battered old leather armchairs, curtains at the windows, a cupboard with tea, coffee and cups. He had a footstool for when he wanted a snooze. He got out biscuits and made tea. It was the tea that did it really, finally. He took time with it, made it with fresh leaves, on a primus stove. We watched the blue flame and listened to the hiss and the echoing shush of the rain. He heated the pot with boiling water and we waited for it to brew. It was dark and delicious, no scum in the cup; it had a taste! We dunked our custard creams and they were ambrosial.

'It struck me that I spent my days staring at a screen, hardly tast-ing the food and drink I ate from cardboard containers; if anyone had asked me what I'd had for lunch I'd be hard put to remember. We sat and sipped and looked out on his rows of runner beans and

124

I knew I was alive. Back home, I told Maeve I wanted to grow and sell vegetables for a living.'

'That must have been quite a shock.'

'She asked me to see the doctor, so I did. I took an antidepressant for a couple of weeks. It made me feel better, as if I was wrapped in a snug jacket, but it didn't improve the office; I just saw the place through a pleasant haze. So in the end we sold up and moved here. We could get a lot more for our money and Eileen's a boon in terms of childcare.'

She folds his hand and tucks it between them. 'Any regrets?'

'None, except the proximity of my mother-in-law but that's a price worth paying.'

She laughs. 'She promotes your produce, especially your spuds. One night I'm going to bake potatoes on the hearth like my grandmother used to. They taste charred, smoky.'

'This is such a lovely place. It's simple, clean lines. Unfussy. Can you feel her here, your grandmother?'

'I can. When I close my eyes I can hear her humming and the *switch switch switch* of her brush as she swept the floor. She'd throw the door open and fling the dust into the hedge, saying, 'good riddance to bad rubbish'. I'm lucky to have this. It succoured me when I came here, weeping after you said goodbye. It's where I came to grieve you and it's where you've come back to me. Have you come back to me?'

'I have no right to, but I have.'

'Yes.' She cups his chin. 'You used to call me Liv-of-my-life. You said that this was it, this was for ever. That was the hardest thing when you told me you were leaving, it was as if all that must have been lies.'

His eyes fill, brimming. 'I wasn't lying, the feelings were real. I took fright, I was young and I became terrified by the statements, the promises I'd made. I was callow and stupid and fascinated by

125

myself, convinced that I was entitled to roam the globe. I have no excuse, only that reason.'

'It's all right,' she says. 'Let's not talk any more about that. You're here, we're here now. I remember the feel of you. Your shoulders are heavier, you're more solid.' She holds him to her, relishing his dense, middle-aged sinews, her lost companion in life. Now she wishes she'd gone after him like a camp follower, pursuing him around the world, refusing to be cast off. After all, she hadn't put up much of a fight, had she? She could have stayed flickering on his radar, waiting to be guided in. As soon as she'd seen Maeve she had known that he'd settled for a woman who was no threat, no challenge and had felt disappointed as well as intrigued.

He is Aidan and yet not Aidan; not the skinny youth she had fitted against, who always had to pull his belt to the tightest notch so that his jeans didn't fall to his hips. She had loved to sleep curled into his back, sniffing the spicy skin of his neck. Now he is bulkier, his eyes crinkled, his jaw wider and she thinks that maybe he too is weighed down by life.

They lie, watching the fire lick and leap, then settle to a steady glow.

'What do you remember most?' he asks.

'The French toast you made for breakfast and the night the bed collapsed; watching our washing go round in that launderette near my place – it seemed so romantic; walking on Parliament Hill Fields. You?'

'The songs you taught me; the night we stayed out in Holland Park till four in the morning, talking and eating chestnuts; the way your freckles got bolder in the sun.'

'Memory lane is an enticing place but not necessarily pleasant. I always come back to that bloody restaurant and the inane music and the gap-toothed waiter who kept smiling nervously while I was crying.'

He takes her hand, kisses it. 'We can erase that memory together, if you want to. Memories don't have to be static, they can alter like everything in life alters. That's the only truth, isn't it – that everything changes?'

'Yes, that's what keeps us sane.'

'I'm going to have to go soon.'

'Just when we're warm and the lamps are lit. Yes, I know.'

'Can I come again?'

'I'd like that.' She pulls him close. 'There's so much I want to tell you, I feel as if I've been storing it up. I have missed you. I pretended I didn't because I had to. It's true that everything changes but some things stay the same.'

He holds her tight. 'You haven't told me if you love me,' he says into her hair, the tart taste of panic in his throat.

She moves back, tracing a finger around his lips. 'I do, Aidan. Indeed I do. And to love you here – to love you here – well, it means everything.'

He stands, raising her with him. 'I'll ring you, then.'

'Ring me and we'll have hearth-baked spuds, Glenkeen style.'

She writes down her number for him and stands at the door, holding a lamp up to light him down the glen, watching as he slowly blends into the deepening evening. The sky is an intense blue, a sickle moon dangling lightly amongst scattered stars. Life is good, she thinks, ambushed by the novelty of the idea.

Chapter three of *Long Ears* has been finished. The little donkey had been taken by the tinkers and the chase was on. Aidan lies on Carmel's bed as she arranges her soft toys to her satisfaction inside the duvet. She is wearing the pink nightie covered in bunches of cherries that he bought her in Dublin last month. His eyes are heavy, his limbs aching with joy; he would love to sleep and hug his joy tight. Maeve is running a freesia-scented bath and pattering quietly between their bedroom and the bathroom.

'What would you do if someone snatched me away, like the tinkers took Long Ears?' Carmel asks buttoning a teddy bear's waistcoat.

'Nobody's going to snatch you away.'

'But if they did, what would you do?'

'I'd find you and bring you home, of course.'

'How would you find me?'

'I'd follow the trail of liquorice allsorts that you'd left, eating them as I went. That Teddy has a saucy glint in his eye, I hope he behaves and doesn't cause trouble with the others.'

Carmel sniggered. 'It's Boris who's naughty, he tried to get out of the cage earlier.'

'He's probably been listening to the "Freedom for Russian Hamsters" broadcast on Radio Moscow. Maybe all the Russian hamsters in Ireland are going to break out and set sail on a stolen ship all the way across the seas to their motherland. Boris is probably their leader, he has a haughty air.'

'What's haughty?'

'Proud, a bit stuck-up.'

'Like Jacinta Rees?'

Jacinta had attended the same school in Manchester. 'That's right.'

'I don't miss her at all!'

'But you do miss some people?'

'Yes, Sonia and Elizabeth. And I miss my uniform and the swimming pool.'

They had sent Carmel to a small private school in their leafy city suburb, one that cost a fortune. The pupils wore a purple and cream uniform. Every morning he would drop her off, sporting her boater hat with purple ribbon. She'd sobbed when they had told her they were moving, and wet the bed for a fortnight. The memory of that always makes him wretched.

'You've made new friends now, though. And the horses up the road, you're loving learning to ride, aren't you? And Granny Eileen worships the ground you tread on, she thinks you're the cat's pyjamas, the icing on the cake, the jam in her sandwich, the silver lining in every cloud – and the greatest child genius of all time.'

Carmel sniggers. 'Don't be daft.'

He tucks her fine, fragrant hair behind her ears. 'Someone has to be daft round here, and I think I have the best qualifications. Time for sleep now, my eyes are almost closing.'

'When are we making the chutney?'

'Soon, one Saturday soon.'

'And we'll call it after me?'

'We will; Carmel's Chutney. It'll sell like hot cakes.'

'Don't be a twit, it's chutney, not cakes!'

'I know, I'm a dimwit. Night night.'

Maeve has left the bathroom door open, an indication that she wants him to wash her back. Standing, he is suddenly drained, light-headed. He pauses outside the door for a moment, then goes in. She is lying up to her neck in bubbles, hair pinned up in a twist. On her face is a green mask, a cucumber cleanser. She looks like a woman in an advertisement for soap or maybe chocolate.

'Has she settled?'

'Yep, she's fine.' He takes up the sponge, rubs soap on.

Maeve sits forward, her plump, soft shoulders traced with foam. He washes her back slowly, with the circular movements she likes, across the birthmark shaped like Malta. Sometimes, when they are making love, she asks if she is his little malteser and he feels a quiver of discomfiture. She likes endearments, calling him her tall giraffe, her rowan tree and sometimes Brad because, she maintains, he has a slow, sexy smile like Brad Pitt's. He knows he

129

disappoints her by not reciprocating with similar sweet nothings. He feels the sponge glide. Everything he is doing now seems fraudulent.

'Did you sort out the deliveries OK?' She has closed her eyes, is smoothing her arms.

'Yes, no problems.'

'It's a lovely night, aren't we lucky after all with the weather?'

'Very. Even if Carmel thinks we're ruining the planet single-handed.'

'I gave her a pain killer after supper, just in case the brace hurts during the night.'

'Good. She seems OK with it. Kids adjust quickly.'

'I remember when I had to wear an eye patch once for a couple of weeks, it seemed in no time at all I'd always had it. In fact, it made me quite a celebrity.' She opens her eyes. 'That's great, sweetheart, thanks.' She lifts her mouth for a kiss.

He bends, closing his eyes now, the flames of Liv's fire tracing under his lids, a flickering memory, a steady glow. 'We've settled in OK here, haven't we?' he asks, leaning back on his heels.

'Yes, I think so. It takes a while.'

'And Carmel, too. I know it was hard for her.'

Maeve touches his nose with a soap bubble. 'Go on, you know you're her idol, she'd have gone to Timbuktu if you'd wanted. She's fine, Aidan, children are adaptable.'

He's both reassured and ill at ease. 'You enjoy your soak. I'll just go down and lock up.'

'Oh, could you make Carmel's sandwich? I don't know where the time went tonight.'

In the kitchen he slices wheaten bread, butters it lightly and lays thin slices of chicken and tomato in neat rows. He tears some basil leaves from a pot on the windowsill and sprinkles them on, then closes the sandwich and slices diagonally. Carmel says it tastes

130

different, better, with a diagonal cut. He places the sandwich in her Bart Simpson lunch box with a banana and a raspberry yogurt and stacks it in the fridge. As he closes the door he pauses and reaches again for the box, hiding two squares of dark orange chocolate under the sandwich.

He pours himself a small slug of whiskey and goes into the hallway to listen. There's no sound of running water yet. He goes back to the kitchen, closing the door firmly, turning the light off so that he can monitor the beam spilling into the garden from the bathroom. He slips his phone from his pocket and dials. The smoky aroma from his glass calms him and he sips, glad of the tang of the spirit.

'Hallo.' She sounds tense.

'I just wanted to say goodnight.'

'Are you at home?'

'Yes. I wish I was still there.'

'Me too. I'm drinking cocoa and toasting bread at the fire.'

'I've some whiskey. It might help me sleep. I love you.'

'I love you. Why did we part?'

'Don't. I wish . . . oh, you know.'

'I wish, I wish, I wish in vain, I wish I was a maid again . . .' She sings the line in her low voice.

'. . . But a maid again I ne'er can be till apples grow on an ivy tree,' he replies.

'How true.'

'I was wondering . . . Douglas – why is he not here with you?'

'He's drying out in a clinic.'

'Ah. He has a drink problem?'

'Yes, which means we both do. Let's not talk about it on the phone. You'd better go. I thought I'd say it before you do this time.'

'Do I detect a hint of tartness?'

131

'Me? I'm full of sweet content right now.'

'What I told you earlier, about the day I sat in the allotment, you're the only person I've said that to. I'd have felt stupid saying it to anyone else.'

'I thought that was the case. My toast is a lovely dark gold. Good night, Aidan.'

He hears the water rushing down outside, sees the light go out in the bathroom. The smallest of movements have now assumed huge significance.

'Sweet dreams. I'll ring in the morning.'

8

The hotel where the birthday party is being held is a place of dark wood and carpets, furnished in fifties-style. A fusty smell pervades it but there are huge bunches of flowers around and the staff are young and seem delighted with everyone. When Liv uses the toilet, the seat wobbles beneath her and she has to clutch the wall for balance.

She has donned the one dress she brought with her, a dark-blue crushed velvet that she bought in Prague while Douglas was attending a convention on skin melanomas. She had loved Prague and the stunning baroque beauty of the churches; Douglas had loved it too and in particular the wine at forty pence a bottle. While he propped up bars she sought solace in churches, listening to choral and organ recitals. She smiled a good deal at people as little English was spoken and the act of smiling, of practising happiness, lifted her spirits. She shakes her head to banish the memory and thinks of Aidan. He is somewhere near, out in the still evening, probably tucking his daughter up in bed. When he speaks of Carmel, his voice softens and his lips curve involuntarily.

'Well,' says Owen, spotting her, 'don't you scrub up nice!'

'You're pretty smart yourself. I like the burgundy jacket.'

'Thank you, ma'am. Come on and I'll do introductions.'

Owen steers her, a protective hand guiding but not touching her back. They are sitting at a table of ten, with him beside her. Lucinda is at the next table in grey silk with one red rose pinned behind her right ear. She waves, using her other hand to cool herself with a bamboo fan. The meal is plain but well cooked and wine pours freely. Liv is asked about herself in a genuine fashion; several people at her table knew her grandmother and speak warmly of her.

A woman opposite has a placid baby about six months old, called Roisin. The baby, replete from a bottle, lies in the crook of the woman's arm and gazes around through grave, pearly eyes while her mother's spoon lifts and falls to her lemon syllabub. In the middle of the hubbub she is centred in her own contented world – adored, safe. The mother is talking to her neighbour but also attentive; at her baby's slightest shift, she moves her arm, nestling her back to comfort. When her father leans towards his daughter to nuzzle the warm curve of her cheek she grabs his hair and turns her steady gaze on him. 'My own little rose,' he croons. He loosens the top of her cardigan, his big fingers fumbling with the buttons. The mother automatically runs her hand over Roisin's downy head, where hair like a chick's is sprouting softly. Then she looks at the father and down; there is an intensity to the three of them, a knowing bond that is almost tangible.

Liv is mesmerized, abruptly sensing the loss of the child that she will probably never have. Douglas has always maintained that he doesn't want children; he states that there are already too many, poor and needy in the world and they should adopt if they really want a family. She used to try and persuade him otherwise at one time but gave up the battle many years ago; what child would want a drunk for a father? It became easier in the end to convince herself that she didn't want a child, she had enough responsibilities in her life. She would like to touch the baby, feel her soft warm scalp. Instead, she holds the palms of her hands together, feels the slick of disappointment and longing on her skin. This must be like emerging from an anaesthetic, glad to be breathing independently but suddenly conscious of the lights, noise and promising, jumbled spill of life. When she looks again at the baby, the father is tracking the mother's palm across her scalp and Liv remembers Aidan's hand and the furry pelt that lies the length of his breastbone. Oh, there's still time, she assures herself.

Over coffee Owen is called on to tell a story. He heaps brown sugar crystals into his cup, pauses for a moment with eyes closed, his arm along the back of Liv's chair, then begins in a conversational tone. 'Well,' he says, leaning back so that the others draw forward, 'did you hear tell of how Cuchulain was married to the Lady Emer but he fell in love with Fand, a lady of the sea and they made a secret tryst and met down on the strand not far from here? But Emer found them out and she came to the strand with an army of women to slay Fand. Cuchulain protected Fand, asking Emer why he should give up his love for a woman who was fair and lovely and could ride the hollows of the ocean. Emer reminded him that everything new is fair, that men worship what they lack and disregard what they have. She appealed to him, full of grief, reminding him of how he had first loved her and grief came over him too. Fand saw this and she knew she had lost him. She told Emer to take Cuchulain back, that though her arms resigned him, she would always long for him and she would go far off to make sure her longing might waste away. And she walked back into the sea.'

There is silence, broken only by the rattle of a teaspoon.

'And did they ever meet again?' Liv asks.

Owen shakes his head. 'No. Cuchulain grieved for months but Emer got an enchanter to give him a potion of forgetfulness and

135

the sea god shook his cloak over Fand so that she would never be able to meet Cuchulain again.'

Everyone at the table is listening, rapt, unaware of talk and laughter from their neighbours. Roisin has gone to sleep, her delicate eyelids translucent and veined like flowers. Liv is conscious of the breathing around her, of the baby's snuffles and her uncle's hand settled on the strut of her chair.

Owen taps the table, breaking the reverie. 'You see, Liv,' he says, 'the Irish love a good tale of sorrow and suffering, longing and loss.'

After coffee the tables are pushed back to the walls and there is dancing to a quartet who sit on a rostrum, middle-aged men with maroon and green waistcoats. Owen and Liv circle the floor. He's a good dancer, easy and light on his feet. Candles have been lit on the tables and the balmy air is laden with scent from the drifts of freesias, roses and carnations that adorn the room.

'Where did you hear that story you told us?' Liv asks.

'I've had it years, I think my mother might have told me it; or maybe I read it once on the radio. I learned a lot of the old tales from my mother, she was a storyteller, a *seannachtai*. Stories help to makes sense of life, I always think.'

'If there's sense to be made of it.'

'Ah, so young and such a cynic. Do you think that maybe deciding it all makes no sense is in a way making sense of it?'

Liv nods, acknowledging the point. 'Were you by any chance educated by the Jesuits?'

He claps a hand to his heart. 'A perceptive cynic! I went to be a priest, I was in the seminary for three years but in the end they threw me out.'

'Why? Did you not have a vocation?'

'That wasn't really the issue. I was extremely devout, first up for Mass and hot on scripture. The issue was that I loved God but I also had an abiding adoration for women and I'm not talking about the mother of God. My own mother was mortified when the priesthood and myself parted company. My standing in the family never really recovered from that time and slid further down the years until my name was mud. I was a complete reprobate, you understand.'

She looks at him, appreciates the attributes of the man and the way he glides confidently on the floor, owning the space in his tailored black trousers and beautifully soft white cotton shirt. When he told the story he had his audience entranced; he could have done the same in a pulpit, using the tale as a parable. After all, priests were actors as well as holy men. She understands that he is one of those rare people who have so many interests and talents, they have to live many lives within the one.

The band strikes up again and she registers a sense of déjà vu, a pang of melancholy.

'This song, "Smoke Gets In Your Eyes", my mother loved it, the version by the Platters, she'd sing it while she was having a fag.'

'Mollie had a good voice, strong. I recall her singing at her wedding party, in this very hotel: "Maybe it's because I'm a Londoner". She had no idea where she'd landed, this place must have seemed like another planet after Haringey. The song was her way of staking her claim. Some people joined in but others didn't; the old guard who thought that your father had let the side down by marrying out. I admired her for it. It's never easy to be an incomer and I think she always had the map of this place upside down.'

She feels bemused and in the dark, presented suddenly with this picture of her mother before she knew her. She tucks the information away to mull over in private. Owen sings as they come to the end of the dance and she joins him: 'When you're your heart's on fire, you must realize, smoke gets in your eyes.'

137

As they move back to their table, Owen stops to talk to a couple and Liv carries on, too warm now, wishing she had a fan like Lucinda's. She catches the eye of a woman sitting near the rostrum, an older woman with greying hair pinned up in a bun. The woman is very still and upright, her eyes keen, dark little berries in a bird-like face. There are two walking sticks leaning against her knees. She nods to Liv, a stately tip of the head, without smiling, then turns to a dark suited man next to her. Liv has the feeling that she's being discussed.

As she pours herself water, Lucinda stops unsteadily beside her chair. 'I do hope you're enjoying the party.' Her speech is slurred.

'Thank you, yes. It's great fun and it's so nice to meet people who knew Nanna.'

'And you've been introduced around, I know Owen's made sure. These events can be a bit daunting if you don't get a sense of who's who.'

'Oh yes, although it's hard to keep all the names in mind. There's a woman over there, Lucinda, near the band, in a navy dress, with walking sticks.'

Lucinda clicks her fan open and shut. It's decorated with a flaunting peacock and yellow petals. 'Oh, that's Edith, you know, Owen's wife.' She bends closer. Liv can smell the wine on her breath and her musky perfume. 'If you watch, you'll see that she keeps a steely eye on him. Pity she didn't manage to do it thirty years ago.' She laughs, taps Liv's shoulder with the fan as the music stops, a birthday cake is wheeled in and everyone applauds.

On the way out, Eileen O'Donovan waves to Liv in the foyer. She's looking glamorous in a floral shift dress with a chunky necklace at her throat. In her hand she carries a small clutch bag. She playfully taps the arm of the priest she's been talking to with the bag and crosses to Liv.

'Everyone seems to be here tonight,' Liv says. 'It's a popular

138

venue.' She fixes a bland smile in place.

'Oh, for sure, there's loads goes on here. Nearly all the weddings, birthdays and such like, and funeral wakes too. I come nearly every Saturday for the whist drive,' Eileen tells her. 'We send any proceeds to the missions. I didn't get here last week because we had a family get-together, Maeve and Aidan and little Carmel. I made Carmel's favourite pudding, raspberry trifle. Maeve tells me you met her on the market?'

'Yes, that's right.'

Eileen is rolling the beads of her necklace between her plump fingers. Liv looks away, uncomfortable. 'I was saying to her how you helped Carmel with her homework. Isn't that little girl just a pet?'

'She's a lovely child, you must be proud of her.' She is aware of an electricity she is carrying in her skin, sparked by Aidan. She believes that Eileen O'Donovan must be aware of it crackling loudly, deafeningly along her nerve endings.

'I'm mad out about her, she's great company for me there in the afternoons after school. You never know the information she's going to come out with; didn't she tell me the other day that the colour of a diamond depends on the impurities in it! I told her, I'll be Einstein before she's finished with me. And she's great with helping count the stock and keeping an eye on what's needed on the shelves. She has the same good nature as her mother. And she's mad out about her daddy – a real daddy's girl, she can twist the poor man around her little finger. I remember you being the same with your own father; he'd bring you into the shop, carrying you on his shoulders and sit you up on the counter while you had your Peggy's leg or sherbet dip. He'd be chatting away to my Tommy, God rest his soul.'

Liv forces herself to look directly at the woman, hoping to stop the flow. 'I must have been very young,' she says. 'I can barely remember.'

'Oh for sure, you were just tiny, with your lovely curls.'

'Well, it's nice to hear those memories, anyway. I'll tell my father when I next see him.'

To Liv's relief, Owen appears, calling goodnights. 'Eileen,' he says with a little bow, 'how nice to see you.'

She nods, sizing him up. 'Aren't you looking the swell tonight. You've both been at the birthday do, I suppose?'

'That's right. And a wonderful time we all had.'

'It must be great to have your niece here, after all these years.'

'It certainly is, she's a darling girl.' He loops his arm through Liv's and she gratefully receives the warmth of the gesture. 'You must excuse us now, we have to find Lucinda and drop her home or we'll all turn into white mice when the clock strikes twelve.'

Eileen gives him an old-fashioned look. 'For sure, Owen, some things never change, no matter how many years flow under the bridge. You and your ladies! Aren't you always squiring the women!'

'Ah well, Eileen, some of us just can't help being irresistible.'

'Thanks for the rescue,' Liv murmurs as they exit.

'You're welcome. She's like a stealthy snake, that one, the kind that mesmerizes you and then bites your head off. Ah, I see Lucinda, having a crafty fag by the rhododendrons. Let's away and Eileen can size up another victim.'

Liv has two letters in the morning post. The postman is coming up the path as she makes her way from the well with a bucket of water. He's a hefty man with a high complexion and brilliantly shiny shoes that squeak as he climbs, panting.

'We meet at last,' he says. 'I'm Pat, Pat Noonan.'

She shakes her head. 'No, you can't really be – not postman Pat!'

'God strike me dead if I lie. Isn't life cruel to some of us?'

She puts the bucket down and takes the letters from him.

'You'll have great muscles soon,' he says, tipping his hat back.

'Either that or a hernia.'

He finds this hilarious. 'Ah, you have your grandmother's sense of humour. I hear you've been swimming.'

'How did you know that?'

He winks. 'A little bird told me. Don't be getting sunburned, the wind off the strand there is deceptive. Oh, and the jellyfish that get swept in on the tides can give you a nasty old sting.'

'Thanks, I know, from when I was a child.'

'Ah, of course, Eileen was telling me you used to be over from London. And one of your letters is from England.' He tilts his head, nodding down at Douglas's even script.

'So it is.' She puts the letters in her pocket, noting his disappointment. 'I'd better get on with my chores, I've had no breakfast yet.'

He squeaks away, his bag flapping against his hip. In the kitchen she makes tea and refills the kettle, then sits by the window and opens the first letter, postmarked Castlegray. It's from Owen. There is what looks like a faint trace of egg yolk at the bottom and she imagines him writing it over a fry-up, sitting at the big round oak table with Toby snoring in the corner.

Dear Liv

I wanted to mull something over with you and it helps sometimes to write things down . . . makes the grey matter sift and shake.

I've been wanting for some time to go and see Edith, try and find out if we could make a go of things again or a least have a friendship. The older I get the more the stand-off between us seems ridiculous and too much like the plot of a play by Synge or a John B. Keane story . . . we're always

141

passing each other or nodding at a distance and we only live a few miles apart. I always regretted that I lost her. I lie awake at night, thinking about it . . . you know, the wee small hours. I suppose I'd like to make my peace with her as I'm heading for my three score and ten. Bridget used to say that the man who made time made plenty of it but on the other hand, Tempus Fugit. And Bridget dying suddenly has made me think about that time flying by.

I've no idea how she would respond. Maybe I'm just a cracked old grey beard with foolish notions . . . what's your woman's take on this? You have a level head on your shoulders and steady eyes and you're from a different generation, one that doesn't seem so keen on feuds and silences. There's no one else I could ask about this without feeling a right eejit.

Any response gratefully accepted, even if you tell me I'm daft as a brush and I need to see a man in a white coat.

Love to yourself and a lick from Toby
Owen

P.S. When you were a baby you used to swing on my ears and call me Nownie.

She opens Douglas's envelope, lays the letter on the table as she cradles her hot cup. The handwriting is less firm, some of the lines uneven.

Dearest Liv,
Thanks for the water from the well. The Glenkeen surgery prescription; at first I wasn't sure should I rub it in, drink it or sprinkle it round the room? No, just joking; send more. It should be on the NHS. It certainly tastes better than the

spinach and quinoa juice I'm getting five times a day. I have a sip every night as I go to bed and think of you. I'm sure I can feel it doing me good, working its magic. There's an extensive library here and I found a book on Irish wells so I'm becoming versed in their significance. Did you know that there are societies in Ireland devoted to their renovation and upkeep and many have been 'lost' with emigration and land development?

It's tough just now; probably the worst bit. The initial adrenalin has worn off so it's a hard slog. Won't go into it, you'll know.

There are at least half a dozen people here whose marriages have already failed. Listening to them, I do understand how much I'm in your debt for sticking with me for so long. I have pathetic moments of feeling sorry for myself and then I recall how bloody lucky I am.

Hope you're having a wonderful rest and some craic. Does the cottage need much doing to it? Once I'm back on my feet, with my limbs calm and my brain in place, I'd love to come and see it, give you a hand. You may remember, from the early days, that I'm quite good at DIY – before I got into Drink It Yourself. Seem to recall that I did a good job on the loft and the cupboards. I know, self praise is no praise!

Liv, I'd like to get to know you again.

She places her hands on the solid, scarred surface of the table. His efforts to keep in touch, stay in her life, keep himself in her line of vision arouse her pity. He had done wonderful things in their house when they'd first bought it, sanding, repairing, loving to fix doors and skirting. He was a good carpenter, a fast worker. They had varnished the floors together, homemaking. Then, the beer or wine in the evening had been a reward for hard graft.

She folds the letter into squares so that the lines won't accuse her. Her thoughts drift to Aidan. She has woken frequently during the night, conscious of him, imagining she can hear his breathing, remembering the rough nubs of skin around his nails, the scab on the index finger of his left hand. Nearly twenty years have passed but now it feels like only yesterday when she last held him, was infused with his taste, his scent. She had buried the memory because it was unbearable after he left; now it's reborn. She thinks of a bulb that's lain under the earth, storing nutrients and energy, stirring itself, pushing up green shoots.

She looks at the bleak grey ashes of the fire and the faded, empty rug. The daylight striking the dresser is too revealing; she wants the subtle lamplight and the flickering turf flames, the secret warmth of their breath in the dusk. And she wants him, his skin, the weight of him in her arms. She presses her hands down to ease the longing.

When her phone rings she starts.

'I was just thinking of you,' she says. 'How are you?'

'Tired, I didn't sleep much and I had to be up at six. Carmel's brace was hurting her so I was reading her a story at 3 a.m. Then I was thinking about you so sleep was evasive.'

'I had broken sleep too. I miss you. Where are you?'

'In Cork, at a suppliers. An organic wholesaler. Are you busy this afternoon? I could come by about 2.30.'

'That would be great.'

'I hope I don't just fall asleep.'

'Well, that makes two of us.'

He laughs. 'Do you remember, on Sundays we used to sleep late and then while I made breakfast you used to run over to the Catholic church to get the papers from the woman in the foyer.'

'Holy Harriet! She used to look at me as if she knew I was a lapsed Catholic who'd just fallen out of bed and a man's arms. I'd

144

look at the pious faces of the congregation filing out and feel so wanton and carefree.' She stops, suddenly near tears. 'Well,' she says, 'those were blissful times.'

'Weren't they?'

'So, half past two it is then.'

'I'll be there.'

She rakes the fire, producing a glow and washes up her breakfast dishes. Those Sunday mornings . . . They had always spent Saturday night in his flat in Stoke Newington because he worked in a bar on the high street during the evening. She sat, eating peanuts and eking out a glass of wine, talking to him between customers. Those Sundays had been languid, love filled, easy. She had pulled clothes on without showering, running across to the church at the end of midday mass, conscious of the scent of their lovemaking while handing Holy Harriet the money. They had read the papers over French toast and bacon, calling out snippets to each other, making a second and third pot of coffee. She liked to dip her spoon filled with demerara sugar into black coffee and hold it for him to sip and crunch.

In the afternoons they had walked in St James's, Regents or Hyde Park, heading for an early evening film followed by curry; they agreed that for some reason, a robust curry was a natural full stop to a Sunday, a fitting tribute to the week lived and the week to come. In a cheap Indian restaurant off Portobello Road they had eaten from a round platter holding separate dishes of lentils, okra, lamb, cauliflower and potato with huge nan breads and a cooling yogurt dip.

Sunday had been the hardest day after he left, long and loveless and arid and pointless and tasteless, a day of tears and sighs and beans on toast and lying in bed but not sleeping. Oh Aidan, what did you do? Think of what and who we could have been now.

She takes the bowl of washing-up water out and throws it over

145

the hedge, wondering if her grandmother had also jettisoned her resentments with the sudsy foam.

It's years since she has cooked properly. Douglas has little interest in meals and she often eats alone, rustling up quick bowls of pasta, grilled meat with vegetables, the kinds of recipes to be found in books called *Ten Minute Suppers*. There is something about Glenkeen that inspires her to bake; certainly, since she's arrived her appetite has been insatiable. Is it the air or the water, she wonders, or maybe just the slow tranquillity of life in the glen that makes her want simple, comfort foods? There is, too, the memory of her grandmother standing over the mixing bowl, her floury hands shaping wheaten breads, scones and barm brack which was best eaten warm with butter. As she sifted the fine flour through her fingers she'd be singing, 'If I'd known you were coming I'd have baked a cake, baked a cake, baked a cake . . .' She had a special red cotton pinafore for cooking, with a design featuring tiny salt and pepper pots that wrapped around and tied at the side. It is still hanging on a hook by the dresser, worn, with fraying seams.

Liv ties it around herself. It smells of wheat and meat gravy. She stands at the table with the same bowl and in the same posture, her back to the light so that it falls full on the creamy butter and snowy flour. She rubs them together to fine crumbs, adding sultanas, dark crumbling sugar and milk, enjoying the magic of the mix binding together into a golden ball. She can't find a pastry cutter so she uses a glass to cut rounds from the rolled mixture and lays them on a greased baking tray. She isn't sure how she knows the recipe for scones, as far as she can remember, she's never made them before; she can only assume that she absorbed the knowledge while she was watching her grandmother. That's also how she must know that you need cool hands to make good pastry, even though she's never tried to.

While she is waiting for them to bake she rings Owen. There is a message on his answerphone instructing callers to ring his mobile.

'I got your letter,' she says when he answers. 'Where are you? There's lots of noise.'

'I'm in Dublin. Got a bit of work doing a voiceover in an insurance ad. They wanted a mature, reassuring man.' He lowers his voice and adopts a steady, comforting tone: "Whatever unexpected turns life takes, we're here to see you through." What do you think, would you take out a policy?'

'Certainly, probably more than one.'

'And what are you up to? You sound chipper.'

Reeling with love, refreshed with kisses, dizzy with anticipation. 'I'm making fruit scones, they're nearly done so I can't talk for long.'

'I didn't think young women went in for that kind of activity these days.'

'I don't, usually. This place is inspiring me. I'm working from memory, from watching Nanna.'

'Oh, she was a great cook, Bridget. Her Christmas cake was to die for and she made the best lamb stew I've ever tasted, loaded with onions and pearl barley. So, what did you think to the letter?'

'I think you should go and see Edith.'

'You do?' He sounds pleased and tentative.

'Absolutely. What's the worst that can happen? If she tells you to go away, you're no worse off than you are now, just a bit of fresh bruising. She might be waiting for you to make a move.'

'She's never given any sign.'

'Maybe, but that doesn't mean you can't try. And she's never asked you for a divorce, has she?'

'No, that's true. How did you know that?'

'Lucinda told me.'

147

'Ah, nothing's a secret west along there; the walls don't just have ears, they have tongues and memories.'

She laughs with him. She wants some of this love that has come flowing to the glen to surge outwards, lap abundantly around other lives. 'It was all a long time ago, whatever happened. People get snarled in old animosities; sometimes they'd give anything to be freed. I think it's worth a go, if you care about her.'

'Well then, I think I will. I'm back tomorrow and I'll screw my courage to the sticking post.'

'Good man.' She opens the oven door and peers in. 'I've got to get my scones out now, let me know how it goes.'

'I will, so. I'll make a real effort, smarten up with a new bib and tucker, trim my eyebrows and smooth them with water. And you, you're not lonely up there in the wild glen, with the ghoulies and the ghosties and things that go bump in the night?'

'No, not at all lonely. I have plenty to occupy me, keep me busy. I'll save you a scone.'

'You smell wonderful,' Aidan says, rolling her on top of him. 'Of warm spices and sugar.'

She sniffs her fingers that smell now of him, too; musky, sweaty. Her hands are supple from the scone mixture. 'Am I sugar and spice and all things nice?'

'Hmm. That would make me rats and snails and puppy dogs' tails.'

They have both been sleeping, the brief, satiated sleep that comes after daytime lovemaking. She looks down on him, laying her arms along the length of him. With his head back, in the afternoon light, he looks younger, his skin ironed of cares and creases. His torso is a deep butternut colour from working outside and tending his garden. He has tiny abrasions on his arms from where nature has fought back. There is a toughness that she likes, a stur-

148

diness from physical work. He brings with him a scent of the outdoors, of earth and vegetation.

She runs her tongue along his forearm. A fearful happiness floods her heart. He was her first love and there is a way in which he can be her only love. The knowledge is woven in the densely packed layers that accumulate as life paces on. She pictures Lucinda's bog paintings, the deep compacted earth that conceals and preserves bones, gold and artefacts, the tokens of human longings.

He has been describing his garden to her; the rows of potatoes, lettuces and onions, the fruit bushes, his plans for hens, his frustration at not having enough land. She can picture it, well tended, fed, weed free. He had always been methodical, thorough in whatever he did; his flat had been much neater and cleaner than hers.

'This is the bed my father was born in,' she tells him. 'That used to fascinate me when I was a child, that he'd been a baby in this bed.'

'I thought he didn't like me when I first met him. He was so quiet. But then, your mother could talk!'

She lies down, her head on his chest. 'I used to think they were happy, well matched but when my mother died he remarried quickly, to a woman completely different to her; an invalid type. She's even quieter than him, there's a kind of hush in their house – in fact it's more silent than my library.'

'Maybe he sought someone as different as possible because he couldn't bear to be reminded of what he'd lost.' He kisses her forehead, arches his back, gives a luxurious groan. 'I'm starving, I could eat for Ireland,' he says.

He had arrived with champagne but it remained unopened in their hurry to shed their clothes and fall into the welcoming bed. He uncorks it while she fetches warm scones, butter, cheese and jam on a tray and they eat a bed picnic, sitting on top of the eiderdown.

'My scones, your jam,' she says, 'a complimentary mixture.'

He raises his glass: 'To us, to this amazing, extraordinary coincidence that's brought us together.'

'To us and to Nanna, who must have been weaving an unknowing spell.' She clinks her glass to his. 'She wouldn't approve, of course, she's probably turning in her grave. Actions and unexpected consequences; she wrote a will and here we are.'

He leans on an elbow, touches her knee. 'Tell me about Douglas.'

She looks at him and down, picking at the flowers on the eiderdown. 'I married him the week after I graduated. He was a locum doctor at the student medical centre on campus. I felt so lucky, to have found love again and so quickly. I think Douglas was always drinking but I didn't notice at first; I didn't read the signs and then there's the golden mist of love. Gradually the drinking came to dominate our marriage. He's tried to give up many times. Now he's booked into a place where he'll be helped. He's hoping it will save our relationship.'

'And you?'

She rolls her glass against her cheek. 'I don't know. I want him to stop drinking but that would still mean I'm married to an alcoholic and I don't know if I can live that life any more. I don't know if I still want that to be my identity. Addiction is a hard taskmaster. I know it inside out, it's my best friend and my worst enemy, it goes to bed with me at night, gets up with me every morning. I've read the books, studied the up to date literature on the Internet. The latest theory is based on genetics and I discovered a few years ago that Douglas's grandfather was a heavy drinker. The subject, the fact of it takes all my energy. It has made me tough in ways that I don't much like. Since I came here I've understood exactly how exhausted I am.'

'Have you any children?'

'No, that's another bit of our life that's gone adrift. In many ways, Douglas is my child; I have to look out for him, protect him, pick up the pieces. You see, his big relationship with drink has robbed us of so much, it's the thief in the night who steals away with your precious things.'

'I'm sorry.'

'Yes. That's all I want to say about my marriage, I don't want to dwell on it. You know,' She touches his hand with her fingertips, 'I feel as if I've been tunnelling for a long time in a dense gloom and now I've finally broken through. Up here in the airy height of the glen, with you, I'm afloat in light.'

He puts the tray on the floor. She moves into the well between his legs and he smoothes his thumbs down her cheekbones. 'I think you have more freckles now. They make you look serious, a woman of the world.' He kisses her face, blowing lightly on her eyelids.

She holds him tight. Sun is spilling into the room, tracing patterns through the lace curtain. The lace, pretty and delicate, reminds her of Maeve. 'I should be serious,' she says. 'This is serious, what we're doing. Your wife, your child – what about them? We're heading for trouble, Aidan, you know that, don't you?' But at the same time she feels that she deserves him and that this reunion had to happen.

'Shh. Don't talk about that now. All I know is that you're Liv-of-my-life. That's what's important, that's all that matters.'

She accepts the loving lie, allowing him, his tempered skin, his breath and warmth to become the world.

'I don't want to go,' he says, looking at his watch.

She doesn't need to see the time; she knows from the movement of the sun, just glancing off the corner of the window, that it's about five.

'I could ring Eileen and ask her to keep Carmel for a bit.

151

Maeve's at an evening class after work.'

'What will you say?'

'That it's a late delivery.'

'Well . . . you know I don't want you to go. There's something I've been wanting to show you.'

He makes the call on his phone, speaking of a last-minute order, stating that he'll be there by 7.30. Carmel comes on the line and he bends into the mouthpiece, reassuring her that he has apples for chutney. 'Carmelita', he says quietly. She wonders if the child detects the false note in his voice.

They look at each other. He rubs the front of his throat, where the lie has snaked from.

'Deceit is awful,' she says. 'It taints everyone, doesn't it?'

'This was meant.' He reaches for her hand, pulls her close. 'I'd lie my way to hell and back not to lose you again.'

She feels claimed, wanted. It's a long time since she's felt that way and it's an exhilarating rush. 'Now,' she says. I'll show you where I get the water, my place of magic.'

Down at the well, lying side by side on their stomachs, they gaze into the depths.

'Do you remember,' he says, 'that caravan we rented near Whitstable? The roof was leaking and we both got food poisoning.'

'From the pot roast in the pub. We said that it must be love, if you've heard the other person groaning on the loo while you were groaning too.'

'There was a foldaway bed but we never folded it away.'

'We needed it too often.'

'You were my world.'

'And you mine. I'm the man who threw the world away.'

'But now it's here. Just us, in this enchanted glen. This well has magical properties, you know.'

152

'How come?'

'It's to do with the power of place. There's been a tradition of that in Ireland since prehistoric times. The Celts believed in earth-centred religion, goddess based. Certain places, particularly wells and natural springs are believed to have curative and regenerative powers. You might, for example, look into the water for inspiration or good luck. My grandmother gave it to people to relieve their ailments.'

'Maybe I should take some to Carmel, her mouth hurts from her brace.'

'Why not? The magic works in all kinds of ways, allegedly, from bestowing wisdom to sorting out headaches and lack of libido. Maybe it brought you to me. I especially wanted you to be here with me, by this well. When I came to Glenkeen after you told me we were over, my grandmother walked me down here and smoothed the water over my face and my heart. I think she wanted the well to ease the hurt and thoughts of you. I humoured her; I was too despondent to resist and it meant so much to her. But maybe there was healing and magic, it was just longer term; it was your return to me.'

'Do you believe that?'

'I believe in now, and you and me and this place. God, Aidan, there's so much I'd like to do with this, my home on the hill. I've got a builder coming, Owen recommended him. I want to talk over some possibilities.'

'Such as?'

'A bathroom, for starters, maybe the smaller bedroom upstairs. A fitted kitchen and a conservatory so that I can have sun without the wind and rain. Not too much, I want to maintain the simplicity. I'd have to take out a small loan, I could manage that.'

'You're definitely keeping the cottage then?'

'Yes. I wasn't sure at first but I know now I need it.'

There is a silence. They are both boldly imagining the life they could have in the glen and are unsettled by this prospect within their reach.

He speaks first, his voice shaky. 'I'm envious of that garden, there's such potential. I've been mapping it out in my head, where I could grow stuff.'

She runs her fingers through the water, splashes her face. 'We could garden in the early morning, sell at the market, swim in the afternoon, cook, eat and make love at night, then water the crops. A simple life.'

He rolls on to his back, sighs contentedly. The sun is a warm blessing, enveloping them in a fond embrace. 'In the winter, we could concentrate on buying from the markets and making home produce.'

'I'd love that; I'm enjoying cooking so much now. You could really branch out.' She sits up. 'Listen, I was thinking in bed last night; you could provide recipes featuring the seasonal vegetables you're selling. Every week, you could give new recipes away with the stuff you sell. Simple, easy to make dishes, no fuss. I bet it would be a real draw; something different.'

He looks at her and sees himself in her eyes; a real person whose labours are significant. 'Liv,' he says. 'Liv.'

'Oh,' she says. 'I'm full of such energy. I could run a marathon and climb a mountain, sail the seven seas and all before breakfast.'

'Will you marry me?' he asks.

She smoothes his hair back, rubs a springy grey curl between her fingers, then pushes firmly back along the top of his head, remembering how he loved to have his head stroked, how it calmed him. His hair smells yeasty, like rising dough. There is a rawness in his eyes and voice that makes her want to shelter him from the rough chafing of the world.

'You have a wife, Aidan. I have a husband.'

154

He takes her hands, cups them in his. 'I know. But will you, when the time is here?'

'Oh yes. There is no other answer.'

9

The builder, Marty Nulty, arrives early, at eight. He is long and thin, with shoulder-length grey hair, small round eyes and a solid expression, as if he would be a hard man to impress. He takes his boots off outside the front door and says he'd shake hands but his are covered in muck. Liv finds this reassuring, and the pencil stuck behind his ear. When she'd got a builder in to rebuild the front wall in London, he'd arrived at night, clothed in spotless denim, smelling of aftershave and he'd taken ages over the job.

Marty accepts a cup of tea and she shows him around, explaining her ideas. He taps walls and presses his hand against them, examines window frames and floors.

'We'd have to run water up, and electricity, of course. You'd need a septic tank dug somewhere out the back.'

'So it all sounds feasible?'

'Oh yes. It's good, the way you want to keep the features. There's plenty now with more money than sense, building monstrosities that wouldn't look out of place in Texas, having jacuzzis and the like. Last year a fella, a cousin of the O'Donovans the other side of Redden's Cross, had a lovely thatched cottage pulled down and put up a ranch house with a hot tub outside.'

'Well, just a bathroom with a shower will do me.'

Outside, they walk the garden. The dew is still fresh, beading the dark rhododendron leaves. It's another cloudless day with a breath of breeze.

'I'd stop by here sometimes and buy eggs from your grandmother,' Marty tells her. 'Her hens laid the best I've ever tasted. She said it was the special mash she made for them. She'd never tell me the secret of it. Smarty Nulty, she used to call me, because I was so good at quizzes.'

'Do you think she'd approve of what I'm planning?'

'I'd say so. She'd appreciate that you're not going to go over the top. The tank could go by the side here so it wouldn't be obtrusive. Then you can have a clear run at your garden. Have you plans for that, too? If you need help, my brother does gardens, he's in Cork but he travels.'

She thinks of Aidan's schemes for the garden, his description of how he would double dig vegetable plots and have espaliers for fruit, apples and pears. On the eiderdown in front of the fire, he'd explained the value of horse muck and how the stables would give it away by the steaming sack full. On a piece of paper, he'd illustrated the twelve months of the year and the labour that would need to be done in each season. It would be hard graft, team work, but satisfying. She'd looked at his roughened fingers, the swift strokes of the pen and blinked to capture the moment, store the image in her memory. She has already composed her letter of resignation to the library in her head. Her explanation to Douglas is harder to formulate, she hears it like a distant train, vibrating faintly. The world has become Aidan; there is no sense or shape to anything now without him.

'I'll deal with the house first,' she says. 'Get that in shape.'

'Very wise, one step at a time.' He takes his pencil from behind his ear and gestures with it. 'You have a lovely spot here, with the land and the sea behind you.'

'I know. I'm blessed.'

'I'll put a quote together for you, so.'

'Lovely. Oh, and the well stays untouched, did I say that?'

'That's fine. No one in their right mind would touch a well, my father would say, on account of the little people and the mysteries within. I stopped by there on my way up, to ask a special favour. I've been suffering with my nerves; my mother has Parkinson's and I'm pretty frazzled,' he confides.

She reappraises him. 'You believe in the powers of the well?'

'Indeed. I've done the circumnambulation a number of times. It never fails.'

'What's that?'

'It was your grandmother who got me into it, as a matter of fact. You walk around the well, clockwise, about, oh, a dozen times, whatever feels enough. You say whatever's bothering you, what you need to resolve. It's worked for me; whether it's the power of the well or my own mind I don't know. I don't care either; it gets the result. I suppose it's just another form of prayer, in a way, asking for your intentions to be granted.'

Only by the earth rather than the heavens, she thinks.

When Marty has gone she goes to the well and stands, studying the water. Now she knows what Nanna was doing the night she'd read the letter from or about Owen, when the heart had been put across her and she'd circled the well, unaware that her grand-daughter was watching her. But what was her prayer and was it granted? Walking back up the path, gazing at the cottage, she visualizes Marty, her unexpectedly spiritual builder, making her wishes come true.

There is a bulkier envelope from Douglas this morning. Inside are sheets of paper headed 'Shame List'. Kia, he says, has encouraged him to write it. He supposes it's a kind of confession, a therapeutic naming of his sins. In no particular order, she reads.

Disappearing at the end of dinner at Mandy & Philip's & being found asleep in the bath. I think we were never invited back.
Going out for postcards in Rome and being escorted back to our hotel room 6 hours later by a kindly bar man.
Vanishing overnight in Nice with that new best friend who stole my credit cards.
Falling down the hotel steps on our wedding anniversary.
Failing to turn up for my own brother's wedding.
Making you miss your grandmother's funeral.

And many more such incidents which you will recall far better than me. I have liked vanishing, haven't I? Evasion has been my forte. I realize that this list is of more use to me than you. I can hear the ring of hollow laughter from your end. I suppose I'm asking for forgiveness, like any penitent.

She reads it calmly, knowing that it has come too late. These words would have meant so much last year, the year before. She is far removed from him now, from that life; it's like reading a letter from a fond acquaintance. The woman who recalls all those occasions is no longer imprisoned by the memories. It's easy to consider forgiveness now, when she is replete with another touch, another voice, her life suddenly brimming with possibility.

Aidan stops in briefly in the late afternoon; he has an hour, just, between hurriedly packing up the stall and calling for Carmel. He turned away a few customers to get a head start, jumbling produce together hastily, chucking boxes into the van. Bertie from the cheese stall had called to him, laughing, 'Is the devil riding your coat tails?'

159

The kitchen is empty. He blinks, coming from the brightness into the shaded room. He sees that Liv has acquired some tall oak shelves where she's put her books and there's a new painting of moorland on the wall opposite the dresser. On the table lies the biography of Dirk Bogarde that she's reading, and a pile of tomatoes and onions. He smiles, breathes. The fire is burning low but intensely and there's a huge pot of water simmering over it. He hears a radio, identifies Paul Simon. There's a banging from upstairs.

'Liv?' he calls.

'Up here!'

He finds her in the bedroom, standing on a chair, trowel in hand, stripping wallpaper, dressed in her swimming costume. She's done half the room and she's covered in grime, her hair dust filled.

'This is a surprise; as you can see, I'm not dressed for visitors.'

'You don't mind? I managed to grab a bit of time. I so much wanted to see you. It's been two days, seems like two years.'

'I know. Why do you think I'm up here, scraping and sneezing? Anything to keep occupied.'

She steps down from the chair, kisses him. She smells of glue and brackish water. Her lips are warm and dry and there's the heat of hard work pulsing from her skin. He feels her biceps. 'I like a strong woman. Why the swimsuit?'

'It seemed most practical; I was going to strip off but then I thought someone might call and I'd be the scandal of the town. Or maybe I'd become the latest TV guru: the Naked Decorator.'

He picks her up and swings her round, smudging himself with debris. 'I love you and your no-nonsense approach to life. When did you decide to do this?'

'After lunch. I reckon if Marty's going to start the renovation soon, I might as well do up this bedroom and sleep in the small

160

one in the meantime before he tears it apart for a bathroom. Then there's one room that'll be liveable while he does his worst. I've excavated four layers of paper; the top and second layers floral, the third geometric and the last brown and green stripes. I had to soak each wall twice, they used glue made to last. I'll finish tomorrow, I was about to have a bath. Want to join me – you're all mucky now.'

'I can't, really. I have to go for Carmel. I've another ten minutes; I'll help you fill the tub.'

He draws the curtains, drags the tub out and fills it while she rinses her hair off outside. Pausing, he looks at her in the sunlight, head bent, spray flying. He watches the lean lines of her, her taut calves and grimy feet. When she has finished washing she'll smooth some moisturizer on her face, nothing else. He is contented with her straightforwardness, her lack of fuss. There is a cool, unruffled quality to her that he finds reassuring; despite whatever travails she's had in her marriage, she moves in her own composed space.

'I like the shelves and the painting,' he tells her as she climbs into the tub and lathers her hands.

'I got the shelves from that house clearance place on the Cork road. The painting I bought from Lucinda, Owen's friend; it was in her exhibition. I like its mystery, the way you can read stories into it.' She lies back in the water. 'I had another letter from Douglas today.'

'Oh. How is he?'

'He says he's doing well. His body is through the worst of the withdrawal now; the sweats and cravings. He seems positive. They have a strict regime but the rules really help him. There's nowhere to skulk and hide, which is what alcoholics do best.' She looks at him, rueful. 'Ironic, isn't it, that just as he's finally doing what I've been begging him to do for years, we meet and his efforts seem

161

less crucial to me.'

'They still are to him, though. He has to do this for himself, surely. He'll benefit, his life might turn around.' This is what Aidan needs to believe; he injects optimism into the words.

'Yes, but I doubt he'd be able to continue with the cure if he could see me here, now, with you. It would probably drive him straight back to the bottle. I write him supportive little notes, supportive, traitorous little notes, saying everything but the truth.'

'We need to talk about how we're going to do this, be honest, start the life we want.'

'I know. We need time for that. More than a furtive hour here and there, looking over our shoulders, drawing the curtains in broad daylight. Your list of lies and excuses must be getting suspiciously long. I don't want to have to lurk around the square in Bantry, getting a glimpse of you at the stall to keep me going, dodging around in case somebody sees me behaving oddly.'

'You've been doing that?'

'A couple of times. You have a lovely way of throwing bananas from one hand to another while you chat. When you drink your tea from your flask and gaze into the distance I imagine you're thinking of me but you're probably gauging the day's takings. Sad, isn't it? I'm like a lovesick teenager, mooning around, playing truant. It's no way for a grown-up to be carrying on.'

'Don't; it's grim and I can't stay. I don't want to leave that hanging in the air. There'll be enough difficulty ahead. Let's not be grim for five minutes.'

She stretches her arms, nods. 'You're right. Will you help me choose a wallpaper for upstairs? I wanted to paint but the plaster's too bad.' She grabs his hand. 'I mean, you'll be looking at it as much as me, won't you?'

He kneels by the tub. 'I will, yes, there's no doubt about that.'

He has to force himself to go out into the bright, revealing sun, hastening down the glen, fumbling with his keys as he sees how the time has flown again, flitting, gone for ever while his back was turned.

Liv is trying her hand at a barm brack, love flowing from her fingers into the mixture. Aidan says they're both going to get fat, that they won't be able to make it up the glen. She can't stop baking; it's such an unusual pleasure to make food as a gift of affection. And the scents of fruits and spices belong in the cottage, nestling into the beams and plaster, breathing back into the air when the fire warms the room.

There is a sharp knock at the door. Wiping her hands down and across her apron she opens it. An oldish, balding man in a black suit, like an undertaker is standing there. He seems vaguely familiar. 'I believe you'd be Miss Liv Callaghan.'

'That's right. And you are?'

'My name is Magee. My sister, Miss Edith Magee, is down with the car and she'd like a word with you. She can't come up here, you understand, because of her disablement.' He has stony eyes, eyes that miss nothing. He's looking at her apron as if he's counting every stain. She takes it off and he is already walking away so that she has no time to wash her hands. His arms swing by his sides in a marching step.

A large silver car is parked by the hedge and beside it is the woman she saw at the birthday party, balancing on her sticks. She is formally dressed in a white blouse and black skirt with a string of pearls at her neck. Her hair is subdued again in a tight bun. On her feet she wears stout black lace-up shoes. Her eyes, unlike her brothers, are moist today, rheumy under crepe lids but they dart still.

'This is your one,' the brother says and he walks away a few yards, studying the hedgerow as if it might reveal a secret to him.

'Good afternoon, Miss Callaghan,' Edith Magee says. 'Thank you for coming down. I didn't like to take the liberty of driving up and as you can see, I have some difficulty walking.' Her voice is surprisingly light and reedy with a hint of whistle on sibilants.

'That's all right. I'm pleased to meet you. I saw you at the hotel the other evening.'

'Indeed. Did you enjoy your dance with your uncle?'

'Yes. He dances well.'

'Oh, he does. He always did.'

'And you, did you enjoy your evening?'

'It was a good entertainment.' She rebalances her sticks, shifts her right hip. 'Miss Callaghan, I haven't come for social chit-chat, I'll get to the point. I don't think either of us wants embarrassment. I had a surprising visit from Owen Farrell recently. Your name was mentioned during our brief conversation. He seemed to think that some kind of renewal of our past relationship might be possible. I had the notion that you had encouraged this idea. Perhaps, being young, you have romantic leanings. I advised Owen Farrell that no such possibility existed and that his visit was most unwelcome.' She makes a little pucker of satisfaction with her lips.

'I see,' Liv says, buying time. She can smell the butter on her fingers, feel the dry powder of the flour in the palms of her hands. The afternoon is softly warm, the sun the colour of a ripened pear, but these visitors are unexpected clouds bruising the sky. 'Owen mentioned that he was thinking of visiting you. I suppose I did encourage him, it seems awful for people not to even speak, to be estranged in such a way. He's still very fond of you, I know that.'

Edith pulls her shoulders sharply inwards, so that they form straight blades. The brother clears his throat and turns a foot sideways, examining the sole of his shoe. 'Miss Callaghan, your opinion is of no interest to me. I do not know you. I do not know why

164

you should wish to intrude on me in such a fashion. I do not want Owen Farrell visiting me and upsetting my household. I hope I make myself clear on this matter.' The voice is sharper, louder, the words rushing out, as if a stream has been undammed.

A small black and white cat has appeared along the verge, picking its way behind Edith. It sits near her, blinks and turns, washing its right flank with a darting pink tongue. Liv imagines it is a friendly caller and feels grateful.

'I'm sorry if you've been upset,' she says, sounding calm although her heart is thumping at this rapid, carefully executed ambush. 'I didn't mean . . '

Edith rests a stick against the car and holds up a hand, palm forwards. 'Please, let us just leave it there. What you may or may not have meant is immaterial. Miss Callaghan, you are a recent arrival here; it is best not to meddle in other people's business. You have no knowledge of the history between Owen Farrell and myself and I regard what has happened as an utter invasion of my privacy. Now, I must bid you good day.' She leans on her sticks and moves slowly to the car. The brother steps forward, opening the door. She gives a little groan as she settles herself in, the brother making sure that her sticks are tucked in beside her. He crosses to the driver's door, opens it and taps the side of his nose with his forefinger at Liv before he gets in.

As they drive away the cat yawns and stretches, approaching Liv. She puts a hand down to stroke it and it smells the butter, rasps her fingers eagerly with its tongue. She watches its neat head and ears. When it has tasted the last buttery trace it turns abruptly and vanishes through the hedge. Slowly, she walks back up to the cottage, reeling from the antagonism. In the kitchen, she finishes the brack and slides it into the oven, hardly aware of her movements. Her breath is light and shallow. 'That's knocked the wind out of his sails', her mother used to remark when she got the

165

better of someone and Liv sinks down by the hearth, observing that Edith is not a woman to cross in good or bad weather.

On Saturdays, Aidan has to get up at six. It's one of the busiest market days and he likes to make sure that everything is looking its best. Always a light sleeper, he wakes just before the alarm and knocks it silent. Maeve slumbers on beside him, on her stomach, her left arm flung sideways. She looks peaceful, far away. Her wedding ring stares at him accusingly. She often refers to the house as their nest but unknown to her, he has flown it. In the past, he has been dubious about the idea that it's possible to love two people simultaneously, believing it to be an excuse for adultery. Now he knows that it's true. He knows that he loves Maeve and Liv but it's Liv that he wants, it's Liv who is his harbour, who makes him feel that he is berthed in his skin. He knows too that it's a love he shouldn't have allowed but he's too far in, the current has got him and he doesn't want to save himself.

He longs to close his eyes again. His life is being spent on the run, every spare hour dedicated to Liv. All his time and thoughts are focused on when he can conceal his van behind the hedge at the bridge and run up the path in the glen. As he weighs and wraps produce, he is calculating with the change the time he can steal between journeys without raising suspicion at home. The deceit and planning brings its own quick energy but it's a terse, nervy vigour, one that makes his bones ache.

When Liv knows he is coming she waits for him at the well and that's where they make most of their love now, protected in the shade of the Hazel tree, cooling each other from the spring. There are bottles of milk and wine staying chilled at the edge, beaded with water. They drink from both and eat her scones and fruit breads and the creamy yellow cheese from a ceramic dish wedged between the bottles. He feeds ravenously, feeling his stomach expand, replenishing his strength; he needs the milk and the food to maintain his energy and his wits. Lying back, he studies the shiny bark and dense foliage of the hazel tree, follows the light dance off the serrated leaves, tracing their deepening autumnal yellow. Reaching out, he tears off a thin strip of bark and tucks it in his pocket, recalling that Liv told him that it purportedly protects from witches and ill deeds. He reckons he needs all the safeguarding he can get, considering the turmoil in his life. Despite his whispering conscience, he feels enchanted, singled out for happiness.

When he can call in the evening, they eat potatoes baked on the hearth, skins rubbed with olive oil and sprinkled with sea salt and then they dance to the records she has found, swaying to big bands, Ella Fitzgerald and Duke Ellington. And always, finally, she puts on her favourite record and holds his face, singing to him, 'so happy in my blue heaven'.

He eases from the bed. For a big man, he is light on his feet, treads softly. He has a quick shower, dons his frayed jeans and a T-shirt and pads downstairs, makes a strong coffee and pulls a face when he tastes it. They mostly buy instant now, instead of the fresh roast he prefers. He accepts the sacrifice, one of the costs of the new life he has introduced them to. As he drinks he looks for his wallet and keys. The dominoes he played last night with Carmel while Maeve watched *EastEnders* are still spilled on the living-room floor. As he sat opposite her on the carpet, cross-legged, he could feel the salt score on his arms from where he had been swimming with Liv. He'd managed to grab some hours in the afternoon on the pretext of seeing his accountant. They'd gone down to the empty strand and floated naked in the sea, fingers linked. He'd felt like a baby in the womb, an aroused baby, all his nerve ends alive, his mind alert, his heart bliss filled. The weight of the waves pushed them against each other, willing them into each other's arms. Silver speckled fish had leaped in the foam, twisting and falling. He'd reeled home, driving too fast, the van skimming the roads, exhausted, drunk on love and salt spray.

Carmel had beaten him in all four games, easily. 'Dad! Where's your brain gone?' She'd ruffled his hair, laughing, crowing to her mother that she'd trounced him. Looking at his daughter, he knew with a dragging heart that he couldn't live without her but neither could he exist now without Liv. Maeve had commented that he looked tired and asked if he was feeling OK; he'd played with his dinner, still full of Liv's baking, defeated by salmon roulade with lemon and watercress.

'A bit exhausted,' he'd acknowledged, giving her a faint smile.

She'd uncurled from the sofa, brought him a bottle of stout, taking the cap off, holding the glass tilted and pouring it carefully so that it maintained a smooth head. 'There,' she'd said, 'that'll put some iron in your blood.'

Carmel had clamoured to have a taste and pulled a face, yuk! Then they had watched him drink, agreeing that they both hated the stuff and he'd flinched at their indulgent, amused faces, despising himself, barely able to swallow.

Later, Maeve had come to him in the kitchen while he was making Carmel's cocoa and asked him if the job was tough at the moment; he seemed tired and his appetite was poor. He'd heard in her voice the anxiety that he might not be making a go of things, that he might have another breakdown. He'd put his arms around her, reassured her that he was just a bit run down, it was a busy time, and not to be a worry wart. He'd felt her tangible relief as her tense limbs relaxed and her shoulders went down, felt that her shape and smell were already becoming strange to him, thought, I'm no good at this, I'm not one of those men who can juggle two women. His chin resting on his wife's head, he envied Liv her solitary sojourn; she wasn't being observed, she had no one to answer to and be responsible for.

He finishes his coffee, takes a croissant from the bread bin to eat en route. The house is silent, the only sound the homely flicker and grumble of the boiler as it kicks in to boost the hot water. He feels like a man who has heard a melancholy tune playing late at night, one of those melodies that tug at your heart and stomach and leave you yearning, regretting what's gone. It's not that I'm unhappy, he thinks, it's not that I was looking for anyone else. If anyone had asked me a month ago, I'd have said I was content. Something happened and I found myself in another place.

Carmel has stuck a purple and green Post-it note on the latch of the front door: 'Message to father – dateline Saturday – apples for chutney'.

He takes his pen and scrawls beneath: 'Yes boss!'

They've pulled the kitchen blinds down because the sun is too hot to work in. The blinds are yellow, so they are surrounded by a wall of warm gold. Carmel sits on a tall stool and carefully chops dates into small, equal-sized segments while he peels, cores and slices cooking apples. His eyes are already watering from the onions he's chopped and now his roughened right index finger smarts from the juice. Carmel has cleaned the jars and they are warming in a low oven. They weigh brown sugar and sultanas and mix them with the dates in the wide ceramic bowl with spoons of ground clove and cinnamon.

'It smells like Christmas,' she says.

'Mmm, Christmas in September, when it's as hot as July. Maybe we should call this Indian summer chutney.'

'Where does that come from, Indian summer?'

'I don't know – maybe from the British in India?'

Carmel gives the dry mixture another turn with the wooden spoon. 'Hang on a min,' she says, and disappears.

169

He knows what she's gone to do. He takes the heavy jam-making pan from the cupboard and puts the chopped apples and onions in, adding a bottle of dark malt vinegar. Now the kitchen smells like Christmas crossed with a chip shop. He sets the pan on the cooker and turns the ring on. He stares into the mixture. He sees Liv sitting by the fire, taking potatoes from the hearth, exclaiming at the crispy skins. She loves simple, unfussy food that you can shove over the flame and forget about while you read a book or dig the garden; casseroles in a pot, left to simmer and thicken, chunky soups that taste earthy. In the cottage, his taste buds have been reinvigorated, his lungs fill with easy air.

Carmel dances back with computer paper, standing by him with her toes pointed out. She is wearing immaculate pink shorts and a yellow top with bees buzzing across it. Her clothes never look dirty; even when she's been riding, her jodhpurs are fresh looking. He wonders suddenly if she has fun. When he was little, he was always covered in mud and bruises.

'An Indian summer,' she tells him, 'is probably a saying that can be traced back to the traditional period when Native Americans would harvest their crops.'

'So really, it should be Native American summer.'

'Maybe. There are other explanations.' She reads more labori-ously, her finger following the words. 'For example, "Indian summer" can apply to anything that blooms late or unexpectedly, a renaissance that comes out of the blue. What's renaissance mean?'

He can hardly speak. He stirs the apple and onion mixture. The fumes from the heating vinegar make his nose run, camouflage unexpected tears. He wipes his eyes with the back of his hand. 'Oh, Carmelita, it means . . . a new beginning, a new start of some kind.'

170

'Like when we moved here?'

'Yes, like when we moved here. Now, this has boiled, I think we're ready for the other ingredients.'

He brings the pan to the work surface, cautioning her to be careful as they add the dates, sultanas and spices. Then she moves her stool over to the cooker and they take turns stirring the thickening mixture, watching it turn a dark brown as it simmers gently with tiny volcanic eruptions.

'Gloop shloop. Gloop shloop,' Carmel laughs.

The kitchen is suffused with a sour sweet scent. Carmel shrieks as a wasp finds its way through the window and floats across the cooker. 'Make it go away!' she flaps, ducking her head, her stool wobbling.

He fetches a tea-towel and catches the wasp in its folds, dropping it outside the back door. 'You should be on the stage, with those dramatics; Carmelita, the Bantry diva!'

'I might be on the stage,' she grins at him. 'The Christmas play auditions are in a couple of weeks; *The Wind in The Willows*. I've been practising with Annie Ryan.'

'Indeed? What's all this?'

'Look.' She climbs down from the stool and takes up a pose in the middle of the floor, singing in her high, fluting voice about the pleasure of being in a boat on the river.

He looks on, amazed. He had no idea that she could sing like this; she looks older, knowing, her movements controlled. When she finishes he claps. She looks flushed and thrilled. Sweat is dripping down his back from the heat of the day and the cooker.

'Brilliant! RADA must be beckoning; I'll be an old man who sits in the cinema watching his daughter up on the screen. Now in the meantime, there's a matter of some chutney here and I think it's just about ready.'

171

He scoops up a teaspoon and they taste the mixture, considering, looking at each other.

'It's good,' Carmel pronounces. She has a shred of apple caught in her brace.

'Mmm, treacly, dark and sharp with a hint of . . .'

'Tar!'

They snigger. Carmel takes the glass jars from the oven and they spoon the thickened mixture in. It's a good batch, fifteen jars. When they are all full he carefully places the waxed paper rounds on the tops and tightens the lids in place. He passes the jars one at a time to his daughter who peels off her sticky labels and fixes them: *Carmel's Chutney – Date & Apple.*

'That's a job well done,' she says and she stands with her hands on hips, the way Maeve does when she's examining a dish she's prepared and is satisfied with the outcome.

He tidies the kitchen while Carmel heads off to the stables with Annie Ryan and her mother. He puts the jars on a tray and places them in the larder to cool. Amidst the warm disorder they have just created, he feels content, slack limbed. Things will work out, he thinks, we'll find a way of sorting this. He knows that Carmel will get on well with Liv, once the initial hurt is over; already, he has considered how Liv's influence will be good for her, encourage her to be less finicky in her ways.

As he rubs sticky traces of chutney he ponders Liv's account of her unpleasant visitors. He's seen Edith Magee about the place, a sharp looking little woman who looks as if she'd harbour a grudge or two. He's heard that the brother drives a hard bargain with the logs he sells from their woodland. He advised Liv to keep well out of the business from now on, tell Owen what happened and leave him to it.

He hears the front door open, Maeve come in, the jingle of her keys as she puts them on the hall stand.

172

'Hallo!' he calls. 'Welcome to chutney mansions!'

There's no reply. He gives the table a final wipe and goes into the hallway. Maeve's bag is on the floor, a couple of magazines rolled inside, telling him that she's been at her mother's. He looks in the living-room. She is sitting in her chair, hands in her lap. She's wearing a skirt and shirt in bands of navy and white, with a striped scarf in those colours around her neck.

'You look nautical today,' he says. 'Have you been shopping? We finished the chutney, we made loads.'

She looks up at him. She is pale and without lipstick. She never goes out without her lipstick. 'Is Carmel out riding?' she asks quietly.

'Yes. Are you OK?'

'OK? Not really.'

He squats down by her chair. 'What's up?'

She moves back into the chair, away from him. Her eyes are tired, with that strained look they have when she gets a migraine. She puts her hands on the chair arms, sits up rigid. 'I wondered, Aidan, if there's anything you want to tell me?'

He smiles foolishly. 'No, I don't think so. Why?'

'You're sure?'

He believes he has kept the two worlds successfully apart, doesn't see the collision coming. 'Yes. What's wrong?'

She presses her lips together, shakes her head at him, her look steady and distant. He knows then, in that gesture, his heart gripping. There's a long moment's silence. The ice-cream van jingles outside, stopping at the dusty patch of green on the corner. 'Greensleeves' plays tinnily in the stillness. The tune means that it's Stefan's van today; he usually has the weekends around here. Doors slam and voices call as children wheedle money from their parents. If Carmel were at home, she'd be heading over for a vanilla ice with sticky caramel sauce.

173

'That's a very apt tune, isn't it?' Maeve says. 'The lyrics just suit this situation. It is a bit wrong and discourteous, isn't it, to swim naked with another woman? Would you say so, Aidan? Would you not agree with me on that point?'

He gets up slowly, stands behind a chair opposite her, holds onto the back. There's a white noise inside his head, a mocking, sneering buzz: what did you expect, did you think you were going to get away with it?

'Let's see,' she says, her knuckles bony on the wooden rests. 'Yesterday, around five o'clock. Oh yes, you phoned and said you had to see your accountant. I fetched Carmel and we made a tasty salmon dinner. I'd gone out especially in my lunch hour for the fish, hurried my sandwich down; fresh Atlantic salmon, none of your farmed rubbish. Now I understand why you didn't have much stomach for it. Swimming would make you hungry, after all. I expect you had an early tea.'

His tongue is closing off his throat. 'How do you know?'

'Pat Noonan saw you down at the cove. He has lobster pots nearby. He informed my mother this morning. She told me. Probably most of Pat's post round know by now. That's nice. You must have felt very safe, out in the sea there, you must have thought I was a real eejit.'

'God, Maeve, I never meant it to be like this . . .'

'To be found out, d'you mean? No, I don't suppose you did.'

'I didn't mean . . .'

She raises her hands, brings them down sharply, a hard slap against the wood. He flinches. 'I don't care what you mean. How long, how long have you been seeing her?'

'Not that long.'

'So were you both having a good laugh at me that day on the market?'

'No, nothing had started then.' Although even that is a lie.

Everything is a lie and now Maeve knows it. He sees the dark knowledge in her face, in the wretched hollowing beneath her eyes.

She looks down at her wedding ring, twists it on her finger. 'How did it start, why? I didn't know you were that unhappy with me.'

'I wasn't, I'm not. Please believe me, it's nothing to do with you. I knew Liv before, it wasn't our first meeting.' He tells her about university, says that they split up.

'So she was your first love.'

'Yes, she was.'

'And you were hers?'

'Yes.'

'I see. You never mentioned her before, you must have wanted to keep her close.'

'It was all a long time before we met, that's all.'

Maeve grasps the knot in her scarf. 'So, when were you going to tell me?'

'Soon. It's been a shock for me . . '

'For you!' She stares at him. 'A shock for poor Aidan. I've been walking for an hour before I came home, piecing things together. Your various trips out in the evenings, the sudden need for journeys to Cork, your exhaustion, the way you've been pacing round the house looking as if you've lost something. And I was a complete fool, worrying about you, thinking you were overdoing it. Overdoing it! That's a laugh and a half! Are you leaving us, are you planning to leave your family for her?' Her speech has become more accented, rural; she sounds as if she's never spent time away from here.

'I hadn't made plans. I want to be with Liv, yes. That's what I want.'

Maeve rises, stumbling from the chair and walks the floor. She

175

places her hands in front of her face, then holds her arms across her body. 'So let me get this straight; you brought us back here to live because you wanted this life and now you want another one with a woman in a cottage who has a husband in England. Are lives that easily rearranged? I had no idea. It's your great fear, isn't it Aidan, that what there is right here and now is it; there's always something shiny for you, some opportunity just out of your reach. The gloss has rubbed off us and she's the dazzling one.'

He's never heard her sound like this; cutting, acerbic. He would have expected tears; he keeps thinking she'll cry but she remains dry-eyed.

'It wasn't anything I intended to happen.'

'And what kind of slut is she, this Liv woman, to want to break up a marriage, to take a father away from his child?'

'Don't. She doesn't want any of those things, this has happened as unexpectedly for her as well.'

'Oh, that makes it all right then. Have you told Carmel?'

'No, of course not.'

'What do you think that little girl is going to make of it? You've already taken her away from one home and friends and now you're abandoning her.'

'Look, Maeve . . .'

'No, no, no.' She shivers. 'You look, you look and you listen, carefully. You can go now and pack a bag and get out of here. Go on, go along to that woman. I don't want you here, lying to me, lying to Carmel, playing your little games, shaming me in front of everyone. You're a weak, selfish man; my mother was right, she always said that you think only about yourself.'

He takes the one opportunity given him. 'Your mother would have an opinion wouldn't she, the interfering busybody.'

'Get out, get out, Aidan.'

He goes slowly upstairs, takes a bag from the landing cupboard,

176

stuffs clothes in. He has disturbed the cushions that Maeve likes to arrange on the bed during the daytime. They are lilac and pink, matching the curtains, carpet and duvet. In the hardware shop in Bantry he has seen the parchment-coloured paper that Liv would like in the cottage bedroom. He places the cushions back in position and takes his toothbrush and shaving gear from the bathroom. He stops by the living-room door on his way out. A sweet warmth still drifts from the kitchen. Maeve is sitting in the chair, staring into space. He wants to enter the room but can't; already, he is an interloper.

'What about Carmel?' he asks. 'I'll need to talk to her.'

'I'll tell her. I'll explain as kindly as I can.'

'Can't you hold off a bit, please? Say I've had to go on a trip for a couple of days, buy us some time.'

'I think there's been plenty enough lies already.' She turns her head and body away from him.

'I'll ring her later, then.'

'No, leave it till tomorrow.' She makes a gesture with her hand.

He makes to protest, stops, closes the front door softly behind him. The cream and yellow ice-cream van is still there on the triangle of green, its motor humming. Stefan waves to him, several lollies in one hand as he serves a queue of noisy children. Carmel has picked up a few words of Polish from him to describe her purchases: *zimny, lody, wanilia.* He waves back, nodding. Stefan arrived from Warsaw at around the same time they moved from Manchester. He has digs in Bantry and sings in the church choir. His landlady, Peggy Murphy, buys from Aidan and has confided that Stefan is too thin, she's hoping to build him up with her lamb stews and fruit pies. He loves it here, he has told Aidan; he's making a decent living and hopes to settle permanently, find a wife, buy his own house. The usual, universal aspirations.

Aidan walks to his van, clutching his bag. It seems unlikely that

177

a marriage can be over so quickly, in the time it takes to buy a cornet or a multi-coloured ice lolly. He looks back at the house; he wouldn't be surprised if it shuddered and collapsed in front of his eyes.

10

Owen has called by on his way to Cork to say that he's sorry about Edith. He's brought Liv a handsome oval bone china serving plate as a token, white with tiny pink roses around the edge. It's nineteenth century, from a little place he knows in Dublin, one of his traders that he 'wheels and deals' with. She places it on the dresser, admires its fine beauty, says she'll probably be too nervous to use it.

'Ah, I never thought Edith would go on like that to you; she usually only wages battles with people she knows. I must have rattled her more than I thought, turning up and yarning about my feelings. I disturbed the status quo as ordered by her, I suppose, shifted the ground from under her feet.' He rolls a cigarette and takes up his usual pose, standing in front of the fire and securing a log in it with his foot. He's looking a bit worn and weary, she thinks and feels the contrasting satisfaction of her own boosted energies.

'Is she speaking to you still?'

'After a fashion. That's her style; a good old barney, a bit of a slanging match, then she sweetens up. Don't take what she said personally, she's argued with more people around here than the

179

Pope's had hot dinners. She's probably forgotten what she said to you by now.'

Sounds tiring, Liv thinks. She can't imagine why Owen would still be fond of such a waspish woman. Where would the tenderness be? 'Well, she didn't get much of a match here anyway, it was more of a monologue.' In retrospect, she thinks, it was a bit like being visited by the mafia; the godmother attended by the heavy, scowling henchman who softens you up for the punch. 'So you reckon you still have some hopes with her?'

'Let's say I haven't thrown in the towel completely. I'm playing the long game at the moment, giving her time to mull it all over. Are those Marty's sketches for the improvements?'

'Yes, he brought them yesterday; just rough ideas while he costs it out.'

'So you're definitely keeping the old place; a holiday hideaway, is it?'

She bends to stir the fire, throw more turf on. 'For now, yes. You never know,' she adds lightly, 'I might take up residence, become a permanent fixture.'

'Well, that beats banagher! That would be a turn up for the books. Is your husband keen on that idea then – does he fancy doctoring here? I believe the pay's better.'

'There are lots of discussions to be had yet.'

'Very wise. That would be a huge decision, living here after London. The winters are long and wet and there's not that much call for librarians. I'd love to have you here, we could gallivant to Cork and Dublin and you could maybe come in on the old antiques with me a bit – it can be quite lucrative, now there's money flowing and people want "instant" family heirlooms. But you're sensible to consider it from all angles.'

She is dazzled by these possibilities, a hermit crab blinking in the light.

180

Owen takes reading glasses from his pocket, holds Marty's plans close up. 'Well,' he says, 'I won't know the old place, it'll be a transformation.'

'You like the ideas?'

'Wonderful, I knew Marty would do the business. As Bridget would have said; it will be as if the golden goose has laid. You'll be sitting pretty in clover, no doubt about it. Your mother would have loved it. She always said that apart from better weather, all Glenkeen needed was to be dragged kicking and screaming into the twentieth century. She didn't go a bundle on rural charm.'

'She was never that fond of coming here, I gathered that much, even as a child. Before we left London, she'd see loads of films, have her hair done, stock up on novels, cosmetics and cigarettes. It was as if she was preparing for a siege. I heard her say to a neighbour once, "I just pretend it's a penance for my sins".'

Owen glances at her. 'Children notice things you'd never credit, and you were always as bright as a button. Mollie just felt a fish out of water here, but it was important to your father, so she made the best of it.'

'It was a shame, then, that we all stopped coming, given that my father liked it here, it was his childhood home. And he had a good relationship with his mother.'

'So did Mollie, you know. She and Bridget had the measure of each other in many ways. But now, well, if she saw these plans, I'd say Mollie would be here in a flash. Even the weather has improved, and there's a wealth of new shops – she'd not have a dull moment.'

She's explaining the conservatory design to him when Aidan shoots past the window, knocks urgently on the door. He's out of breath, pale and holding a red sports bag. 'I need to talk to you,' he blurts. There's perspiration on his forehead and she can smell the sharp whiff of anxiety.

181

'Oh, yes,' she says. 'Owen is here, looking at the plans with me. He brought me a lovely plate, come in and see it.'

'Well, Aidan,' Owen greets him, putting Marty's sketches down. 'Good to see you. How's your vegetable kingdom?'

'Fine, thanks, fine.' He catches his breath, holds his side. 'I've a stitch, sorry.'

'Now, I didn't know until a pub quiz a few months ago, that a stitch is caused by your organs putting pressure on your diaphragm,' Owen tells them. 'Marty knew, of course, he's a demon with the answers. And that reminds me, Liv, would you like to join our quiz team, once a month in the Drift Net, just out the road from Redden's Cross?'

'I'll think it over,' she says, aware of Aidan's laboured breathing and the bag that has a slip of striped shirt sticking through the zip.

'Good.' Owen looks at them carefully, his wild eyebrows meeting. He buttons his jacket, pulls down his shirt cuffs. 'Well, so, I'll be away, I must be in Cork for an early supper – I'm promised prawns and crème brûlée – and the roads can be busy on a Saturday evening.'

She bolts the door after him, something she has never done. The bolt sticks and she has to tug so that it shoots into place with a heavy groan. A pain shoots through her wrist. She turns, guessing what she is about to hear. 'What is it?'

'Maeve knows. Pat Noonan saw us swimming yesterday and told her mother. She threw me out.'

She holds on to the bolt, hands behind her. 'I'm sorry, that was my stupidity. I should have thought – Pat mentioned one day that he knew I swam down at the cove. I'd forgotten it – I've met so many people recently and so much has been happening. I should have been more careful.'

He shakes his head. 'Someone, sometime, was going to see us, unless we stayed inside and grew pale in the half light.' He's still gripping the bag with both hands; she eases it from him, puts it on the floor.

'Sit down. My God, this is sudden.'

He slumps into a chair. She crouches down by him, holds his knee, the thin denim covered in a cloth patch stitched by his wife. He smells vinegary.

'Did you have chips for lunch?'

'Hmm? No, no. I made chutney with Carmel.' It already seems another life, another era, stirring the thickening mixture while his daughter balanced on one skinny leg beside him, fingering her brace.

'Does she know?'

'No, she was at the stables when Maeve came back.'

'And Maeve, how was she?'

'Cold, very cold and angry. She told me to get out. I was honest, at last, after I'd been found out. I said I wanted to be with you. So she told me to come here. I drove around for a while. I didn't know who I was or where I was. I imagined I might just keep on driving, on and on until I ran out of road. You know, like one of those people you read about; they turn up in a place and no one knows why, or who they are. I think I stopped in a couple of places, I can't really remember.' He covers her hand. 'Well, it had to happen, I suppose, that someone would notice. We'd been living on luck, hadn't we?'

'Yes. This place seems so safe; a sanctuary away from the world. There was never going to be an easy way to do it.'

'I wanted time with Carmel, that's the worst bit.' He shudders. 'Have you anything to drink? I could do with a courage booster. Any whiskey?'

'Just red wine, I think, in the cupboard.' She'd bought it planning a chicken casserole for a special supper when he could get away, thinking of the onions and carrots and chopped garlic, with

183

dense white bread to dip in the juices. Now they can have as many suppers as they want.

She fumbles with the corkscrew and hands it to him but he's no better; it takes him several attempts to open the wine. They drink, taking strength.

'Here's to us,' he says. 'I don't think there'll be anyone else wishing us well.'

'Here's to us.' A toast doesn't seem right, though. She's thinking of Maeve and the child. And there is Douglas. It's all too rapid, she can't think straight.

He looks at her, sees that her eyes are dazed. 'Listen,' he says, 'I know this is unexpected. I don't have to stay here – I could go to a bed and breakfast. What I mean is, I don't want you to be hurried into anything because of what's happened.'

'What do you want to do?'

'Be here, with you.'

'And that's what I want. There's a relief, in a way, that it's been brought out. We need to stay close now, be united. There are going to be slings and arrows.'

He unlaces his boots, kicks them off. 'I could sleep for a week. I don't know what's keeping my eyes open. It's just as well this cottage stands high in the glen. We'll be able to see our enemies coming, prepare our ammunition.'

'Have you anyone in particular in mind?'

'Eileen, for sure.'

They laugh, exchanging guilty glances.

He frowns, pushes his glasses up his forehead. 'I think Owen guessed.'

'I'm sure he did. It doesn't matter now, though, does it? In fact . . .' She goes to the door, draws back the bolt, throws it wide. The sun is fading, casting a farewell blush on the glen. The heaviness of the day dwindles with it, making way for the light fingers of dusk. The evening is tranquil for now, until the birds start their busy twilight rituals, calling, flitting from tree to tree.

'There,' she says. 'No more secrets. That's something to toast.' She looks at him, sees his weariness, wants to cover him with a soft blanket and sing him to sleep.

He pours more wine. He pulls her on to his lap and they sit by the purring fire's leaping shadows, holding each other, looking through the door at the honeyed light spilling on the world outside.

In the night they lie close, nesting on a mattress in the small bedroom; the main one is still in a state of peeling chaos, awaiting the wallpaper that has arrived and is stacked in rolls. They've dragged in a wardrobe, hung up the few clothes he's brought beside hers. His shaving kit is on the washstand. A chair acts as a bedside table. They bump into each other whenever they move and smile at their jostling and squeezing. The room looks like a rough drawing, a preparatory work. He says it reminds him of her bedsit when they first met, when she also had a mattress on the floor. There's an exhilaration in the disorder; they could be eighteen and twenty-one again, swapping stories about lectures, scribbling essay notes, cutting coupons from the papers for cut-price meals and cinema tickets.

By the candlelight, they create animal shapes on the wall, rabbits, deer, flapping birds, rearing horses and elephants. With joined fingers they make a deep winged eagle, gliding swiftly across the shadow-pocked wall. They talk themselves hoarse, spreading out the real, here and now life they will start building; repairing the cottage, planning the business, preparing the garden. They decide they'll need another room, a study that can also serve as a guest room when Carmel stays. It could be added at the back and maybe another toilet. Marty will have to be consulted again, drawings reviewed. Herbs, she says suddenly, clapping her hands together; she loves them, is good at growing them – she'd like eventually to make them a feature of the stall. He'll have to see a solicitor as soon as possible, get things sorted with Maeve. They agree that he should sign the house over to her, no question about that. It's a great relief now, they tell each other, that they can be honest and move on. Brimming with plans, excited by their own boldness, they sink back and discover all over again how well they fit, how together, with a hand here, a caress there, skin kissing skin, they make sense of the world's mayhem.

In the small hours, Aidan wakes and is confused for a moment, looking for his alarm clock. Then he feels the satin of Liv's thigh, looks down at her angular shoulders. He weaves his fingers through her hair, breathes in deeply of her scents of turf and sea. The silence is deep and astonishing. In the house in Castlegray, there is always some sound – a distant car alarm, a foraging cat, a sleepless neighbour. He thinks of his daughter, lying amongst her soft toys. He hopes her brace isn't hurting. He'd promised her the next chapter of *Long Ears*. As he stares into the darkness his mobile chirps a message. He sits bolt upright. Liv sleeps on. He reaches for his jeans, slides the mobile from his pocket and opens his text inbox. The message is from Carmel, glowing greenly at him: *Daddy, come home.* He lies back, the mobile held to his chest. He doesn't care what Maeve says, he'll see her soon, he has a right to see her, explain to her. He puts his hand on Liv's waist for reassurance. He recalls what she used to say to him when he was agonizing over his looming study deadlines: 'All shall be well and all shall be well, and all manner of thing shall be well.' She sighs and murmurs in her sleep, shifts on to her side, facing away from him. He pulls his lumpy pillow under his neck, trying to find a comfortable spot and nestles into her back, fitting his knee into the crook of hers.

*

Liv hears the van pull away and takes out her notepaper to write to Douglas. They have agreed that he will see his daughter and she will tell her husband. She feels bereft and anxious with Aidan gone away from the fastness of the glen, back into that other hostile territory. There is so much to do and yet they've only had just over a week together. At the same time, it seems as if all the years in between have fallen away, insignificant now. 'Douglas, I have to tell you . . .' she writes and looks at his name. The clock ticks loudly on the dresser and the measure of time passing seems menacing. She gets up and put the clock in a drawer, face down. Now she can hear her own breathing, feel the pumping of her surging heart. What if the sight of Maeve and Carmel, the tears and sadness make him change his mind? She couldn't blame him if his mind was changed; he is, in the end, making the bigger sacrifice. She dries the breakfast dishes and sweeps the floor, scrubs the table. Now and again she glances; 'Douglas'. She throws the dust out; the day is hot and bright outside, beckoning.

She is digging the garden fast, turning the soil on the bed they have marked for carrots, wanting to speed the morning along, when Owen calls a greeting. 'I've been trying to ring,' he says, 'but your phone goes to message.'

'Sorry, I've been a bit preoccupied.'

He takes his hat off, dusts it against his forearm, like a cowboy. 'So I hear, so I hear.'

She pushes the fork in, rests her foot on the top. 'You know, then?'

'I imagine there aren't many people who don't know, except maybe the natives of the upper Amazon. Once Eileen has information, you might as well broadcast it on the news.' He bends a knee and rests his forearm across his thigh, scans the horizon.

She rubs her hands together slowly, feeling the ridges of the fork handle imprinted on her palms. He touches her arm. She

puts a hand over his, patting it, as if it's he who needs reassurance. 'It's all been very sudden, Owen. I knew Aidan a long time
ago. What we had has been rekindled, unexpectedly, amazingly. I
didn't mean any of this to happen.'

'No. And is he moving in here now?'

'Yes. We were found out and that pre-empted everything. His
wife told him to leave. He's gone to see Carmel.'

He nods, takes his tobacco tin out, extracts a roll-up. 'Your
peace that you had here is vanished so.'

'For now. We'll rebuild it.'

He looks at her, a kind, knowing glance, then into the flare of
his lighter. 'As with all stories, there are different versions around
the place. One is the predator account, that you came here on
purpose to seek him out.'

'That's rubbish. I had no idea that Aidan lived here. Who's
saying that?'

'I had it from the butcher who had it third-hand from someone
unnamed. It doesn't matter, it's being said and you might as well
try and stop the tide coming in as attempt to stem the talk. Worse
will be said, you can be sure of that. You're an outsider and you've
thrown pebbles in the pond.' He draws deep on his cigarette. A
robin hops nearby, grabbing one of the worms she's turned up.
There's still a haze in the day that will join the cooling mists of the
afternoon. The sun is slowly losing its strength and the evenings
are falling faster. She remembers her mother wandering the
garden, avoiding the nettles and cowpats from the odd heifer that
strayed through, saying 'Sometimes this place feels like the edge
of the universe.'

'I love him, Owen. He's all I want in life.'

'I'm sure. He's a good man. Look after yourself, Liv, that's all.
The world's a cold place when you're an outsider.'

'We know it won't be easy. Nothing worth having is, is it?'

'True enough. But explaining that to Carmel; there's the rub. Have you told your husband?'

'I've just written to him. He's staying somewhere at the moment where I can't ring him.'

'Ah, well, at least that'll give him time to absorb the shock.' He runs a hand through his hair. 'Bridget must be spinning beyond in her grave. That robin there's a bold fellow, this must be his territory.'

They watch the bird hopping and pausing for juicy snacks. She looks at Owen's creased face, the slight droop of his shoulders. She takes his hat from his hand and neatens the brim. 'At least you don't disapprove of me?' She tilts her face to him, jaw up.

He laughs, coughing, rolling his eyes back. 'If I did, it would be a definite case of pots and kettles! I have no moral high ground, Liv, I'm like the robin; I just patrol my own bit of ground and watch the world go by.'

She reaches up and places his hat on his head, taps it down. 'You'll have a cup of tea with me then, even though I'm a Jezebel?'

'Lead the way, scarlet woman, I've a thirst on me that would drink an oasis dry.'

She wedges the fork into the earth, dusts her hands off. As she brews up she tells him of the wallpaper they're going to start putting up later in the afternoon, the design they've done for the garden, the new, more extensive plans for the cottage, the message she's left for Marty. Bent over the fire, her back to him, she doesn't see the anxious flickering of his eyes, the twitch of tension around his mouth.

Aidan takes his key out of his pocket but then thinks better of it, rings the doorbell to his own house. The street is hushed and he can't help feeling that there are eyes at windows. Cooking smells

189

float on the air – frying onions and the darker whiff of meat. This is still a country where there are some women at home making a hot midday meal. Eileen opens the door after a long pause, looks him up and down, then turns abruptly and goes back into the living-room, leaving him to shut the door and follow her. He might have known she'd be here, should have expected it but his head was too full of seeing his daughter, rehearsing what he'd say.

Maeve is sitting in the same chair he last saw her in. She's wearing an old T-shirt and jeans, the clothes she wears for doing housework. She's ashen, no make-up, her hair drawn tightly back into a ponytail. She hasn't washed it, he can see, it's lank and lustreless. Without cosmetics, the blue veins are apparent beneath her fine skin. Eileen looks robust, dressed in a red skirt with a wide leather belt, the light of battle in her eyes. She has pulled a chair up to sit beside her daughter and he stands before them. It reminds him of being called to the headmaster's study.

'Where's Carmel?' he asks.

'She's at a friend's,' Eileen replies.

He looks at Maeve. 'I thought we'd agreed I could see her this morning, take her for a walk, get a bite to eat.'

Eileen reaches out and takes one of Maeve's hands between her own, patting it. 'Maeve has talked it over with me. There's no question of you taking Carmel out anywhere. You can see her here or not at all. I'd say Maeve is being very kind, letting you see her anyway. But I suppose at the end of the day you are her father, even if you're not much of one.'

'Is that what you want, Maeve?'

She looks through him. 'Yes.'

'And Mr Riordan is going to act for Maeve,' Eileen continues, as if neither of them had spoken. 'For sure, you're going to be held to account for all of this – and you'll pay your whack, too. There'll be sleepless nights for you ahead, me bucko, and for that

190

one over in her little love nest. Here, pet.' She hands Maeve a tissue.

He rubs his tongue against the roof of his mouth, tries to moisten his lips. 'Maeve, you can have the house, there's no question of that.'

She looks down, flinches. Her mother snorts, folding her arms. Her stony eyes and mouth flash disgust. 'That's very generous of you, very big of you. The house is just the start of it, there's maintenance for your family too, and other expenses. Riordan will be in touch, you'll be getting a letter.'

He tries again. 'Maeve, do we have to start this solicitor stuff so soon? We can talk to each other first, can't we?'

'Oh for sure, you'd like that,' Eileen laughs. 'You think you can get Maeve to agree to things being your way, work on her while she's half out of her mind? Well, you can think again so put that in your pipe and smoke it.' She nods and slaps her knee.

'All right, Eileen,' he says. 'I get the message.'

'Oh do you, indeed. A lovely situation you've created here; Maeve and myself off work, Carmel not at school. It's well for you of course, with your woman and her inheritance, I suppose you're planning to be a gentleman of leisure.'

He makes a hopeless gesture with his hands, goes and props himself against the wall, runs his fingers through his hair. He has been written into a story now and he doesn't know where the plot is going; all he knows is that he's the villain. He is reminded of one of those books Carmel has, where you are offered several options at the end of each chapter and you can choose how the narrative will proceed.

Maeve stirs, folds her hands in her lap. She is wearing slippers with no socks and her feet look naked, bony and chilled. She always has cold feet; his job has been to warm them at night, tucked between his calves. He can't bear to look at them, they

191

speak to him of misery more than her face or her puffy eyes or the box of tissues at her elbow. 'Can you fetch Carmel, Mummy.' Her voice is dull, barely audible.

Eileen rises. 'I'll only be a couple of minutes.' She walks in front of Aidan, shoves her face close to his so that he can smell her milky breath. 'You might find your woman in the cottage has bitten off more than she can chew. There's more ways than one to skin a cat.'

He recoils, seeing the two red spots in her cheeks; her blood is up.

'Oh yes, mister, you should be worried.' She holds a finger up to him. 'Don't you be upsetting my daughter while I'm gone.'

He registers that as she goes out, Eileen leaves the front door ajar, as if he's some kind of thief or desperado, not to be trusted. Maybe, he thinks, she'll put *Wanted* posters up in the town. He walks over to the hamster cage, softly taps the side. Boris emerges sleepily from under a pile of sawdust and looks at him, nose twitching. He's glad of what seems a friendly glance. He angles the water nozzle lower, for something to do. Maeve blows her nose, sighs. He suddenly recalls the day they moved into the house and ate fish and chips sitting on the carpet, before the removal lorry arrived. They'd all been ravenous; it was the best meal they'd ever had, he and Maeve had agreed later.

'Maeve, I'm sorry.'

She rises, picks up the tissues. 'I'm going upstairs. You can have one hour with Carmel, down here. Don't say anything to cause her any more distress. It would help if you could get her to eat something, she's off her food. My mother will see you out.'

'We will need to talk at some point, sort out when I'll see Carmel. I've had four text messages from her. She needs me; whatever fights or recriminations we're going to have, she needs me.'

192

Maeve hugs the tissue box, rocks it like a baby. When she speaks it's in a faraway voice, as if she's preoccupied. 'Carmel does need you, that's certainly true. She's needed you since the day she was born. You've always been able to make her smile. I can't do that, I haven't got that talent. But none of that seems to be your priority now.'

'Carmel will always be a priority, I think you know that. I'm talking about the arrangements we'll need to make based on the future, on my living at Glenkeen.' He hears his voice rushing out roughly, swallows to moderate it.

'Glenkeen; beautiful glen. Isn't it funny how places can be completely misnamed? What would I call it? I think, I think it would be . . . Greasan Breag.'

'And that means?'

'That means web of deceit. It would be more suitable, I'd say.'

'Maeve, please – it doesn't help, being like this.'

'No?' She glances his way then, her eyes sliding across him. 'Well, any more talking can be done through Mr Riordan. I understand that's the best way. He'll draw up a plan about Carmel, too. Now I'm so tired, I must lie down for a bit.' She leaves the room silently, feeling her way through the door like a blind person. He bears down on the back of the nearest chair for support, squeezing his hands against the wooden frame, closing his eyes tight and seeing a conflagration of leaping colours. Then he hears the clatter of speeding feet and his daughter flies into the room, throws her arms around his waist, nearly knocking him off balance. They clutch each other, the only sound her ragged breathing.

Eileen has gone upstairs, her tread heavy and warning: I've got my eye on you, it says. He's persuaded Carmel to share a tin of tomato soup with him and for her to make toast while he stirs the comforting red liquid.

'I don't know what it is about canned tomato soup,' he says, 'but it always hits the spot when you're under the weather. I recommend it to the clientele in my restaurant any time, when they're looking a bit peaky. I call it the Back On Your Feet menu.'

She's playing along with him, pretending things are normal. She keeps looking towards the door. 'Do you want your toast light, mid or very brown, sir?'

'Oh, *very*, I think. It goes better with the colour of the soup and I do feel it enhances the flavour. Shall we be really naughty and have trays on our laps?'

'OK.' Her movements are listless and she has her hair in tangled bunches. One of her socks is cream, the other white.

'Now, you remember the secret to delicious tomato soup?'

She shakes her head, digging the knife into the butter so that it screeches on the dish.

'Never let it boil, just heat very slowly to good and warm.'

They sit in the living-room with their trays, sipping in silence. She dips her toast in her soup, spattering some.

'I hope Boris has been behaving. He looks perky.'

She shrugs. 'I think so.'

'Is it just today you've been off school?' he asks.

'Yes. Mummy said it would be best to stay here because you were coming. I'm missing my French test. I'd learned all the tenses of *Manger* and *Avoir*.'

'I'm sorry about that. The learning won't be wasted, though. I got your text messages, Carmel.'

'I thought you'd send me one but you didn't.'

'No, I wanted to see you.'

She raises her large, limpid eyes to him, spoon hovering mid-air. 'Don't you want to live with us any more?'

At that moment, he can't take a breath, thinks that his heart might have stopped. Her eyes were the first thing he noticed the moment she was born. The midwife had raised her up and she

194

had looked straight at him as if to say, I know you. He gives up the pretence of eating, puts his tray down. 'It's not that, Carmelita. I love someone. Her name is Liv, she's the lady you've met a couple of times, the one who helped you that night with your homework.'

'Don't you love Mummy?'

'Yes, I do. But I want to be with Liv. It's complicated, but I'll sort it out, I promise. You can come and stay with us, when the time is right. I'm not far away, you know, only about ten miles.'

She scuffs her heel on the carpet, rocking the tray. 'But I want you to live here. I don't like it without you. Mummy cries and she's cross with me.'

He leans forward in his chair. 'Mummy's not cross with you, she's just upset. It's me she's cross with. It will be OK, I promise.'

Her face crumples. 'I want you to come home.'

'Carmelita . . .' He gets up to go and cuddle her, take her on his knee, tell her she's his best girl but she lets out a wail and jerks the tray in the air. A red waterfall sprays to the carpet, the bowl flying across the room and shattering against the fireplace. He ignores the mess, grabs his sobbing daughter in a tight hug as Eileen and Maeve run into the room. Eileen's skirt and the soup are the same colour and he thinks that it's a handy coincidence as she stoops to pick up the smashed china, her hem dipping in the liquid. He looks at Maeve over his daughter's head and is alarmed by the blank, fixed desolation in her usually serene eyes.

195

11

They lie in the bath in front of the fire. It is filled almost to the brim, the steaming water pine scented with salts to ease their grumbling muscles, exercised by an afternoon's digging. They have prepared beds for early spring sowing and cut back straggling bushes, removed stones, set up a compost stack, working easily around each other, talking only occasionally, stopping now and then to consult, exchange kisses or a touch. Now and again one would glance at the other, checking, confirming, reassuring. They like to keep in each other's sights. They worked until the sun was fading and the mauve evening hastening towards them on a gathering breeze that worried at their bare arms.

'That's the dying of the year now, you can feel it in the wind and see the tired dimness in the sky. The sun is growing shy.'

Aidan had put his arm around her as he spoke and she was glad of his body heat. A shiver of melancholy ran along her spine when she sniffed the sourness that came from the earth as it cooled, thought of the long winter nights stacking before them. It was the end of October when her mother died and that same tart tang had clung to the clods in the rain-blown cemetery. Since that afternoon, she has felt a falling in her heart, like an ominous minor chord, when the evenings draw in. For the fist time, she wonders

196

what her father will say when he hears the news from the glen but she pushes the thought away; she hasn't the wit or inclination to deal with that just now.

They have not spoken about the solicitor's letter delivered that morning. The postman is unseen now, he has started bringing the mail early, leaving it on the front doorstep and vanishing, no word spoken, no merry quips. They just fit in the tub, as long as she tucks her legs around his waist and he props his feet behind her shoulders. The evenings are cooling rapidly, brisk draughts nagging under the front and back doors and through the windows; they have built the fire up and the lamps are lit. A stew thickened with carrots and shallots is simmering slowly at the back of the fireplace. They link fingers on his knees.

'It'll be lovely to have a proper bathroom but I'll miss this tub. There's a curious harmony to watching your dinner cook while you bathe.' he says.

'That's if we ever have a bathroom. Marty hasn't returned any of my calls. I suppose I shouldn't be surprised; he knows Eileen.'

He rubs his thumbs over her knuckles. 'Probably best to forget about him. We'll contact some builders in Cork.'

'People who don't know that our social standing is rather low?'

'Exactly. People beyond the west Cork Cosa Nostra. There's plenty out there. We'll get a phone book, make a list – or go to the Internet café tomorrow.'

'It's a shame, though; Marty knows this place, was in sympathy with my ideas.'

Aidan shrugs with a nonchalance he doesn't feel. 'I know. Never mind, we'll find someone else who can translate what we want. We did well today, didn't we?'

'We did, we shifted loads.'

'We'll be well prepared for early planting next year. Once we've a greenhouse we can start our own stuff from seed. I was thinking

197

that we should look for one in January, we can get the standing organized by then.'

'It's a pity Maeve won't let you have any produce from the garden there. It seems so petty, she can't use it all.'

He agrees but he doesn't want to criticize Maeve to Liv. That would seem like a double betrayal. He busies himself with the sponge and soap.

'Do you think some of this business will be settled soon?' She gestures at Riordan's letter, lying on the table. It states in that officious, pedantic style that solicitors always employ that there can be no divorce for four years but that an interim settlement will be sought. Property, pension and lump payments are mentioned in separate paragraphs but it is the last section that caused Aidan to slump over his breakfast, pushing his plate aside. Access to his daughter, it warns him, will be allowed for one afternoon each weekend but only in her own home and with her mother or grandmother present. He had handed the letter to Liv without speaking and gone outside, returning with bleary eyes.

'I hardly think so. I'll see a solicitor this week myself, find out where I stand. Carmel's the main issue.'

She leans forward, cradles his head, massaging his temples. 'I'm sure that weekend business can't be allowed, they're just trying it on. Maeve's angry, I know, she's out to punish you but that's not fair on Carmel. You have rights as a father.'

'Well, we'll see. Like I said, I need some legal advice. I'm not sure fairness will come into it just yet.'

'Would you like me to come with you to a solicitor?'

'No, that's OK. Eventually, yes, but I think it's best if I handle this bit on my own.'

'But you will say that you want Carmel to be able to come here, to visit us in our home?'

'I will, yes, but I have to think about her, first and foremost. If it's too much for her now, I'll have to play along. I don't want her to feel torn between myself and Maeve.'

There's a silence; they both know that she will be torn whatever is arranged.

'It's just,' Liv says carefully, 'that I want to be able to get to know her. And I don't want to feel like the wicked witch, murmuring my spells in the glen while you see your daughter. There's an implication in that letter that our home is somehow unfit.'

'I know, I know. You have to give this time though, Liv. Up till recently, that was my home. It just needs time.'

He sees the concern in her face and can't stand talking about it any more, he's worried that he'll blurt out to her that he gets several text messages from Carmel every day, saying over and over, *Daddy, come home* and he wants to spare her that knowledge. If he loads that on to her, there's a danger that he might tell her about the market and how some of the traders, the locals who are part of Eileen's network, are ignoring him or giving him the chill cabinet treatment, shoulders turning. He doesn't want to burden her with these things that she can do nothing about; she has her own heartache, anxiously awaiting a reply from her husband. He has to do his best to ride the troubles and balance this precarious seesaw they're all perched on. 'You've got to roll with the punches', his boss used to say when things went pear-shaped.

Liv closes her eyes, sees her parents dancing in this room to the hissing gramophone, her mother winking at her over her father's shoulder, singing in her surprisingly powerful, tuneful voice, '. . . a little nest that's nestled where the roses bloom . . .' She sits forward, inching towards him so that the water won't overflow.

'Aren't we cosy,' she says, 'tucked away here with the fire and the lamps and a bottle of good red wine uncorked and warming? Could two people ask for anything more in the whole wide world?'

He encircles her with his arms. 'We're as snug as bugs in a rug,' he confirms. 'Now let's get dried; I'm a starving man and that stew smells wonderful.'

It's pouring with rain as Liv drives into Cork and there is a strong westerly blowing, buffeting the car. She opens the window to welcome the wind in, hoping it might clear the mist in her head, sucking in the deep gusts. Her phone rings and she pulls over, tears of relief in her eyes that it's Aidan at last.

'Where on earth have you been?' she asks. 'I left three messages. I was worried something had happened to you.' She tries to control the panic in her voice, sits up straight.

'I know, I'm sorry, I had a puncture and while I was sorting it out my bloody phone slipped behind some boxes. I've only just found it. What's up?'

'Douglas rang me this morning, he's in Cork, asking to meet me.'

'What, so fast, with no warning?'

She stares at the trees bending and dripping in the wind. 'He had a letter before mine, from Eileen, informing him of my activities.'

'What?'

'She must have remembered his address from the things I posted to him, or copied it. The postal service and its officers have featured significantly in our lives recently, haven't they?'

'Oh, Liv, Liv. I'll come back straightaway, we'll . . .'

'No, no, I'm in Cork now. I'm on my way to see him.'

There's a pause. 'Oh. Are you OK, I mean, how did he sound?'

'I'm better now I've heard your voice. I didn't want to see him without you knowing. He sounded all right, quite calm in fact.'

'I just can't believe that Eileen did that.'

'Can't you? It seems in keeping with everything else. She wants to protect her family.'

'But you must have had a terrible shock. Oh God, I'm so sorry you couldn't get me.'

'Yes. I thought he was ringing from England, obviously. No worse than the shock he's had, I suppose. I'd better go, I said I'd be there at three. I'll be home later.'

'I'll be there. This is the worst part, remember. It will be OK, I promise you. I love you, Liv.'

'And I love you. Wish me luck.' She shivers and closes the window. Her hair is damp from spray. Wasn't that what Douglas had said to her when he told her about Hyde House? *Wish me luck.*

During those hours after she'd heard from Douglas and couldn't contact Aidan, she had felt a terrible desperation, a sense of being trapped in some barren, gloomy landscape. She'd paced the kitchen and garden, convincing herself that Aidan was being worked on by Eileen, playing the good cop after the bad, that he was never going to return to her. She could hear Eileen's voice. 'For sure, you've been a fool but you know Maeve will have you back and think of poor Carmel, what's she going to do without her Daddy? Come on back now and no one will say another word about it.'

After she had left the third message she ran down to the well just as the rain was starting, drifting mistily, dimpling the surface. There she had kicked her sandals off and done the circumnambulation in her bare feet so that she would be known by every pebble, every crumb of earth and patch of moss, treading over and over around the rim. She had whispered without knowing who she might be sending her pleas to. 'Let him come back to me, let this work out.'

The chill of the rain has entered her bones and her breath has misted the windscreen. Braver now that she has heard from him, bolstered by his voice, she turns the heater to the blower and drives on. The hotel, Douglas said, is by the river, the Dromore. He'd added very little, just asked if she would meet him, have a cup of tea. Yes, she'd replied, of course, dazed, amazed at Eileen's canny outflanking. Afterwards, puzzling, she'd realized that the call had bewildered her too because his voice was quiet and distinct; no fumbling for words, no stuttering.

There's a gravel car park at the side of the hotel, a handsome Edwardian building with palm trees in wide tubs. The wind has abated or maybe this avenue by the river is sheltered; certainly the water is calm. At reception, she asks for him and the young woman rings his room.

'Dr Hood says would you like to go up or meet in the lounge?' she asks.

'In the lounge, please.' How odd, how formal, she thinks.

The woman confirms and smiles at her. 'If you'd like to go through, so, Dr Hood says he'll be down in a minute. The lounge is in there, to the right. Would you like refreshments?'

'Yes, please, a pot of tea. Dr Hood usually likes black coffee, with sugar.'

In the empty lounge she sits in a dark leather armchair with velvet armrests, glad that the nearby chunky radiator is warm, drawing the chair closer to it. It's a pleasant, old-fashioned hotel, unpretentious, the pictures and paintings all a little skewed on walls of panelled wood. There are books and magazines on the coffee tables and a massive grandfather clock between the sash windows. It's the kind of place they've both always liked, the kind of hotel they would have chosen together. She wonders if he has selected it deliberately with this in mind but dismisses the thought, acknowledging that Eileen's activities have left her paranoid. She places her hands on the radiator. The skin on her palms is roughened from digging and she's glad of that, proud that she shares this evidence of their hard work with Aidan. She has removed her wedding ring, it's in the dresser drawer at Glenkeen. Her left hand looks bare without it, a ring of pale skin on the third finger. If he is sober, and he seems to be, he will notice but it would have been the worst kind of pretence to have put it back on.

He comes in swiftly, a newspaper rolled under his arm and sits opposite her, his back to the window. He's wearing clothes she's never seen before, jeans and striped shirt, crisp and pressed with newness. She can smell soap, the muskiness of sandalwood. Her feet are still gritty from the ground by the well, her sandals darkened from the drenched grasses. The push and pull of the day is sitting tight behind her eyes. She puts her hand up to her temple to shield them from the grey, insistent light.

'Hallo, Liv. You found it OK, then?'

'Yes, no trouble. Cork's pretty easy to navigate.'

'I can see that. It took no time from the airport. Seems a handsome place.'

'I don't know it that well, it's really always been an arrival and departure point.' A waiter approaches with a tray, china rattling. 'I ordered drinks, coffee for you if that's OK.'

'Lovely.'

She looks at him covertly as the waiter bends, setting out cups and jugs. She is used to checking him out, taking in the important features in one assessing glance. He has lost weight, his face no longer puffy and more defined, the high colour toned to a mere hint of rosiness. His hair has been cut short and has a spiky look; she thinks he must have some kind of gel on it. He looks more adult. But it's his eyes that impress her most; the bags have reduced and his pupils are brighter. They busy themselves with their drinks. She notes that he pushes the sugar away, foregoing his usual three spoons. He still has a slight tremor in his fingers but his nails are unbitten and smooth.

When the waiter has gone he holds his hands out to her; he hasn't missed her scrutiny and that's unusual in itself. 'The trembling will take a while to go but there's a big improvement. And look at my nails, aren't they smart? I've had manicures and pedicures and massages and seaweed heat treatments and Indian head rubs and mud body wraps. I've been pummelled and scraped and steamed. I'm the cleanest and neatest I've ever been, outside and in. It's all been part of holistic care, making me feel good about myself, like a baby does. I felt just like a big infant when I was swaddled in towels. I can bear to do more than glance in a mirror now.' He laughs self-deprecatingly, taps the side of his chair.

She sips her tea, glad of the weight of the cup and saucer. 'I'm glad, I'm so glad for you.'

'Yes, I think you are. I was doing it for you as well, you know.'

She looks down, shakes her head. 'Douglas, I'm sorry that you had to find out about me and Aidan in this way. I had no idea that that woman might write to you.'

'It was certainly unusual. Nobody has ever told me that I should "see to my wife". Sounds like *Othello*. I didn't know what to make of it, I thought maybe she was the local madwoman whom you'd crossed in some way. I got your letter the next day. Then I did forty desperate lengths in the pool, had a sauna and decided to come, not to come, to come . . .'

'Did my letter, her letter, make you want a drink? That's the only reason I put off writing, I thought you'd reach for a bottle.'

'Yes, your letter did. I thought of it. Then I reminded myself that that was what had brought me to where I was, with my wife seeking love elsewhere. I fought the beast of craving down. I call him Joe, after Stalin – he has that heavy, meaty look and vicious 'tache and I aim to banish him for ever to the frozen tundra, where he had me exiled. It helped, of course, that I was in a hermetically sealed environment. The real test was at the airport, on the plane here, in the bar and at lunch. So many alcohol outlets, so many possibilities! I've won, so far.' He taps his head with the paper. 'That's a little trick I've learned, a reprogramming; when Joe swings into operation I give myself a reminder, tap tap, that I can outsmart him.'

She stares at him. The words he is speaking make sense, coming out in a coherent order. There is a shape to him that is more than the sum of physical improvement and new clothing. 'This is so strange, it's the longest conversation we've had for ages. I never imagined a scene like this.'

'It is hard to believe. I'm taken aback by my own renaissance. But back to your letter; you're in love, then. And with the man who jilted you before we met.'

She presses her abraded palms together, senses, summons Aidan. 'I am, yes. Very much. Unexpectedly and extraordinarily in love. I know that must be hurtful but I have to be honest. There's no point in not being, is there?'

'No. And who am I to complain about hurt? I've put you through hell, over the years.' He takes his spoon and dips it in his coffee, laughs at himself. 'I'd forgotten, I don't take sugar any more.'

'Is that deliberate, something to do with your treatment?'

'Yes and no. It's not mandatory, is what I mean. I've just found that my palate is changing in odd ways. Sugar tastes sickly to me now. It's to do with metabolism, I suppose. I'm glad of it, I think it means I'm finally tasting life instead of substitutes.'

'You look a lot better. You look aware.'

'I know. It's surprising to find a Douglas I'd forgotten. Nice to know he's still there, not completely squandered. I've discovered a reserve tank I didn't know I had. You look good but strained. There's colour in your cheeks that's misleading. If I was your doctor I'd check under your eyelids for anaemia.'

She sits back, considers him. 'You're taking this news very well.'

He closes his eyes momentarily, nods. 'You're not the only one with news, Liv. I didn't rush to contact you when I got the admirable Eileen's letter and I pounded up and down the pool when I'd read yours because I'm no angel. I've been unfaithful to you in the last weeks. I've had a relationship too. So I can hardly point the finger at you, can I – even if Eileen whatever-her-name-is would love me to.'

She sets her cup down, settles it in the saucer. 'Well, and there was me thinking that you were concentrating on being abstemious.'

He smiles. 'It's almost too predictable, it wouldn't take you long to work it out if you thought it over. I've been sleeping with Kia, my energetic, bountiful Tasmanian.'

'Oh, I see.'

'No, no you don't, at all. It's not love. She's a good woman, cheerful, optimistic, kind. It was against the rules but then she's a bit of a rebel. I could, so I did, it's as simple as that. I was checking myself out, to see how I'd feel. You'd gone off to your glen and I resented it. It's the first time I've ever been unfaithful to you but that won't surprise you; how could a man who couldn't find his way home find another woman?'

She realizes that her main feeling is of relief, a purely selfish relief; maybe now, she's off the hook. 'Douglas,' she says, 'you don't have to explain . . .'

'But I do and I want to. Kia was part of seeing myself in a new way, experiencing myself differently. And I wanted you to sit up and take proper notice of me, there was a good pinch of attention seeking in there too. I may be confused and daft but I know that. There wasn't one minute when I believed that I wanted to be with her rather than with you. But I realize that you might not want to accept that. So, you see, I haven't come here for recriminations and guilt. All the cards are on the table, Liv. We've both been duplicitous but in a way I've behaved more badly – and there's a surprise! At least you've fallen honest-to-goodness in love.'

Oh, she thinks, if only you knew! Eileen and Maeve wouldn't give me any credit for how I've behaved. Honest-to-goodness love; was such a thing possible once there were splintered marriages and desolate children to consider? Sitting in this pleasant hotel with the radiators humming and the rainy sun on the windows, the comforting echo of pans from an unseen kitchen, preparing the evening menu, she hears the nagging whisper in her ear, 'honest-to-goodness love is what you and Aidan had all those years ago, just the two of you when it was simple and straightforward but not now, not now when there are people who will be damaged in the storm you've created.'

'You're being too kind, Douglas,' is all she says.

He looks at his hands, examines them as if wondering that they can be his and she thinks of the enormous change he has under-gone and if it has left him feeling as shaky and astonished as she has been in these last weeks. His world has turned too, like one of those globes you played with at school, spinning it on its axis to see where it would stop.

He takes the sugar bowl and tinkers with it, heaping drifts of brown crystals with the tiny spoon. 'I thought I'd lost you when you decided to come to your cottage. Had I already lost you then?'

'I don't know. Probably. I felt lost, you know, abandoned by you. I wasn't looking for anyone – at least I don't think I was. I've gone through my own changes while you've been undergoing your renaissance. That must always be a danger for a couple, mustn't it, when they have simultaneous but completely different experiences? I think that maybe a relationship can only take one person changing at a time.'

'Well. Perhaps you're right.' He yawns, his eyes watering,

clears his throat and squints up at the window behind him. 'The downpour seems to have stopped. I haven't had much air today. Fancy a bit of a walk by the river?' He jerks his chair back and she can see that he's struggling to keep this mask of restraint that he's managed to present.

She looks at her watch. 'OK, just a stroll. I don't want to leave it too late before I head back.'

They walk a little way in silence on the damp pavement, skirting puddles and then stop, resting elbows on the river wall. Lights are switching on in houses as people return from work and they refract on the shifting water. Nearer to him, in the air, she can smell a sharp scent of fear from him. She steels herself not to be moved by it. He whistles a few bars of a tune, 'Waltzing Matilda' and she knows from experience that he's searching for control.

'Aidan is living in the cottage with you, is he?'

'Yes.'

'And you're planning to stay here?'

'Yes.'

'What will you do for money?'

'There's my savings and he has a business. We want to make it a joint venture.'

'I can see his attractions; a sober man who wants to share his days with you.'

'That's right.'

'Have you resigned from your job?'

'I posted the letter at the same time as yours. We'll have to sort out the house but there's no great rush. I'll come back to see my father and pack stuff up once things are more settled here.'

'Liv.' He hasn't spoken her name up to now. It comes as a shock. She's grown used to hearing Aidan say it in his lighter, softer tone. He isn't looking at her but at the river. 'I don't want you to leave me, but I know it's probably all too late. I want to be your husband again, your proper, full-time, fully present partner in life. But I'll understand if that can't be.'

She's filled with a sharp spurt of angry remorse, turning suddenly towards him. 'Stop this, Douglas.' She smacks the wall with her hand, hurting the already tender skin. 'When I think of all the times I've pleaded with you, begged you, talked for hours to you, rescued you, covered up for you, dragged you home. And now, after so many years, when I've found a smattering of happiness, you tell me a long tale of sobriety and massages and pampering and Joe Stalin, of brand new reserve-tank Douglas, new clothes and I'm all you ever wanted! I admire the timing, the mistiming. Oh, and of course you mix in the usual haven't-I-been-terrible-but-I-can-change blackmail. My God, what you've put me through!' She's shouting, reckless, nothing left to lose.

He props himself against the wall, hugs his jacket together. 'I can only tell you how sorry I am. It's not much but it can be a start. It has to be the start.'

She walks away from him to calm herself, rubs at her furious heart and the rigid anger in her face, paces slowly back. In the lighted window of a house behind them, a man stands holding a cup, his hand raised to draw the curtains. To his side is a woman flicking through letters and a little boy kneeling, watching television, a brightly coloured cartoon. Enough now, she decides. 'I wanted a child,' she says, speaking intently, urgently to his lowered head, 'but I never had one because you frittered away my opportunities. I wanted a marriage and a husband who was there but I never could have that either. You're a selfish, self-absorbed man. Like all addicts, you can't think beyond your own needs. You weren't the only one Joe exiled to the tundra, you know, he had me confined in my own private salt mine. Give me one reason, one, why I should believe a word you say, all your fine, lavish, deluded promises about never again and this is it.'

209

He buttons his jacket, stands up. 'I can't. There's no reason why you should for one moment believe me. All I can tell you is that I love you and that what I've gone through recently has changed me; no, I've changed myself. And even if you stay here I'll still stay changed. No blackmail, you see.'

A misting rain starts again. She thinks of Aidan back in the cottage, raking the fire, looking anxiously at the clock. He'll have brought home the details of some builders around the city, they've planned to discuss them after supper. She's so tired of the past that's standing next to her with all the old stories and spoiled intentions.

She pulls up the hood of her coat. 'For the first time in years, there's someone I'm longing to get home to and who will see me when I walk through the door. I wish you well. I have to go.'

'I'll walk you to your car.'

They tread silently, the rising hum of evening traffic masking their steps. She walks fast, keeping her eyes forward. As she unlocks the car he moves back. 'I regret the wasted years, Liv, I regret the waste of you.'

She can't speak any more, shakes her head. As she drives away he stands, watching. He doesn't wave.

12

Aidan has set a lamp in the window, inside the curtains, a steady yellow beacon to guide her home. She stands by the car for a moment, looking at the single flame and then up at the sky and the dark moon in the hanging stars. Her life is full of such unsought riches. She is almost reluctant to go in and break this magic, this sense of belonging.

The door opens and he hurries out, wearing his old fleece jacket that smells of mulched forest leaves. He opens his arms and they stand, pressed close. The rain has stopped and the air is drowned and soft with moisture. She feels it on her skin like a balm.

'How was it?' he asks finally, tentatively.

She takes folds of his jacket into her hands, squeezes them, buries her nose in his weft and weave. She would like to climb inside his skin with him. 'Not so bad. Douglas seems to have kicked the booze. He was looking much better.'

'Was he angry?'

'No. He's been having a fling with a therapist so he was also feeling guilty. I was the one who got angry. I thought of all the years gone and the squandered time made me livid.'

'I suppose he wants you back.'

'That's what he said.'

'Were you tempted?'

'No. Were you worried I might not come back?'

'For one panicky moment. I was thinking of the night I came here to you and you were dancing by yourself, carefree. I've brought trouble to you, made you careworn.'

'Are *you* tempted, when you read the solicitor's letters and think of the rocks ahead?'

'No. I'm thinking of the long, content future with you. Has Douglas gone back?'

'He said he was on a late flight.'

'Well, that's another difficult bit done.'

She can feel him trembling with relief. 'Aidan, can we go down to the well, just for five minutes?'

'Of course. I've a big fire going so we can dry off inside.'

He fetches a torch and they pick their way down through the moist dripping of ferns and bushes. He pulls his fleece around them, settling the torch so that it shines on the water. The hazel tree is a sturdy, consoling presence.

'Nobody would ever know we were in here, tucked away,' she says.

'It doesn't get much better than this little sanctuary. Even the shadows are friendly in here.' He feels for her hand. 'I rang a solicitor today, a specialist in family law. I gave her a brief outline and she said she'd take me on. I've an appointment tomorrow. So, we're on our way.'

She rests back against him. 'Why is the moon so dark? You know, sometimes you suddenly realize how little you know. There's the moon, suspended in the sky and I don't understand why it has different shapes and colours. I know that it controls the tides and that poets are inspired by it.'

'That's a new moon. The sun and moon are in conjunction, which is why it's so dark. In folklore, it's supposed to mean a time

212

of renewal and hope.'

'Are you inventing that last bit, to make me feel better?' She looks up at him, kisses his chin.

'No, not at all.' He pulls her closer, tucks the fleece more firmly around her. 'I was helping Carmel with her homework a while ago, a project on the night sky. I learned all kinds of fascinating things. It's also a symbol of female strength, the new moon, and it affects the movement of fluids in plants, because it influences the water table. And it's a good time to sow seeds, under this moon. There are books about planting gardens in conjunction with the moon's phases. According to lunar planting lore, root plants should be put in the ground during a waning moon, because that's when moisture content in the soil is low.'

'Maybe we should try it, lunar planting. We could have a test area and compare it with our other crops.'

'Good idea, then we could sell moon vegetables; loony leeks.'

'Potty parsnips.'

'Crazy carrots.'

'What a life we're going to have.'

'What a life.'

She throws a stone into the well, watches the ripples in the torchlight. 'Did you hear from anyone in Castlegray today, from Maeve or Carmel?' She crosses her fingers as she asks.

He hesitates for a moment, spinning the torch beam across the water. 'No,' he lies. Why spoil this?

'I wonder, does the new moon signal an urgent need for love-making?' She kneels up on the damp earth, eases back the fleece, tastes the chill dew on his warm lips.

Aidan is the lighter sleeper and he wakes first, just after midnight, aware of a different and familiar scent in the room. Apples, he registers, shoving the eiderdown away from his face, glancing at his mobile phone to see the time. The new moon casts no light through the thin curtains but the blue glow from his phone picks out her shadow. He sits up slowly, peering upwards.

Maeve is there, standing at the end of the mattress. He can just make out her hair, fanning over her shoulders, recently washed. She's wearing a light belted cream jacket with wide sleeves that adds to her ghost-like appearance. 'Hallo, Aidan. I was wondering how long it would be before you woke up. You always heard a pin drop. You sleep more soundly here. That surprises me.'

'What are you doing here? How did you get in?'

'You left your back door open. I walked in.'

Liv is waking, turning on to one elbow. 'What is it?'

'Maeve,' he says. 'It's Maeve.'

'What?' She looks at him, then turns her head, sits up.

'You have a visitor,' Maeve says. She switches on the tiny but powerful pencil torch she's carrying, flashes it around the room. 'It's a bit basic,' she says, tapping the torch against her knee so that the beam plays back and forth across the end of the mattress and Aidan's bare feet.

Aidan stretches for his jumper and jeans, pulls them on. Liv's clothes aren't within reach. She hoists the sheet around her shoulders. Aidan switches their torch on, lays it on the floor so that it's pointing at the wall, back lighting.

'What are you doing here, Maeve? Who's with Carmel?' He kneels on the bed, finding his glasses, focusing.

Maeve has that tight, fixed look. 'Oh, nice of you to be worried about Carmel. You didn't reply to her phone calls today, though.'

Liv glances at him. He keeps his gaze on Maeve. 'Why are you here?' he asks again.

'I just wanted to see. I wanted to see what's better than us. I was in bed, our bed, what used to be our bed, and I had a hankering to see your new home. It's hard sleeping when you keep thinking

214

of your husband with another woman. It tends to stop you sleeping, actually. Has that ever happened to you?' she asks Liv, swiftly pointing the torch at her.

Liv blinks, shades her eyes. 'No, that hasn't happened to me.'

'Lucky you.' She shifts her bag on her shoulder. 'Yes, lucky old you.'

'Where is Carmel?' Aidan asks again.

'What do you care? She was in tears this evening, wanted her daddy. She has a gum infection from the brace so we had to go back to the dentist today. She's on antibiotics. The poor little girl's feeling lousy. She wanted her daddy but he wasn't there. Daddy had switched his phone off, or wasn't answering.' Maeve sways a little, side to side.

Liv shivers. She wonders if Maeve has been drinking but there's no smell of booze, just a soapy scent. She's speaking in a matter of fact monotone, almost as if she's talking about other people, another family entirely. The torch is hurting Liv's eyes as the beam swings across the room. 'I think it would be best if we all went downstairs,' she says.

'Oh, do you?' Maeve asks and it's as if she's revved up, changed gear suddenly. Her voice surges with power. 'Who asked your opinion? I was talking to my husband. I suppose you'll allow that?'

'Look . . .'

'No, you look. I've looked, I've seen enough, standing here waiting for you two to wake up. It's foolish to leave a door unlocked, even around here, you could be murdered in your bed.'

'Maeve, Maeve,' says Aidan. 'Don't do this, this isn't like you, saying such things, acting this way.'

'Isn't it? Maybe not. Maybe you don't really know yourself or what you can do until the chips are down, the fat's in the fire.' She claws her bag from her shoulder, snatches at the clasp and takes out a long, thin knife, a vegetable knife, points it at Liv. 'Why do you want to take my husband? Haven't you one of your own back in England or are you greedy, do you need two? Look at you, you never expected this, did you? It's not so easy having to face the person you've stolen from.'

Aidan stands, holds his hands out, palms downwards. 'Maeve, stop this. This is no way to go on, it solves nothing.'

She looks at him, head on one side. 'Doesn't it? It'd solve a lot if I shoved this into your woman there. That's what I'd like to do, all right. Then *she* could feel some pain. At least I'd be stabbing her in the front, not the back.'

He takes a step towards her. 'If you're going to stick it anyone, stick it in me. I'm the one who chose to leave. I'm the one who has run out on you, taken advantage of your kind nature, left you in an empty, lonely bed. I'm the one, Maeve, aren't I?'

She waves the knife at him and makes a noise in her throat, her mouth working, distorting, shaking her head. Her whole body starts trembling. Bending, falling to her knees, she holds the knife in her two hands, stabbing again and again into the mattress. And as she stabs she starts moaning, an awful enraged noise. You would never have thought that such a howling could come from such a petite, softly spoken woman.

Liv feels the pounding of the mattress jar through her bones, as if the blade has indeed sliced into her. As Maeve finally collapses over the knife she comes to her senses, finds and fumbles on her dressing gown. Aidan kneels by his wife, extricates the knife and throws it behind him. It clatters against the skirting and comes to rest in the shadows. He takes the sobbing Maeve in his arms and rocks her. 'Shh, shh, shh,' he says, 'no harm done, shh.'

Liv watches, leaning against the washstand. She recollects the first time she saw Maeve in the market, busy with her shopping, linking with her husband, smiling, leaning into him. She has never before seen someone's face collapse, crumple in misery. There is a kind of heat in the room, the fever of despair. Liv tastes it in her throat, a thick, rancid coating. She can't look any more. It feels as if she's been standing there for hours. Turning away, she lights a lamp, finds their torch and switches it off. Maeve's has shattered from where she let it fall. She stands, the lamp in her hand as Maeve's sobbing slows. Aidan looks at her over his wife's head, his eyes blank, lost.

'I don't know how Maeve got here,' Liv says quietly, 'but you'd better take her home, Aidan and see to her and Carmel. You should probably call a doctor.'

He swallows, nods. 'Maeve, how did you get here?'

'Taxi,' she whispers.

'Come on, then,' he says. 'Come on now. Time to go home.'

Liv follows them down the stairs, fetches him a coat. Maeve opens the front door and drifts outside, as if they're not there, a spectre against the dark green bushes, like one of the spirits that Nanna believed roamed in the glen.

Aidan holds Liv's shoulder. His eyes are full. 'I'll ring you in the morning. Are you all right?'

She nods. 'Just look after them. And look after yourself. Drive carefully.'

She tugs on some clothes, finds the bottle of strong red wine they opened earlier when they got back from the well, three hours ago, a lifetime ago, pours herself a large glass and drinks. A long shiver passes through her body. She knows that until her dying day, she will never forget Maeve's face dissolving and her savage cry. The thought of going back to bed is impossible. No one in that other house will get much sleep tonight; why should she?

She can't bear being alone with her fears. Crouching before the fire, she rings Owen's number. He answers quickly.

'I'm sorry to wake you,' she says.

'Liv! You didn't, I just got in from a bridge party west along,

217

literally walked through the door. What's up?'

'Is there any chance you could come over? I'm in trouble here. I could do with your company.'

'I'll be there in half an hour. You'll be all right?'

'Yes, thanks.'

While she waits for him she stirs the fire, gazes into its depths. 'Oh Nanna, what's happened here?' Her words fly into the corners of the room, crouch and watch her. She can't get warm, moves her chair into the hearth, holds her palms out. No harm done, Aidan had told his wife. Hardly. Hardly.

Owen brings with him strong, old-fashioned scents of good dining and rich cigars. She is grateful for them, for his big hands holding hers as he asks how she is. 'You look as if you saw the devil on the wind's back,' he says as he makes them both hot whiskey, producing a hip flask, finding cloves and brown sugar in the dresser. When the kettle boils he measures the liquids and stirs briskly. As he hands it to her it smells like medicine. She doesn't care for whiskey but she sips it, bolstered by its fire. He draws a stool up and listens in silence as she spills out her tale, gazing into his glass. He is pale, his face still.

'That's a sad state of affairs,' he says, rolling the whiskey between his hands. 'Maeve is besotted with Aidan, you know. I believe he's the one, she had no other relationships to speak of before him. She'll have taken it hard.'

Liv gazes at him. 'You know I didn't mean for this to happen.'

He nods. 'What are you going to do?'

'I'm not sure. Maeve can't handle this, that's all I know for definite after tonight. The woman is out of her mind with loss.'

'You feel responsible.'

'Yes.' She stirs the fire, adds turf. 'Someone has to do something here to put an end to this chaos and it seems it's me.'

He puts his glass down carefully, brings his hands up and joins them under his chin. His breathing is nasal and laboured. 'I'm going to tell you something now that I never thought I'd tell you, a story that hasn't been told for a long time, but I believe the circumstances call for it.'

She looks at his profile, his eyebrows like wild mountain ledges. His voice is rolling and a little sing-song, the way it was when he told the tale at the birthday party. 'Is this about someone I know?'

'Yes, unfortunately.' He sits upright, folds his arms across his chest. 'Ah Liv, the things we do, the things we do. The reason I lost my marriage and was persona non grata in the glen and with my family for a long time was because I had an affair. The person I had that affair with was your mother.' He looks at her. She stares back, drinks from her glass, pressing it to her lips.

'I was in love with Mollie and she loved me. We didn't mean it either. It just happened. It lasted nearly a year. I came to London and we'd meet in hotels. She got pregnant and thought the baby might be mine. That's when she told your father, while you were all here and then she miscarried. The anxiety was too much for her, I'd say. Shall I make another one of those?'

She holds the glass out to him, watches as he pours again. Already she can see them together, imagine how well they suited each other, two live wires setting London alight, linking arms as they sauntered along.

'That would have been the summer when my father took my mother home and I was left here with Nanna.'

'That's right.'

'Did people here know?'

'No one knew the details except your parents, me and your nanna. There's been plenty of speculation over the years about who I'd been adulterous with. I told Edith I'd had an affair but not who with. She thought it was someone in Dublin, an actress. I can say to you that Mollie was the love of my life. I don't know if I was

219

hers, that would be for her to say and she's gone now. But we caused havoc. We didn't mean to but we did. Your father is a man with a generous heart and he said little. He never said a word to me.'

'He suffered, though,' she says, thinking of her father's resigned look, his air of lingering unhappiness, the tainting of his homeland. No wonder he likes the safety and predictability of his cottage hospital at home and a wife who's never going to go out without him. 'He lost this place, even if he didn't lose his wife. And his mother lost his company, his regular visits.'

'All of that. And you lost your contact with your nanna. You see, I've thought of all the angles over the years; and then there's the lost child, too. Everyone lost, that's the truth of it. And we never meant any of it.'

'I always wanted a brother or sister,' she says. 'I used to envy other children who had siblings. Did you and my mother plan to be together?'

'We talked of it, of course. But I don't believe she could ever have left you and she wouldn't have taken you from your father. We'd go round in hopeless circles, discussing it.' Owen drains his glass, reaches up and sets it on the mantelpiece. 'The day you opened that door to me I thought I was seeing a ghost, you look so like Mollie with your freckles and that hair. You sound just like her, that quick, precise way of talking. Maybe I should have stayed away from you but I couldn't. I liked you as a child and I liked the woman I found. I don't want to lose you now. If you want a refuge with me, you're welcome. But after what I've just told you, I'd understand if you never wanted to see me again.'

She shakes her head at him, manages a faint smile even. 'There's been enough of that over the years, don't you think? Absences, silences, shoulder turning. An old wound that can't be mended now. It's not about us now, anyway.' She pulls sharply on

220

her fingers, cracking the knuckles. 'Carmel is around the age that I was that summer when my mother had the miscarriage. That ten days without my parents seemed an eternity to me, even though Nanna couldn't have been kinder.'

Owen takes her hand, pats it. 'You're right, you have more pressing worries now. I'm sorry, Liv. I regret the past although I can't regret loving Mollie.'

'Yes, but I can't help thinking of my father and the way he would look bewildered, as if there was something he'd misplaced and couldn't find.'

'Mollie loved him, you know, she never had a bad word to say about him. Is he happy now, do you think?'

She considers her answer. 'He's found a way of being content, yes.'

It's five o'clock when Owen leaves, the night dense and thick, hugging its secrets before the dawn. No point in trying to sleep now, she thinks. She washes her face in cold water, dunking her head right in, rubbing hard. Her hands are curiously steady, her mind clear and intent, her heart desolate. She mustn't stop now, best to keep going, leave no space or time for doubts or hesitation. There are griefs that have to be borne. Her mother, she understands, must have been distraught back then but she never stopped cooking the dinners, doing the shopping, ironing the sheets.

She tidies the cottage, secures the windows, packs her cases and takes them to the car. Her head is down, her manner brisk. If she looks around at Aidan's belongings, his jumpers, boots and garden plans she might falter, start thinking that there is some other way. She throws the bread and scones that are left out for the birds. The whiskey glasses she shatters in the fireplace, wanting the noise and finality of the splintering crash. Then she sweeps them into a glittering pyramid and pours water on the embers to

221

make sure that all is quenched and cold.

At six, the hour when her father has never failed to get up, she rings him. He hates the phone, always has, answers it in a hesitant voice, as if it might bite him.

'I got your postcards,' he says. 'I liked the one of the town centre, it's looking prosperous. This is early enough for you, isn't it?'

'It is. How are you?'

'Oh, fine, you know, getting by. I just put a few rashers of bacon on. Hazel managed to sit downstairs the last couple of nights and we watched a bit of telly, one of those glam dance competitions, fellows swanning about in tight trousers.'

'Good.' She swallows. His mild, steady voice makes her want to weep. 'I'm standing at the cottage door,' she says. 'It's been raining during the night but it's stopped now. Do you remember you used to carry me down the glen on your shoulders when it had been raining, in case I slipped?'

'I do remember, of course. That's a long time ago now, you're a bit older and I'm a lot more wrinkled!'

'Dad, I'm coming back today.'

'To London?'

'Yes.'

'That's a bit soon, isn't it? I thought you said you were having work done on Glenkeen?'

'I was. I've changed my mind.'

'Oh. I suppose Douglas will be pleased, anyway, to have you back sooner, I'm sure he'll have missed you.'

She sighs, covers the phone.

'Is everything all right, Livvie?'

'No. I'll tell you when I see you. I've had some trouble here, I think it's best that I leave.'

'What kind of trouble?'

She can't reply, grips the phone. 'Dad, what do you do when you've messed up and everything is just one huge, horrible disaster, how do you get through?'

'Has this got anything to do with Owen Farrell?' he asks, his voice tightening. 'If that man has said something . . .'

'No. It's all my own doing. I can't tell you now, I'll come and talk to you when I get back.'

'I see.' She hears a pan rattling, can imagine him flipping the bacon over, one-handed. 'Well,' he says at last, 'in answer to your question, I suppose you just try to live a good life.'

She puts the key under a stone by the front door; she will ask Owen to collect it and ask Aidan for his. Before leaving she takes the knife that Maeve had wielded to the well and drops it in, hoping, in her final request of this place, that it falls deep enough for misery to be washed away. She parts the foliage and turns her torch beam on to the white pebbles that spell Mollie and Fintan, places her palm over them, then covers them carefully with an extra layer of stones and ferns.

The day is bright now, with a watery sky and a sharp breeze. A good day for sailing, for feeling the surge of the wind-whipped waves. She wishes that the boat was about to set its course for some faraway, unknown destination that would take weeks to reach, a place across oceans, continents and time zones. She sees it, an island on the fringes of the world where she could be an anonymous, reinvented woman with no onerous history. Disembarking, she would ask the way to a small hotel and give another, unburdened name, find herself a job in a café or a bookshop maybe. Then she would rent a quiet room, living a brand new existence, a scoured, sparkling and polished life that would glint in the sun. After all, Douglas has laundered his life, rinsed and

223

refreshed his body and his spirit. It can be done. The ship blasts two loud, derisive hoots.

She moves out of the way as several children clatter past her and steps into the shelter of a doorway. She takes her phone from her pocket and holds it, weighing it in her hand. Scrolling through, she sends a text message to Douglas, pausing as she presses the letters, carefully trying to measure the words. It would be cruel now to raise false hopes and she has none to offer, none even for herself. *Have left cottage, not returning. Will be back in London alone this evening. Please don't expect anything. I don't know what I'm going to do.* She watches the tiny envelope flutter momentarily on the screen and wing across the Irish sea; *message sent.*

She waits until the bow doors have clanged shut, like a huge shell closing and the ferry has cast off, moving towards the open sea before she raises her phone again and calls up Aidan's number. She watches Ireland slip away from her, bracing herself against the rail as she hears him answer, a faint, lost voice.